FIVE WOMEN AND THE STAR

A JACK SAGE WESTERN - BOOK 5

DONALD L. ROBERTSON

COPYRIGHT

Five Women and the Star

Copyright © 2024 Donald L. Robertson
CM Publishing

All rights reserved. No part of this publication may be reproduced, distributed or transmitted in any form or by any means, including photocopying, recording, or other electronic or mechanical methods, without the prior written permission of the publisher, except in the case of brief quotations embodied in critical reviews and certain other noncommercial uses permitted by copyright law.

Publisher's Note: This is a work of fiction. Names, characters, and incidents are a product of the author's imagination. Locales and public names are sometimes used for atmospheric purposes. Any resemblance to actual people, living or dead, or to businesses, companies, or events, is completely coincidental. For information contact:

Books@DonaldLRobertson.com

ISBN: 979-8-9912601-1-4

❦ Created with Vellum

1

Spring, 1873

Jack Sage halted Pepper inside the treeline. The smell of the ponderosa pines filled his nostrils. Two black and white magpies fussed at him. A long, grass-covered valley stretched into the distance, with a primitive road dividing it westward, the direction he was traveling.

Through the clear mountain air, he could see a wagon stopped. Supplies filled the wagon bed. Two harnessed horses cropped at the thick grass. Jack waited. He saw no one around the wagon. He was about to ride forward when a head lifted into view from the opposite side of the wagon. It rose only to the edge of the wagon's sideboard, looked inside, and was joined by two arms.

Jack frowned. It looked like a kid. "Pepper, what's a kid doing out here by himself?"

The big chestnut shook his head as if he had no idea, snorted, and pulled on the reins. Jack's frown turned into a grin. "Sometimes, I think you boys can understand every word I say." The other two horses and mule ignored him, staring toward the wagon.

"All right, let's go have a look."

Jack clucked. Pepper stepped forward while the other three, on long leads, trailed behind.

Making his way down the gentle slope, Jack saw the boy's head turn toward him as soon as he broke out from the treeline. "The boy's alert, Smokey," Jack said to the trailing grulla.

He could see the youngster turn and look toward where he had been behind the side of the wagon. *Somebody's with him,* Jack thought.

Immediately, a woman rose from behind the wagon side. Standing, she lifted a Winchester and laid the barrel across the wagon's sideboard, the muzzle pointed in his general direction. Her gloved right hand casually held the small of the stock. Her left hand lifted to push a strand of long blonde hair back under the wide-brimmed flop hat.

Reaching the wagon, Jack pulled Pepper to a stop, his other animals drifting to his side. "Howdy, ma'am."

Tension pulled at the corners of her eyes and mouth. "What are you doing out here?"

Jack was taken aback at the abruptness of her question. He was used to the easygoing ways of the west, not sharp inquiries. He gave her a wry grin. "Reckon it's a free country, ma'am. The politicians tell us that's why we fought the war." He could see her wrist tense, and the rifle barrel moved along the sideboard until the muzzle aligned with him. He noted that her finger was still not resting on the trigger. *I guess I can be thankful for that,* he thought.

Her green eyes narrowed. "Davy, get behind me."

Perplexed, the boy looked up at his ma as if he was about to argue.

Her voice hardened. "Now."

The boy looked up at Jack, shook his head, and trudged around the wagon until he stood behind her.

Once her son was behind her, her eyes locked on Jack's. "I

asked you a question, mister. There's only one reason to be riding this trail, and that is to reach the D Bar J ranch. Why are you going there?"

Jack knew the woman was leery of him, maybe even scared, though she handled it well. He had recognized her as soon as she stood and needed to calm her fears, especially since the muzzle of her rifle was pointed toward him. He held his hands up, palms toward her, and eased his coat back, exposing the U.S. Marshal's badge on his chest. "Amy, I mean you no harm. You're right, I am headed for the D Bar J. I'm Marshal Jack Sage, and—"

"Jack?" She leaned toward him, looking past the wrinkles, scars, and changes time had pressed upon him. "Jack Sage, is that really you?"

He could see relief flood the woman's young face. "Yes, ma'am. That would be me. A few years have passed since I last saw you."

"President Grant sent you?"

"Yes, ma'am. He sure did." He let a wide smile drift across his sun- and wind-darkened face. "Now, would it be too much to ask if you pointed your Winchester in another direction? Pepper here"—he patted the red horse on the neck—"doesn't much care for rifles pointed at him."

She shook her head in frustration with herself, sending the stray blonde strand out from under her hat, to fall across her cheek and the corner of her full lips. "Oh, yes. I am so sorry." She lifted the rifle from across the wagon's side, took three steps forward, and slid it into the scabbard fastened next to the seat.

Turning back to Jack, her words came out in a rush. "I am sorry, Jack, Marshal Sage. It's just . . . we've lost cattle and horses. We know there are rustlers around, but we have yet to see any riders. Someone had to make a run to Laramie for supplies, and it seemed like I was the best choice, but I must tell you, I have been so frightened. And then in town, and now this." She swung her hand toward the wheel before it jerked to her face. She turned so her son couldn't see the tears well up in her eyes. "Jack, I'm just glad you're here."

Jack swung down from Pepper, looping the reins over the wagon tailgate latch, and stepped toward her. "Now, Amy, there's nothing to be concerned about. Why, with this strong young fella here, we'll have this wheel fixed in no time, and you'll be on your way."

She blinked the tears back, making her eyes glisten like wet grass after a spring rain. She placed her hand on her son's shoulder. "This is David Warren Franklin."

"Call me Davy, Marshal." He stepped forward and thrust out a small hand.

"Reckon I will, Davy. Glad to meet you. That's a mighty fine name." The boy's hand disappeared in Jack's huge paw. "Let's take a look at this contrary wheel and see what needs to be done to fix it."

Davy's chest swelled at the compliment, and he stood as tall as his nine-year-old body would allow.

"It was my fault," Amy said.

She nodded at the road behind her. A shallow ditch cut a path across the road. "I hit it going too fast. The sudden jolt broke it." She shook her head in irritation. "What I don't understand, it was a new wheel. I just bought it in town."

Jack knelt and examined the wheel. "You say this is a new wheel?"

"Yes, I bought it today. The wheelwright, Mr. Toler, put it on for me just before we loaded the wagon to return to the ranch."

Jack stood and looked in the wagon bed. Under the supplies, he could see the old wheel. He began moving supplies. "Davy, why don't you jump up here and pull some of those boxes off that wheel. We'll take a look at it. Maybe it'll last to the ranch."

He turned to Amy. "How far to the ranch?"

She pointed to the distant tree line where the road disappeared. "It's about three miles beyond the turn."

Jack knelt and ran his hands along the three broken spokes. "It wasn't your fault." He removed his Barlow, opened the blade, and picked at the rotten wood, then nodded toward the ditch. "You should've been able to hit that little ditch at a dead run and just bounce over. You were sold a useless old wheel. Not only old, but rotten. I'm surprised it lasted this far."

Suspicion rising, he stood and looked back down the road in the direction Amy and Davy had traveled from town. Sure enough, he could see a cloud of dust moving toward them. "Ma'am, listen close to me. This is a setup. This wheel was supposed to break. That dust cloud is coming from several riders heading your way. I want you to do something for me. I want you and Davy to climb up on that chestnut, his name is Pepper, and hightail it to your ranch. I'm going to explain to these boys their mistake."

"But—"

"No buts, ma'am. Time's wasting." He pulled the Winchester from its scabbard on the wagon and walked her over to Pepper. Once she was mounted, he handed her the rifle, tossed Davy up behind her, stepped around Pepper, and pulled his Winchester from the scabbard. "I'd be obliged if you'll take my animals along with you. I'll be along shortly."

"Marshal, you don't know how many men—"

"Ma'am, it don't rightly matter. You go on now. I'll see you in a bit." He slapped Pepper on the rump, and the big horse leaped away, almost yanking Davy from his back when the leads of the other animals grew taut, but the boy hung on. For once, Stonewall didn't balk, and Jack watched them race away. Turning, he dropped the tailgate of the wagon, loosed the leather loops holding his two Smith & Wesson .44-caliber Americans in their holsters, and laid his Winchester in the wagon bed. His handguns would do the job, but if he needed the rifle, it would be there.

He could feel the old feeling. It had started to rise when he realized the wheelwright had sold this fine lady and her son a worn-out wagon wheel, lying to her and selling it for new. Jack had at first thought it had been done for the age-old reason, greed, but with the dust cloud moving toward him, he realized the man had intentionally put this woman's and her son's lives in danger. With his realization, his anger grew. It wasn't a wild and crazy anger, but a cold, calculating fury. He knew if he let it grow, it could lead to a bout of unpleasantness for those approaching.

The riders came into view. Five. *They needed five for a woman and a boy?* he thought. *They should have brought more.*

The riders neared. At the sight of him calmly sitting on the back of the wagon bed, they slowed to a walk. He could see them talking. Jack knew they were trying to figure out where Amy and Davy were and who the dickens he was. His mouth spread in a cold, mirthless grin. They were going to find out.

The horsemen stopped their animals twenty feet from Jack. They were a contemptible-looking bunch. Even the leader, or at least the man at the center of this ragtag group, looked like he had just been dragged out of a two-bit saloon. He spoke. "Who the blazes are you?"

Jack locked him in a cold glare. "Marshal Jack Sage. Who are you?"

The man snorted, and the others started laughing. "You ain't no marshal. I know all the city marshals around here, and you ain't one of them. But it don't matter. You wouldn't have no say out here, anyway."

"Yeah," several of the men shouted in agreement while nodding and laughing.

Jack stood and scanned the miserable-looking group. "United States, and I asked you your name."

They stopped laughing. The leader's eyes narrowed. "What'd you say?"

Jack, shaking his head, let out a long exasperated sigh, noticing a flock of buzzards circling overhead. The mountain air had been crisp and sweet until this bunch had ridden up, but their stench had arrived with them. No wonder the buzzards were circling. "I said, what is your name? Are you deaf?"

The leader's face scrunched into a frown. "No, I ain't deaf."

"Then tell me your name, or I'm jerking you out of that saddle and ripping it out of you."

"Mister, you could get dead talking to Leander Hull like that."

"I'm going to ease my coat back, boys. Don't get itchy." Jack watched the five lean forward in their saddles, their gun hands hovering over their sixguns. He exposed his badge and turned his eyes back to Hull. "I'm no city marshal, fellas, I'm a U.S. Marshal, and I'm telling you to either drop your hoglegs or fill your hands." His smile again creased his face, exposing shiny white teeth, much like a wolf about to pounce.

One of the gang turned to Hull. "He's a U.S. Marshal, Leander. I didn't hire on to go up against a U.S. Marshal. Maybe we should ride on out of here."

Before Hull could answer, Jack shook his head. "Not on the menu, boys. The only two choices you have are to drop those guns or use them."

Another of the gang spoke, his voice tense and high. "Cain't you count, mister. They's five of us and only one of you."

Jack's grin widened. "The more I hear, see, and smell you fellas, the better I like the odds. Nobody who looks or smells as bad as you could be any kind of threat, except maybe your stink choking a person to death. Unfasten those gunbelts. The first person who makes a twitch toward a gun butt, I'm blowing out of the saddle."

"The hell you say. Git him, boys!" Hull went for his gun.

Hull had turned slightly. He was positioned behind a good portion of his horse's neck. The only exposed area was the man's left shoulder and his head. Jack would have to fire between the ears of the horse to hit the man in the head. He opted for the shoulder.

When Jack fired, Hull's revolver was barely clear of his

holster. The .44-caliber chunk of lead slammed into the joint of Hull's left shoulder, fragmenting everything that got in its way. It exited carrying bone splinters, muscle, and tendons and blasting them onto the rider next to him. The injured leader never fired a shot, dropping the weapon from his right hand and clutching at his shoulder as he crashed to the ground.

Jack stood, both weapons drawn. The remaining four made no move toward their revolvers or rifles. They had either grabbed their saddle horns with both hands or sat with hands thrust high in the air.

Hull rolled on the ground in pain, blood shooting from his shoulder.

Jack waved his guns at the remaining four men. "One of you get down and help your friend."

A lanky rider began to swing from the saddle.

"Hold it."

The man froze, his right leg in midair.

Jack, using his left sixgun, motioned to the man's gunbelt. "Gun first."

The rider eased back into the saddle and unfastened his gunbelt, letting it drop to the ground. He looked questioningly at Jack.

"That'll do. Now see to your friend."

While the man swung down, Jack turned his attention to the remaining three riders. "What'd I tell you to do?"

Two of the three men rushed to unfasten their gunbelts and drop them unceremoniously to the ground. The third, younger, stared insolently at Jack, slowly unbelted his sixgun, and lowered it to the ground. Once all their belt guns were gone, Jack motioned again. "Alright, get down—carefully—and gather up at the back of this wagon."

He watched them swing from their saddles. "I'm going to holster my guns. You've seen what I can do with them, so don't give me a reason to draw." He pointed to the short stocky rider.

"You pick up the gunbelts and guns, including Hull's. Stack them in front by the wagon seat. Then join your pardners."

Once the guns were picked up and stacked and the three men gathered behind the wagon, Jack moved to where Hull lay moaning on the ground. The tall rider looked up and shook his head. Hull was slowly losing consciousness. The blood spurting from his shoulder had lost much of its force, and his face, beneath the dirt and sun-weathered skin, was pale.

Jack knelt and leaned down. "Hull, what was your plan?"

The man tried to talk, coughed, and in a low whisper said, "We was supposed to take her wagon and supplies. Make her and the boy walk home."

Jack shook his head. "I don't believe you. None of you were wearing masks. She could have identified you. You're dying. You want to meet your maker with a lie on your lips?"

Hull lay silent, breathing in short rapid gasps. His bloodshot eyes followed the buzzards circling overhead. "Don't let them . . . buzzards . . . eat me."

Jack leaned close so he could look Hull in the eyes. "Tell me the truth, or I'll leave you out here for the buzzards and grizzlies and whatever else comes along."

"Take her. I swear. He wanted us to take her. We was supposed to grab her and the boy and the supplies. I didn't want to, but he insisted. He . . . made . . . me . . . promise."

The man's voice was getting weaker. Jack leaned closer. "Who? Who wanted you to do this? Did you kill David and Warren Franklin?"

Hull closed his eyes.

Jack slapped him hard enough to cause his head to jerk.

The man's eyes opened, and a weak smile drifted across his face. From somewhere he mustered enough strength to grab Jack's coat collar and pull him close. Jack's ear was against his mouth. "He'll kill you."

His grip relaxed, and he fell back, blank eyes still staring at the buzzards overhead. Jack glanced around, accounting for all four men. They were motionless, watching. The tall man, he had been the closest, watched with a blank face. Evidently he had heard none of the shooter's whispered last words. Looking at them, Jack couldn't believe these men were going to take this woman and her child. They didn't look like men who would abduct a woman, not in this country. Taking a woman in the west would get you shot or hanged, if you were lucky. He knew of at least one occasion where the guilty man had been burned alive. These men looked exactly like what they were, down-and-out rowdies looking to make enough for another drink, but would they have stopped Hull? No, he didn't think so. They would have been surprised, even shocked, but they were followers. They would have complained, maybe argued, but none of them would have made a move to stop the man who lay dead on the ground.

A terrible anger rode on his heart. If he weren't representing the law, he might just turn loose the wolf. But he was.

2

Jack turned cold gray eyes on each of the remaining four kidnappers. "I'm going to ask you a few questions. I expect truthful answers. Believe me when I tell you I'll know if you're lying. I've been doing this for a long time."

The short chunky fella spoke up. "Marshal, we was just coming out here to hoorah the lady and take her supplies. That's the gospel truth. Didn't Leander tell you? We meant her no harm. We was just going to scare her a bit."

Jack glared at the man. "What's your name?"

The man glanced at his partners. "It's Holt Maize."

"You honestly want me to believe you weren't going to harm Mrs. Franklin and her boy?"

"I swear, Marshal, we ain't planned on anything 'ceptin' scarin' her a bit." He looked at each of the men again, and they were all vigorously nodding their heads.

Jack asked each man, and each confirmed the first man's statement.

"Are you men crazy or just stupid? Since you weren't wearing masks, what do you think would've happened when she described you to the sheriff? I don't know what it's like here in

Wyoming Territory, but where I come from, townsfolk are just as liable to burn a man as hang him for harming a woman."

The four men's faces reflected shock at what Jack had just said. Then one feebly replied, "We was just gonna hoorah her a bit. They wouldn't hang us for that, would they?"

But Jack could see the realization slowly coming over them, and with it fear, and he believed them. He believed they were drunk and stupid, but had not intended to murder or kidnap Amy Franklin or her son. He had questioned killers and thieves, and every man of this bunch came across as telling the truth.

He turned to the lanky rider. "Tell me your name."

"Yes, sir, Marshal. My name's Robert Deeds. I go by Slim."

Jack stood at least five inches over Slim. He stepped forward and glared down at the man. "Why should I believe any of you?"

Slim held his stare. "I can only speak for myself, Marshal. I ain't never harmed no woman in my life. The best I've ever been treated was by my mama. My pa treated her like the gold that she was. I swear, may I be struck dead, the onliest thing we was gonna do was scare her a bit and take those supplies."

Jack continued to stare at the man. "So tell me, Slim, how do you suppose your mama or your pa would feel if they knew what you had planned to do?"

At the question, the man broke eye contact and stared down at his boots. "Reckon Pa would disown me, and it would break my mama's heart."

Jack stepped back from the four, even turning his back on them as he stared across the valley. The wind had picked up, sliding down from the mountain peaks. The sweet pine smell was strong. An eagle screamed in the distance, and he watched a herd of mule deer move along the edge of the trees he had emerged from earlier. This was pretty country, and here he had killed his first man in Wyoming. He had just asked a man what his mama would think about his actions, but now Jack wondered what his would think. He watched the buzzards circling, lower now with the smell of death.

He turned back to the riders. "Who hired you?"

The question had come as a surprise to them. Almost as one they said, "Hull."

"That's right, Marshal," Holt Maize said. "We was all having a drink, and he came in, set 'em up, and asked us if we wanted to make ten bucks. We said sure. I mean, why not? We was a little turned off at the job, but ten bucks is ten bucks, and like we said, we was just gonna scare her a bit."

Jack made up his mind. "Slim, you and Maize bury Hull. You other two pull that wheel out of the bed. We're changing it."

Jack started for the wagon, but stopped and turned when Maize spoke.

"We ain't got a shovel."

"You have a stick, a knife, hands?"

Maize shook his head. "I don't want to mess up my knife diggin' in the dirt with it."

"Then get a stick, but get the hole dug and Hull buried."

Maize turned and kicked through the tall grass until he found a suitable stick. Jack watched him and Slim until they had begun digging, then turned back to the other two men. They already had the wheel out of the wagon and were loosening the hub. He could see one of the men knew what he was doing. Jack moved up and grasped the back of the wagon and lifted. With the other three wheels on the ground, the corner rose effortlessly for the big man.

Quickly, the two men had the broken wheel off and the old one back on. The older man fastened the hub and nodded to Jack, who carefully lowered the weight of the wagon onto the old wheel. Jack nodded at the man who had fastened the wheel. "What's your name?"

"Beau Clark, Marshal."

"You made short work of that wheel."

"I spent some time in the army as a wheelwright."

"You're good at it. You should start your own business."

Clark shook his head. "I hate the work, but Marshal, that wheel oughta be fine. I'd say it's good for quite a bit of travel."

Jack nodded, his face grim, realizing the wheelwright in Laramie had changed out a perfectly good wheel for a rotten one. "You two go help your friends with the hole."

With the four of them digging, even though they were all using sticks, the work went pretty fast. Nearing completion, Slim dropped his stick and began to gather large stones, stacking them near the hole. They had managed to dig to a depth of about three feet before hitting a rock layer that wouldn't be penetrated without a pick or sledge.

Jack walked over and took a look. "That'll have to do. Once you get those rocks piled on him, I don't think anything will bother him except maybe a grizzly. Put him in and get him covered."

The four men bent to pick up Hull.

"Wait," Jack said. He walked over to the body of the kidnapper and went through his pockets, pulling out a leather sack that clinked. Opening the sack, he dumped the contents into his big hand. Ten shiny double eagles lay exposed in the bright sun. He held it for the men to see. "Do you think Hull was paid two hundred dollars to only scare Amy Franklin and her son?"

Moments passed while they stared at the money. Then the youngest of the bunch spoke up. Beneath the dirt and pimples, it was questionable if he had yet passed his twentieth birthday. "Hull's dead. You gonna split that with us?"

Jack couldn't believe what he'd heard. The kid had missed his point entirely. He only had gold on his mind. The expressions of the other men showed their surprise at the kid's question. Jack hefted the coins in his hand, ignoring the kid's question. "No one gets paid two hundred dollars to scare a person. All of you would have been implicated in her kidnapping, and I promise you, there would have been a rope waiting for each one of you." He poured the coins back into the leather bag, pulled the drawstring shut, and dropped the bag into his coat pocket.

The kid's greedy eyes followed the bag to his pocket, then looked up at Jack.

He could see hate flaming behind those eyes. Keeping his eyes on the kid, Jack nodded toward the body. "Alright, go ahead and put Hull in his grave."

The kid hesitated, then with the others stooped, lifted Hull's body, and moved him to the hole, where they dropped him unceremoniously. Hull's right arm stretched over the edge of the hole. Maize kicked it from the edge, the forearm dropping across his bloody body.

Without being told, they began pushing the piled dirt on top of the outlaw. Once covered, the rocks were stacked, forming a rock mound.

When they were finished, Slim slapped his hands together to knock the dirt off. "He ain't got a marker."

Jack walked to the wagon and closed the tailgate, then turned back to look at Slim. "He doesn't deserve a marker. Now you boys shuck your rifles from the scabbards and put them in the wagon bed."

The pimply-faced kid glared at Jack. "You got our gold, and you got our sidearms, now you want our rifles? What if we run into Injuns? What are we gonna do then?"

Jack examined the face. Under the dirt, pimples, and sparse beard, the kid looked stubborn and mean. "First, this isn't your gold. You're lucky I don't take that ten dollars Hull gave you. I don't owe you an explanation, kid, but this gold is going to the woman Hull was going to kidnap. As far as the Indians, was I you, I'd run, but barring that, I'd suggest you be a good talker. Shuck those rifles."

The other three men had stopped with the younger man's

argument. Now they moved to their horses and pulled their rifles from the scabbards.

This was a touchy moment, but Jack was ready. Any one of the three could decide to open the ball. If one tried, they might all follow, but each stepped to the wagon and laid their rifles in the bed. All except the kid. He stood solid.

"What's your name?"

"Jinks Murray, but I'm known as Kid Murray, and I'm gonna keep my rifle."

Jack palmed his right revolver. "Here's your choice, Jinks Murray, you can give up your rifle or go for it. You're young to die, but that happens in this country all the time. Death doesn't care about age or wisdom or wealth. You go ahead and make your move."

Slim stepped to the boy's horse and, from the opposite side, pulled the rifle from its scabbard. "Don't be a fool, Jinks. I think this here marshal is about to give us a chance." He tossed the rifle to Jack, who caught it with his left hand, his right filled and steady with the Smith & Wesson.

Jinks glared at Slim. "I'll make you pay for this, you'll see. You're gonna regret takin' my rifle."

Jack laid the rifle in the bed of the wagon with the others. "Slim's right, boy. Get on your horse." He pointed toward the horses with his revolver. "That goes for all of you. Mount up. I'm giving you this one chance. Ride out of this country. I'd recommend south. I don't want to see you again. You get a break today, but this is the first and the last one from me. Leave Hull's horse where it stands. It doesn't look like much, but maybe the Franklins can use it."

"Looky yonder," Maize cried, pointing in the direction Amy and Davy Franklin had ridden. A group of riders were flogging horses toward them.

"Get out of here," Jack yelled.

The four men needed no further urging. They spun their

horses and slammed the spurs to them. The animals leaped forward, heading eastbound. Jack watched them grow smaller in the distance, finally hidden by the dust. He turned in time to greet the four women and two men.

Everyone was armed. All of the women wore pants and sat in the western saddles like they'd been born to them. Jack recognized Amy and the oldest, Josephine, the wife of dead General Franklin. In the lead, she was holding a Spencer and wearing a belt gun.

"Howdy, Amy, glad to see you made it alright. How's Davy?"

She gave Jack a smile. "He's fine. He was upset he couldn't come with us, but he stayed back at the ranch with Flo. Your horses are there relaxing."

Jack nodded. "Thanks." He turned to the general's widow. "Howdy, ma'am. Sorry to hear about the general and your son."

Her response was abrupt. "Thank you, Jack. Who were those riders, and why did they race out of here at our arrival?"

"Long story, ma'am. We can get started to the ranch, and I'll fill you in on the way."

Josephine turned to the younger man in the group. "Blaze, bring the wagon."

The cowhand swung down from his gray. "Yes, ma'am." He tied his horse to the back of the wagon and checked the wheel, then looked up at Amy. "Ma'am, this wheel don't look bad. Weren't no need to replace it." He then looked at the rotten replacement in the wagon and muttered something under his breath.

Josephine had been watching Jack. Her head snapped toward Blaze. "There'll be no swearing in my presence, young man. Do you understand me?"

Blaze ducked his head and nodded. "Yes, ma'am. Reckon I didn't think anyone could hear me."

"I can hear quite well. Forget about the wheel for now, and let's get started back to the ranch." She turned to the older man.

"Tripp, take Dot with you, and check the cattle over toward the south fork. You don't need to go all the way to the river. Plan on being back for supper."

Tripp nodded to Josephine, glanced at Dot, and turned his horse south, departing at a ground-eating lope. Dot gave Jack a smile before reining her horse after the departing cowhand.

Jack remembered Dorothy from the time he had visited the Franklins' ranch back east, midway through the war. He couldn't help but remember the black-haired young woman, a striking beauty in her white bridal gown. If he remembered correctly, she'd married a young lieutenant. The years hadn't hurt her. If anything, she had grown more beautiful. He grinned to himself as he thought, *Though she looks a mite different in those pants, and she does fill out that shirt proper like.* He reined his thoughts in. *Easy, Jack Sage, you're amongst a passel of women, and she's married. Put a bridle on your thoughts.* He stepped to Hull's horse, a tired-looking buckskin, took a moment to lengthen the stirrups and check the girth, then swung into the saddle.

Josephine turned back to the ranch and glanced over her shoulder at him. "Ride with me, Jack."

He bumped the buckskin in the flanks and eased up next to her.

"Tell me about those men," she said, "and the fresh grave."

Jack gave a short nod. "The one in the grave is Leander Hull. He decided to press his argument with his gun."

The older woman gave Jack an appraising look. "You don't seem to have changed much from the times you visited. David thought highly of you and your belief in justice. It's only fitting you now represent the law. I'm glad you're here. Now tell me what happened."

Jack explained what had transpired after Amy and Davy's departure.

"You don't think those men knew the plan was to kidnap Amy and my grandson?"

Jack shook his head. "Nope, I don't think they had any idea. Hull paid them ten bucks. None of those men would have planned on going any further than stealing the supplies and frightening her for ten dollars." His thoughts drifted to the kid. *I'm sure he didn't know, but I'm not too sure that young fella is above harming anything or anyone if the money's right. I hope I did right releasing him, but dad-gum it, a man can't be hanged for what he might do.*

"Jack!"

He turned to Josephine. "Yes, ma'am?"

"I asked you if they gave you any idea of who might have put them up to this."

"Oh, sorry. No, I think Hull was the only one who dealt with the money man, and he didn't tell them. They also didn't see him talking to anyone. He came into the saloon and hired them. I think most of them were drunk when they left town, all except Hull."

It was Josephine Franklin's turn to ride in silent thought. Jack welcomed it. He wanted to get his thoughts together, for he would have to question her, the women, and the men working for her. Hopefully, someone would be able to give him some direction. All he had found out so far was what he had been told by Carter Schofield, President Grant's liaison, and that wasn't much.

Another thing he hadn't figured out was why Josephine Franklin had decided to travel west and bring her entire family. This was dangerous country. Even if there weren't special circumstances like the Franklin men's murders, this was hard country, with hard men, Indians, and deadly weather. Why would she leave a successful ranch back east to start over out here, especially at her age? It was puzzling. Maybe the answer to that question would help answer some of the others.

They had been riding in a valley along a long timbered ridge extending east from the mountain range ahead. At the junction of the finger with the mountain's slope, he could make out a ranch house, bunkhouse, barn, and corrals. He could see all of the buildings were made with rough-hewn timbers, but were neatly chinked to keep out the winter wind. Out from the buildings about a hundred yards, a fence had been constructed. Riding through the gate, he let his eyes drift over the fence—solid. Whoever did the building knew what they were doing.

Down a slope from the house, a stream of clear water danced over rocks, gurgling its way into the valley. After pulling up at the water trough, in front of the barn, Jack remained in the saddle, examining the ranch headquarters. He turned to Josephine, who had also remained seated while the others stepped down. "How long have you folks been here?"

"We came out shortly after David and Warren. We've been here almost a year. I took the girls back for only a short time to complete the sale of our ranch back east, but we came right back, in the dead of winter."

"From what I hear of this country, you couldn't have come at a worse time."

Josephine swung down, and Jack followed.

"It was bad, Jack, but you've got to remember, we're from the northeast. We're used to cold weather, though it was pretty tough."

A cowhand, stocky, maybe eight inches over five feet tall, stepped up, took Josephine's reins, and motioned for Jack's.

"Jack, this is Monty," Josephine said.

Jack handed the man the reins with his left hand and extended his right. "Howdy. Jack Sage."

The man took his hand and grinned. "You must take a passel of feeding."

Jack returned the grin. "Now there's a fact." He joined Josephine as she strode toward the house. "These structures have been up for a while."

Davy and a blonde-headed girl of about nine years dashed from the stand of trees behind the house.

Josephine's stern countenance softened, and she broke into a smile. "You've met my grandson, Davy. The little girl with him is my youngest daughter, Flossie. We call her Flo. She was a surprise to both David and me." She knelt and swept the two into her arms. "What trouble have you two been up to?"

"Mama," Flossie said breathlessly, "we saw a baby mule deer, a fawn. It still has its spots. They are so pretty." She broke away from her mother and looked up at Jack, her head tilted back so she could see his face. "Mister, you are really tall. The only people I've seen as tall as you are the Cheyenne braves. They're taller than Tripp or Monty."

Davy extended his hand again. "Howdy, Marshal Sage. This here is my aunt Flo. I don't much understand that, because we're about the same age, but that's what Grammy and Mama tell me."

Jack laughed. "Yep, I agree with you, boy. Families can get a mite confusing sometimes."

Davy nodded. "But I don't call her aunt. I just call her Flo."

Flo put her hands on her hips. "That's because you aren't proper, David Warren Franklin, that's why."

The boy frowned for a second, then grinned. "You're funning me, Flo. I can tell."

The little girl broke into a grin. "You deserve it."

A soft but firm voice spoke behind Jack. "Don't tease your nephew, Flo. That's not nice."

Jack turned to find a young brown-eyed woman he didn't recognize.

3

He hadn't really noticed the other women riding with them because he had been intent on Josephine and her stern appearance, carrying her rifle and sidearm. But this young woman removed her hat as Jack turned, and shook her head. Shoulder-length, soft brown hair cascaded from under her hat and around her face. He was surprised. Which daughter was this?

"You don't remember me, do you?"

Jack shook his head. "I know I should, but I'm sorry, I don't."

Flo chimed in with a yell, "That's Lilly, Mr. Sage," her blue eyes dancing.

Josephine added, "You wouldn't remember her, Jack. The last time you visited was at Dot's wedding, and Lilly was only thirteen."

Jack, a wry grin on his face, cocked his head. "She's sure not thirteen now."

The matriarch of the family gave a soft, rich chuckle. "No, all my girls except Flo are grown and have become beautiful women, and when you add in Amy . . . Let me just say, it makes it very difficult for men to keep their minds about them. Now come inside. Teresa will have a pot of fresh coffee waiting, and I imagine there will be something good to go along with it. We have much to talk about."

Jack stepped aside to let Lilly proceed ahead of him, and followed the entourage into the house. Davy and Flo turned and race back toward the trees.

Lilly called after them, "Be careful out there. Keep your eyes open." She looked up at Jack and smiled. "They are always in the woods. We should probably bell them."

Jack laughed. "Aren't you concerned about Indians? I'm new to this part of the country, but I've heard there's trouble with the Cheyenne."

"We keep watch. We can't keep those free spirits locked in the house all the time." She stepped through the door and hung her hat on the hatrack, motioning for him to do the same. He followed her example and proceeded into the kitchen behind her. There, cups were steaming with coffee, and a large basin sat in the middle of the table, rounded over with fresh doughnuts. Cream and sugar beckoned to him from next to the coffeepot alongside the doughnuts.

Jack waited for Josephine and Lilly to sit. Josephine sat at the head of the table and motioned him next to her, while Lilly turned to help the young woman cooking at the stove.

"Jack," Josephine said, "this is Teresa, the best cook this side of the Canadian line. Stay on her good side, and she'll put at least twenty-five pounds on that skinny frame of yours."

"Sounds like a good plan, ma'am." Jack pulled the chair out and waited a moment more for Lilly before realizing she would be occupied in the kitchen. He lowered himself into his chair. "Pleased to meet you, Teresa."

"And you, *señor*. It is my pleasure."

"Help yourself, Jack," Josephine said.

With that, Jack reached for the sugar and cream. He dumped four spoons of sugar into his cup and filled the remaining space with cream. He stirred it gently so it wouldn't spill over the edge and took a sip. It was delicious.

"Jack, you drink your coffee just the way my son, Warren, did. In cold weather, that boy said it was the only way he could keep his energy up."

Jack grinned. "I used to say the same thing. Guess I didn't want to admit I just liked it that way. If a man hasn't eaten for a while, you can almost get a full meal with cream and sugar in your coffee." He reached for a doughnut. "Of course, I'd never turn down one of these, especially hot and fresh from the pot."

Josephine was quiet while Jack finished his first coffee and doughnuts. He watched Lilly move briskly about the kitchen. She reminded him of his long-dead wife, the same spirited yet graceful movements, and with the thoughts of his wife came the sweet smell and delicate feel of his long-dead son. The tightness in his chest began.

He gave an almost imperceptible shake of his head, forcing himself back to the present. His mind back on business, he turned to Josephine. She was watching him. He gave her a self-deprecating smile. "Sorry, your daughter reminded me of someone else, a long time ago."

Her return smile was gentle, unlike the woman he had seen ride up to him at the wagon. "Yes, I could see you had left us for a moment. She must have been very important to you."

You've got work to do, Jack thought, chastising himself. *These women are in trouble. Get yourself back on the trail.* "Yes, ma'am, she was, but that was a long time ago. Your troubles are what's important now."

Her face took on the stern look she had been wearing when Jack first saw her on the range. "You're right. Let's talk about what has happened and your plans." She focused her pale gray eyes on him.

Lilly stopped what she was doing, spoke to Teresa in Spanish, wiped her hands, and came to the table. She took the chair directly across from Jack.

Jack began. "Mrs. Franklin, I was given two orders from the president. Find the killers of the general and your son, and make sure you folks are safe."

"First, Jack, call me Jo. Mrs. Franklin was the general's wife. Unfortunately he is gone, and we are no longer back east. Second, up until now, I would have told you we were safe. During the last part of the winter, we helped out the Cheyenne. They're a proud people, but the snow was bad. We gave them a few head when I heard they were having a hard time finding game. I expect no trouble from them.

"The sheriff tried to tell us the murders were done by Blackfeet, but David was one of the few who were on good terms with them, and they range much farther north except when the buffalo are running. After David's and Warren's murders, there has been no attempt at violence toward anyone on the ranch."

"Until now," Jack said.

She leaned toward Jack, laid her forearms on the table, and clasped her hands together. "Yes, until now. I admit, things have become somewhat more difficult. We have lost a few head of cattle to rustlers, but I think the losses are spread throughout all of the ranches, not just us. There is one ranch owner who does not believe women should be running a ranch, but I don't give a dropped flapjack for his opinion. We are here. Here we'll stay, and I believe all of the girls are with me on this."

"Have you seen any strangers on your land, any drifters riding through? Is there a possibility the other ranchers may have gotten together to run you off your ranch?"

She shook her head. "No, to all three. I definitely don't think the rancher who feels I have taken on more than I can handle would harm us. In fact, though he thinks we should be back east, I'm sure he and his sons would help us if we needed it."

Lilly spoke up. "He might help, Mama, but they are a strange lot. Mr. Poling has spoken quite forcefully about us being out of here. I heard him in town say we were taking up good land, and we should all go back east or get married."

Jo shook her head. "He's just a crotchety old frontiersman looking for wives for his boys."

Lilly laughed. "He'll be looking a long time if he's expecting one of us to volunteer. Have you seen his sons? A bar of lye soap would scare them worse than a gun."

A grin tugged at the matriarch's face, but she suppressed it. "Be kind, Lilly. Those boys don't know any better. They grew up with their papa after their mama died."

Lilly nodded. "You're right, Mama. I should be more considerate." A tiny shudder ran through her body. "But they really smell bad."

Jack laughed. "There's been times I've been pretty ripe myself."

Lilly's face turned red. "I'm so sorry. I didn't mean to insinuate anything. I . . ."

Jack saw his comment had flustered the young woman. "Ma'am, I took no offense from what you said. I'm mighty sorry if my words were hurtful."

Lilly shook her head, her brown hair floating around her shoulders. "No. I knew you meant nothing. It just gave me a moment to realize how harsh my comment sounded. I'm the one who should be sorry."

"No one need be sorry," Jo said, bringing the conversation back, and directing her gaze to Jack. "A fact is a fact. They do smell bad, but it doesn't make them bad people. I do not suspect them. In fact, I don't know whom to suspect. The other rancher is German, and I believe he is extremely honest, if a little headstrong. His mother lives with him. They both came over from the old country. She strikes me as a very respectable lady." Jo lifted her right shoulder in a small shrug. "It looks like if there are any answers to be found, you'll have to dig them out."

Lilly gave a small giggle. "Mr. Schmidt is quite taken with Amy."

Her comment brought a smile to Jo's lips. "Yes, I believe he is. He has been down here several times on the pretext to see how we are managing with the loss of the general and Warren, but I get the feeling his interests lie in Amy's direction."

Lilly giggled again. "Oh, yes, they do, and Davy seems to also like him."

Jo's face switched back to that of the stern ranch owner. "Let's not gossip, Lilly. We'll have to wait and see how Amy proceeds."

Jack took another sip of his coffee and turned the conversation back on track. "I'm here to find the guilty party or parties, and that's what I'll do, ma'am. There's a lot of territory for me to cover, looking and asking questions. I want to talk to both of the ranchers. When I'm done, I'll head back to town. There's a wheelwright who might be able to shed some light on the subject before he leaves town."

Wrinkles furrowed Lilly's brow, her eyes seeking Jack's. "Is he leaving town?"

"He will after I talk to him."

Realization of what Jack meant flooded her face, clearing her brow and bringing a twinkle to her brown eyes. "Oh, I see."

"His name is Toler, Jack, and I have to admit to being uncomfortable around him." Jo said. "We've used him several times, but he's always seemed a little obsequious."

"I've noticed that too, Mama, and I don't like the way he looks at us, or Flo." At the mention of Flo, Jo's head snapped toward her daughter. "Has he made any moves toward your sister?"

"No, Mama, he just stares at her."

The corners of Jo's eyes pulled together, and her jaw set while contemplating Lilly's comment. "I think I shall have a conversation with Mr. Toler the next time we go to town."

Mr. Toler won't be in town by then, Jack thought.

Jo stood. "Bring your coffee into the parlor, Jack. Teresa and

Lilly need to start supper. Dot and Tripp should be getting back soon, and I expect Amy will be in with the children any time. Dark comes fast in these mountains. Supper will give you the opportunity to meet the rest of the hands. We have only two more. Your things have been put in the bunkhouse. If we had more room, we'd love to have you in the main house, but unfortunately, it's not quite large enough yet. I hope you don't mind."

Jack stood. "Teresa, those were about the best doughnuts this old lawman has ever eaten. I'm much obliged."

Beaming, Teresa turned to Jack. "I'm glad you like them, *señor*. There are plenty more. When I make them, I have to make very many. Everyone likes them, especially the cowhands."

"I can understand why." He nodded and turned to follow Jo. "Ma'am, the bunkhouse is just right for me. I'm grateful for the bed, roof and especially the meals. In fact, I have a favor to ask."

Jo Franklin lowered herself into a soft-cushioned cowhide chair. "Before you begin, Jack, I need to tell you something. You might have been looking for Dot's husband, Bill. He is no longer with us. Like so many others, the poor boy was killed in the war shortly after he and Dot were married. She is recovering, faster now thanks to Monty, but I wouldn't want a question about him coming up. Not yet."

Stunned, Jack shook his head. " Jo, I hadn't heard. I am sure sorry. I only met him at the wedding, but he seemed like a mighty nice fella."

"He was, but life goes on. You had a question for me?" Jo's posture signaled her desire to change the subject.

Jack gave a single nod. "As I said, I'm going to be covering a lot of this country. I'd be obliged if I could make this my base of operations. I'll be needing to leave what animals I don't use and switch out when I come back through. That means they'll be using your facilities and your feed. If that's not too presumptive of me. I'll reimburse you for your expenses."

Jo smiled. "Of course you and your animals are welcome here

as long as you'd like to stay. No need for reimbursement. You're looking for the killers who took a large piece of my life. You are most welcome."

"Thanks, Jo, but I'd like to reimburse you what I'd pay if I were staying in a hotel and the animals in a stable. It comes from the government, and they can darn well afford to pay."

Jo Franklin's face turned stern, and her voice was sharp. "Now listen to me, Marshal, you will not pay me for my hospitality. It is given freely. Do you understand?"

Jack grinned. "Mighty clear, ma'am. Now what I'd like to do is check on my stock and clean up a mite."

She smiled back. "That'll be fine, Jack. We'll see you at supper. We can talk more then."

Jack took his hat from the rack, stepped outside, and leveled it on his head. It was a new, gray Stetson he had picked up in Denver. It seemed he was harder on hats than anything else.

He stepped from the last step of the porch as Amy walked to the house from the woods, each hand clasping a child's hand. Flo and Davy appeared less than thrilled to be returning home.

"It ain't dark yet, Ma. I don't see why we have to come in."

"It'll be dark soon. I wouldn't want you two to run into an ornery old grizzly out there in the twilight."

Flo looked up at her sister-in-law. "We'd be careful, Amy. I promise we would."

"I'm sure you would, but both of you have your chores to take care of before supper, or have you forgotten?"

They both shook their head, and Davy responded, "No, ma'am. We remember." He looked up and saw Jack. His face lit up. "Hi, Marshal Sage. Are you going to catch Grandpa David's and Pa's killers?"

Jack knelt where he could more easily look into the intense, matching blue eyes of the two children. "I sure am, and they'll be severely punished."

Flo pointed at his two Smith & Wessons. "By those?"

"Well, now, I have to admit, I don't rightly know. My goal is to arrest the person or persons who are guilty and take them in to stand trial, but if they put up an argument, I might have to use these." His hands drifted unconsciously to touch the butts of the revolvers.

Davy stared at the guns. "Then I hope they argue. I hope they argue real bad. I hope they argue so much you have to kill them like they killed Pa and Grandpa Franklin."

Amy squeezed her son's hand. "That isn't right, Davy. You shouldn't wish someone dead."

Davy looked up at Amy, his youthful forehead wrinkled in puzzlement. "But you do, Ma. I heard you tell Grammy you wished you could shoot whoever murdered Grandpa Franklin and Pa."

Amy glanced at Jack, rolling her eyes, then looked back down at her son. "I was upset when I said that. I'm sorry you heard me. It's not right for me to wish someone else dead either. Now don't you have some work to do?"

Davy stared up at his ma, his young face still wrinkled with confusion, but his eyes trusting. Then making up his mind, he released Amy's hand, said, "Yes, ma'am," and raced to the barn.

The door from the kitchen opened, and Lilly stepped out, carrying a basket. She saw Flo. "I'm glad you made it back. I was beginning to wonder. Are you going to help me? We need to pick up the eggs, then feed and lock up the chickens, or the varmints might get them."

Flo's face broke into a wide grin. "I'm ready. Let's go see the little biddies." She raced up the stairs, across the porch, and thrust her tiny hand into her sister's.

Jack watched the two of them leap from the porch and over the steps at the side of the house. A smile spread across his face, and he shook his head. "One minute dejected, and the next minute racing away with excitement. Kids are amazing."

Amy smiled. "Yes, they are, but Davy has had a difficult time with the loss of his father, more so, I think, than Flo. She seems to have adjusted much better. I wonder if women aren't better at handling loss than men."

Jack thought of Yasmina and his baby again. His smile disappeared, and the corners of his mouth edged almost imperceptibly down. "Yes, I think maybe you're right." He took a deep breath. "But girl or boy, they're resilient. They'll both recover, and it looks like they are well on their way."

He turned to Amy. "It's none of my business, but how are you doing? This must be really hard on you. Not only have you lost your husband, but you're out here far away from your family."

She placed a hand on his arm. "Thank you for asking, Jack. I'm doing well. I have a wonderful family here. Mama Franklin took me in like her own daughter.

"I really couldn't stay back east. My family there is wonderful, but they were much too obliging, and I felt Davy needed the strength of the west. When Mama Franklin invited Davy and me to join them, I was happy and relieved to say yes. I love it out here. Though my parents and sisters cannot understand what I see in this wilderness."

Her hand had remained on his arm through her response. Jack felt the light weight through his coat. He saw her recognize it was still there. She jerked it away.

"I'm sorry. I didn't mean . . ."

"That's alright, ma'am. I understand losing someone important, and I definitely can relate to being around folks when they're set on helping. It becomes downright smothering."

She threw her head back, exposing a long graceful neck, and let out a single laugh that rang through the trees. "Yes, that is exactly what it is, smothering." Her eyes glanced to his neck for a moment, her smile dropped, and she looked away. "I've got to be getting inside. I need to clean up and help with supper. There'll be some big appetites showing up before long. Thank you, Jack."

"Think nothing of it."

After she passed, his hand went up to his bandanna where it had loosened on his neck.

His bandanna had exposed a portion of the healed, but still proud flesh from a rope. The scarred flesh circled his neck, exposing the fact that once, someone had attempted to hang him. There were moments, like now, he could still feel the rope draw tight around his neck. *The scar is part of me,* Jack thought, *as much as a leg or hand.* He tightened the bandanna, coughed, and started for the barn to check on his animals.

Halfway to the barn, Jack stopped and checked to ensure his revolvers were loose. Rounding the point, still at least a mile away, three riders approached the ranch. "Riders approaching," Jack called, to alert those in and out of the house.

4

Monty stepped out of the barn with the man who had taken his horse and one other. Davy was alongside. Monty gazed at the approaching riders. "Tripp, Dot, and the dude from Laramie. Name's Bowden Jessup. He's a lawyer. Supposed to be helpin' Jo with legal papers."

The other, an older cowhand, spit and, with his left hand, wiped tobacco juice from his goatee. "Too blamed slick for me."

Jack looked him over. In his forties, run-over boots, an old Stetson, wrinkled and stained with sweat. He looked to be about six inches taller than five feet. His shirt hung off shoulders too wide for his height. While Jack looked the older man over, he was returning the examination.

He spit again and repeated the action with his left hand. "I'd sure hate to be yore horse, pardner. My back would never stop hurtin'."

"I'd hate to be yours, getting that tobacco juice on me all the time."

The man's flinty, light brown eyes held his gaze for another second, and he extended his hand. "Name's Quint Mason." He nodded at Jack's revolvers. "You any good with those, or they just on your hips to slow your growth?"

"I get by." He took Quint's big gnarly hand in his and felt the hard calluses begin to tighten like a rope pulling tight around a bull's head. He saw Monty shaking his head from the corner of his eye, and Davy grinning.

All right, Mr. Quint Mason, Jack thought, *you're a big talker. Let's just see if you can back it up.* Jack began squeezing only enough to match the cowhand's increasing grip. As they squeezed, the riders neared. Jack could see the oncoming Tripp had joined Monty in the headshaking and had said something to Dot. She looked at the hands locked together and grinned with Davy.

The big hand of Quint's slowly tightened against Jack's grip. The mountain air was growing cool, but Jack could see a fine sheen of perspiration over Quint's bent and damaged nose.

Finally the pressure ceased to tighten, and Jack gave a mental sigh of relief. There for a minute, he thought the older man was going to outdo him. *All right, Quint,* he thought, *it's time for a few words from the good book.* An almost invisible smile touched his lips as he began to tighten against Quint's hand. He could feel his opponent's fingers, clenched though they were, begin to squeeze together. A second later, he felt the man's index finger roll, and knew the pain it must have brought Quint, but the cowhand wouldn't give up.

At the last minute, knowing he was about to break the older man's hand, Jack turned loose and jerked his hand away. Both men stood rubbing their aching hands. "Not a bad grip you've got there, *old-timer,*" Jack said with a grin.

Quint faked a glare at Jack, but he could see the gratitude in the older man's eyes. "Careful, young feller, the last man who called me an old-timer is still laid up in Denver's fancy hospital. I will say that paw of yourn can pull mighty tight. Keep practicing, and maybe one day you'll be able to handle a man's grip."

Everyone laughed at Quint's bravado, for all but Davy had seen the surprised desperation in his eyes only moments before.

Tripp had stepped down from his horse and glanced at Jessup, who was giving Dot a hand down. He walked forward to Jack. "We didn't get a chance to meet on the trail. I'd like to thank you for saving Miss Amy and Davy. I'm Tripp Singletary." He extended his hand.

Jack, still rubbing his, looked down at the offered hand. "Am I safe? I don't think my hand'll take any more punishment." At that, everyone laughed again. Jack shook the man's hand. He had joked, but his hand ached like the blazes. He could just imagine what Quint Mason's must be feeling like. The older man stood nonchalantly, his thumbs hooked into his gunbelt.

Dot stepped forward and flung her arms around Jack's neck, planting a big kiss on his dirty cheek. She dropped her arms and stepped back, unfazed by her action. "Thank you so much for saving Amy and Davy. I'm just so glad you were there." Her face darkened. "I'd like to have been there myself. I would've sent a few of those owlhoots to accompany their friend."

Monty nodded. "She'd a done it, too. You should see that girl shoot."

Jack saw Dot's face instantly flush. He glanced at Monty, who, though it was hard to tell under the sun- and windburn, was showing a little red from his outburst.

"Well, yes, I just imagine she would," the newcomer said, stepping forward to shake Jack's hand. "My name is Bowden Jessup, attorney at law. Let me add my gratitude to Miss Franklin's. Your timely arrival thwarted the brigands' attack."

Jack took the man's hand. It was a firm handshake that hinted at the promise of reserve strength biding its time in the smooth hands. The man was a couple of inches over six feet and filled the unpadded shoulders of his coat, the sleeves effectively tailored to allow bulging biceps to hide in the loose cloth. The lawyer wore a

Colt on his right hip, barrel extending slightly below his sheepskin-collared riding coat. "Thanks, Jessup. Nice to meet you." Jack turned from the lawyer and addressed the group. "If you folks will forgive me, I've got to find some horse liniment to rub on my hand, and then take care of my animals. I'll see you for supper."

Davy turned to go with him, but Dot said, "Davy, shouldn't you get cleaned up for supper. Your mama might be upset if you show up at the table smelling of horse apples."

"Aw, Aunt Dot." He turned and trudged dejectedly toward the house.

Tripp glanced at Jessup. "If you like, I'll take your horse into the barn."

Jessup, unhesitatingly, passed the reins to the foreman and turned to Dot, offering his arm. "Miss Dot, would you accompany me? I have business with your mother."

Monty stepped forward to grasp the reins of her horse. Jack didn't miss the touching of Dot's and Monty's hands as they transferred the reins. The two didn't notice because they were both looking at each other, faint smiles visible. Jack also saw that Jessup didn't miss the interchange, and the lawyer's face darkened. Jack thought, *It might be well to check out this attorney and his business.*

Stepping into the barn, he spotted his four animals eating in stalls on the west side. He headed for Smokey first. The big grulla turned his head toward him and let out a low whinny. At the sound, Stonewall, his mule, turned, spotted Jack, and watched him approach. Pepper, his chestnut gelding, and Thunder, his gray gelding, both ignored him. Their heads were down in their troughs, munching oats someone had given them. Jack stopped at each one, talking to them and rubbing their sides and necks.

Quint, unsaddling and giving a rubdown to Jessup's horse, called over, "Those are some fine animals you've got there. Don't usually see a man keep a string with him, specially one including a mule."

"Long story. Smokey and my mule, Stonewall, have been with me the longest, but the other two, Pepper and Thunder, have been around for a couple of years." Jack looked towards Tripp, who had fed and was brushing down his horse. "How'd you know the general?"

There was quiet in the barn. All that could be heard were the brushes on the horses and the animals chewing. After a while Tripp spoke. "He bought a herd from me in Kansas and then hired me to drive them out here. We pushed 'em here with the same ten drovers who hired on in Uvalde. Quint, Monty, Blaze, and me hung around, at General Franklin's request. The others took their pay and a bonus, for getting them cattle all the way here, and took off for warmer country. I think we made the right decision to hang around. Of course, everybody liked him and his son."

"So the six of you took care of the cattle and built these buildings?"

Quint cleared his throat and looked at Tripp. The man nodded, and Quint said, his Texas drawl heavy, "Not just six. All the women came out, almost right from the start. They pitched in and worked about as hard as any man. Even little Flo and Davy were fetchin' and totin' from can to cain't. Late in the afternoon, you'd find the little tykes all worn out. They'd be curled up in a corner, sound asleep. That whole family's hard workers. We was just finishin' when the general and Warren got killed. It's a dirty shame. Like to have broken Mrs. Franklin's heart."

Jack shook his head. "Warren's wife?"

Tripp responded, "No, sir, the general's wife. I've never seen a woman as strong as she is, but when we brought the general in, I surely thought she might try to join him. She was torn up. She did some almighty praying during that time. Through the window, we could see her on her knees in her room, day after day. Then one day she gets up, wipes her eyes, and goes back to work.

It was a thing to see. I swear there ain't no man stronger than either of those two women."

Monty stopped brushing Dot's horse, straightened, and shoved his hat to the back of his head. "I'll tell you, Marshal Sage, I've seen a lot of death and families torn apart, but this is about the strongest family I've ever seen. If it's possible for a bunch of women to make a go of ranching, this'll be the ones."

Tripp cleared his throat and continued, "Miss Amy mourned, but she never fell apart. I suspect she was holding it together for Davy. Whatever the reason, she pushed head-on into the work around here, taking up the slack for Mrs. Franklin, Jo, until she was ready to take the reins again. She done real good."

Jack looked at each of the solemn men. "Who found them?"

Monty pitched in, "Me and Tripp. They hadn't shown up for dinner. We didn't think much of it. We'd finished all of the buildings, and they had gone out to get an elk. We figured they'd just spent the night out, but come noon the next day and they hadn't shown up, we rode out to see if they needed any help. We still didn't expect what we found. Both of them shot dead. A single bullet in the forehead. There they lay, bushwhacked. The horses were grazing nearby. I'm astonished the buzzards or coyotes hadn't bothered them, but they ain't. They were just stretched out in the grass."

Quint spit. "I seen that kind of work before. We all have. You was in the war, too." It wasn't a question.

Jack nodded.

"Was a sniper did it. We all rode out and looked around beyond where they'd fallen. They were in a tallgrass area of the valley. A rock outcropping jutted out from the mountainside about two hundred yards in front of them. That's where the sniper, the dirty bushwhacker, laid up and waited. They never knowed nothing, never had a chance."

Jack had moved over to Quint and was helping him finish. "Did you find anything?"

Tripp spoke again. "We did. We found tracks, an unshod horse's tracks and moccasin tracks. There was a Blackfeet arrow lying next to where the shooter had fired from, so naturally our fine sheriff declares they was killed by Blackfeet Indians. A five-year-old could tell it was a setup. There's no way this was an Indian's doing. I don't know why they were murdered, but I know who it wasn't. It dang sure wasn't Indians."

Suddenly a dinner bell began ringing. The piercing clang of metal against metal carried down the valley.

Tripp grinned. "Teresa can bang that triangle about as loud as any man cook I've ever known. Let's go eat."

"Thanks for the information."

Quint spit, wiped his goatee, and nodded at Jack's revolvers. "No problem, Marshal. We want the lowlife who did this brought to justice. A gun or a rope will do just fine."

Jack followed the men into the kitchen through the side door. He hadn't had time to get cleaned up, and he knew he was grimy, but he fit in with the other men except for Jessup, who had changed clothes and looked like he'd just stepped out of one of the new Montgomery Ward catalogues.

All of the women had managed to clean up. Jack looked around at each. Jo was right. She had a bevy of beauties, and they'd also caught Davy. He looked like he'd been dragged through a tub. Someone had tried to comb his unruly black hair, but a cowlick still pointed in all directions.

Jack pulled out a chair at the far end of the table with the rest of the cowhands, but Jo wouldn't have it. "Come up here and sit by me, Jack, across from Flo. Don't worry about dirt. We've all eaten with dirt. Shoot, we live with it every day."

He smiled at Teresa as he sat to Jo's left. Davy sat to his left, and just past him was an open chair, where Jack figured Amy would sit, and next was Dot. Beside Dot, Monty had managed to grab the chair. Across from Amy was another empty chair. Jessup sat across the table from Dot. The cowhands crowded in, leaving an open seat for Teresa. Amy and Lilly were up helping Teresa with the food. Once it was all placed on the table, everyone sat.

Once the group was seated, Jo said, "Jack, you're new here. We say grace before every meal." She looked at her grandson. "Davy, would you do the honors tonight?"

Davy nodded to his grandmother. "Yes, ma'am." He bowed his head, along with everyone else. "Lord, we're mighty thankful for this food you've set before us. We're asking you to bless it to our health, and Lord, we've got a special guest with us tonight, Marshal Sage. He's here to find the killers of my pa and my grandpa. Please help him find them and help him send them where they won't do no more harm to anyone. Amen."

Before anyone could say anything, Tripp spoke up. "That was a mighty righteous prayer, Davy. I'm sure the Good Lord heard every word and will show Marshal Sage the way."

Davy looked down the table at Tripp. "I sure hope so, Mr. Tripp. I surely do."

Jack patted the boy on his shoulder. "Son, I agree with Tripp. That was an excellent prayer, and I thank you for it."

The boy beamed up at Jack. "Thank you, sir."

Jo looked around the table. "Alright, boys, dig in. It's way too late to pretend you have manners."

Laughter rippled around the table, breaking the spell. Dishes began to clink, and conversation picked up between the chewing. Amy looked Jack's way. "Will you leave in the morning?"

"I plan on it. Of course, I planned on getting cleaned up before supper. Look how that worked out."

She smiled back at him. "You're not that bad, Jack. You should have seen us when the buildings were going up. We were all filthy every night. If it weren't for Mama Franklin, we'd never have bathed, but she kept us civilized."

Jack shook his head. "I can't imagine you ever being dirty."

Davy giggled and looked at his ma. She tried to give him a warning look through her smiling face. He turned to Jack. "Marshal Sage, you didn't see Ma when the barn was being built. Why, she got about as dirty as Mr. Quint."

Jack heard a foot make contact with a small leg.

Davy let out a fake cry. "Ow, Ma. Why'd you kick me?"

Flo giggled from across the table. "Marshal Sage, you should have seen Davy and Mr. Quint. They looked like great big mud balls." The mental picture set her off, and she burst out laughing. Her laugh was infectious. Everyone joined in.

Quint growled at Flo and Davy, "You young'uns best be careful. When I need to spit this chewin' tobacco, there's no tellin' what direction I may fire it in."

Davy laughed again, and Flo shuddered.

Jo looked at Jack. "Welcome to the Franklin family, Jack. Unruly at all ages."

"It's mighty fine, ma'am. I like hearing laughter. In my line of work, I don't often hear it."

"Yes, I can imagine. Amy told me she noticed a scar on your neck. Do you mind talking about it?"

"No, ma'am. I surely don't." He reached up, untied his bandanna, and pulled it off. Flo gasped, and quiet took over the table.

Quint broke the awkward silence. "Looks like you got on the wrong end of a rope, but you're still around. Most folks with those kinds of scars don't have another opportunity to say a word."

Jack looked at Quint and then around the table. All the looks he saw were curious and concerned except for Jessup. A look of disdain momentarily appeared in his wrinkled brow and pursed lips before he controlled it and returned to his normal haughty gaze.

"Quint, you speak gospel. It was my fault. I was trailing a bunch of killers, down Silver City way. I got a little too complacent, and they waylaid me and did their best to hang me, which was almost good enough. However, I had a rotten limb and a bit of luck on my side."

Davy stared up at Jack's neck. "That don't look too lucky to me."

Again Quint spoke up. "He's sittin' here talking to you, boy. I'd call that mighty lucky."

Davy couldn't take his eyes off the scar. "Can I touch it, Marshal Sage?"

5

Amy, her eyes wide with shock, said, "David Franklin, don't be so rude."
Jack shook his head. "He's not rude, ma'am, he's just curious. Sure, button, you can touch it."

Davy stretched to reach Jack's neck and gently ran his fingers over the twisted flesh. "Does it hurt?"

"Not a bit," Jack lied, for there were days it still burned like fire.

"Did you catch up with them?"

Jack nodded and glanced down the table at Quint. He was developing a real liking for the older man. "I sure did, Davy."

"Now that's enough, Davy," Jo said. "Your food is getting cold."

The matriarch had spoken, and the spell was broken. Jack wrapped the bandanna around his neck, tied it, and went back to eating.

Jo asked, "So, when did you hear about us?"

"While I was in New Mexico. A representative of the president contacted me. President Grant thought very highly of General Franklin and is concerned about you running a ranch in this territory."

"Believe me, Jack, I also have my concerns, but this is what David thought was best for the family, as do I. We can make a good life here, and I plan on doing it, concerns or no."

Jack was looking at Jo when the bullet crashed through the window, clipped the black bow in Jo's hair, and plowed into the cabinet behind her. Following the crash of the bullet, the distant boom of a big rifle rocked through the house.

"Get down!" Jack yelled as he dove for Jo. He was airborne, his body flying over the top of the table, his arms and chest contacting and covering her when the second bullet arrived. The report was not so loud, sounding more like a Winchester. He felt the sting of the lead burning across his back at the second shot. His momentum carried Jo over backwards, Jack's big right hand wrapped around the back of her head to give her protection and cushion her crash against the floor. He heard the whoosh of air escape her lungs when the weight of his one-hundred-and-ninety-pound body landed on top of her.

Quint leaped to close the shutters of the window, but no third shot sounded. Tripp led the charge out the door and into the dark, making themselves perfect targets for anyone who might be out there, but there was only the sound of a running horse.

Davy and Flo were thrust under the table by Amy and Teresa. Jessup was able to get there with no help from anyone. He slipped out from under the heavy pine table, along with the kids. He stood and straightened his coat. Everyone was rushing to check on Jo. The crash and loss of air had dazed her. Jack stood, lifting her in his arms.

Amy grabbed his arm as she felt her mother-in-law's forehead. "This way, Jack. You can put her on her bed."

Jo began blinking, took a deep breath, and looked up. "Put me down, Jack. I'm fine."

He continued to hold her while following Amy toward her bedroom. "Maybe you should lie down for a while. You took a nasty fall."

She slapped him on his shoulder. "Nonsense. Put me down."

He grinned at her. "It's not often I get to hold a beautiful woman in my arms. Maybe I should just hang on."

Her eyes narrowed in mock anger. "Jack Sage, if you don't put me down right now, I'll draw my derringer."

Jack had made his way to the chair she had chosen earlier in the parlor. "I sure don't want you in trouble with the law for shooting a marshal." He lowered her into the chair.

Amy knelt next to her, with the other women gathered around. Flo, tears streaming down her little face, ran to her and leaped into her arms. "Mama, are you all right? I was so worried about you."

She hugged her daughter close. "There, there, my little sweet. I am just fine." With a twinkle in her eye, she looked at Jack. "I was doing quite well until this buffalo-sized man fell on me. Goodness sakes alive, Jack. You about smashed me like a tumblebug."

Quint moseyed up with the other men. He looked at the blood soaking through Jack's shirt. "I reckon we all didn't escape unhurt."

Amy turned to look at Quint, who nodded at Jack's back. She grabbed his arm and pulled him around so she and everyone else could see. Above his shoulder blades, where his thick neck joined, his shirt was sliced as if by a knife. The bullet had cut along his neck for about six inches, leaving a shallow channel from which blood ran down his back. She turned him around and started unbuttoning his shirt.

"Whoa now, hold on, little lady. There's no call to be undressing me here in front of the whole world."

Jo had seen Jack's wound. "That was close, boy. You could've been killed."

Jack grinned at her. "Ma'am, I'm a lucky man. You wouldn't believe how many times that's been said to me."

Lilly was standing next to her mama. Jo pushed against her

arm. "Lilly, go get the bullet-wound kit. We'll get this fixed up right now."

Jack shook his head. "Ma'am, that's not necessary. I imagine Tripp or Quint could do the job in the bunkhouse. There isn't any use for me to get undressed here in your living room and get blood all over your house."

Jack glanced at Quint for help, but found the wide-shouldered cowhand grinning at his discomfort.

Amy continued to unbutton his shirt. "Look, Jack. Let us fix this. We've dealt with bullet wounds before. You don't want it to get infected, do you?"

He knew he was painted into a corner. Realizing the shortest amount of misery would be in allowing these women to fuss over him, he reluctantly consented. "Alright, but does everyone need to be here?"

Jo looked around the room.

Tripp spoke up. "Come on, boys. Let's see if we can find any sign of that feller."

Quint was the last one out of the house. Stepping to the door, he turned. "Miss Amy, you take good care of that young feller. He seems to be mighty fragile."

Jack's eyes narrowed while he watch Quint's shoulders jerking in laughter, but he said nothing. Teresa brought a basin of hot water and several strips of clean linen, placing them on a side table.

Amy unbuttoned his long john top and pulled the sleeves down his arms, baring his thick back and chest and exposing the scars.

Jo remained seated, though she appeared to be feeling much better. The parlor was still full of people, though the cowhands had left. The matriarch of the family began directing her brood. "Flo, you and Davy go get ready for bed. Teresa, you, Lilly, and Dot get started on the kitchen."

"Yes, *señora*," Teresa said, and with the other two women

hurried to the next room. Within minutes dishes were clinking, mixed with whispering and the occasional giggle. Amy was busy at Jack's back.

When she wiped the clean wet cloth across Jack's wound, the water burned like fire in the bullet's crease.

Jack winced in surprise at the first touch, then relaxed. "From the feel of it, I can tell it's not deep. I appreciate you cleaning it up, but it should heal pretty fast."

While Amy's one hand held the wet cloth and cleansed the wound, the fingers of the other hand gently caressed his damaged neck and the puckered bullet scar in his left shoulder. "You've taken some punishment, Jack. Now you're going to have another scar across your shoulders."

Jo thoughtfully watched as Amy patched up the thick-chested man. "Jack, you know you saved my life."

"Mrs. Franklin, if I did, it was my greatest pleasure. I hope you aren't too sore from that fall I caused."

"I will forever be in your debt. Because of you, I'll be able to watch my youngest join her sisters and hopefully marry a strong man like you. You did me a great service this night. One I shall never forget."

Amy patted his shoulder. "I think we've got you fixed up for tonight. See me before you leave tomorrow, and I'll check the wound again to make sure there's no infection setting in."

Jack quickly slipped his long john top over his shoulders and buttoned it. He reached for his shirt, but Amy jerked it away.

"We'll darn it tonight. It'll be good as new in the morning."

Jack grinned at her. "My goodness, ma'am, you didn't take me to raise."

She gave him a sweet, almost sad smile. "Somebody should."

He felt the sincerity and concern from her dark green eyes. An emotion he had tamped down on occasion in the past rose in his chest. Standing before him was a beautiful woman, her blonde hair falling past her shoulders, slightly tousled now, around a wide honest face. "Well . . . uh . . . many thanks." He turned to head out the door for the bunkhouse and caught sight of Jessup sitting in a wingback chair in a dark corner of the house. He stood when Jack saw him.

"Mrs. Franklin, I'll speak with you tomorrow about those legal papers. I'm glad you're safe."

"Thank you, Bowden. I'm hoping tomorrow will be much less exciting than today."

Jessup nodded, took his hat, and preceded Jack through the door.

Jack grabbed his Stetson and stepped outside to the porch. There was a light rain falling, as was the temperature. It would be chilly tonight. This was a good night not to be on the trail. A real bed would be welcome. He took a deep breath, inhaling the sweet, sharp fragrance of the wet pines. The smell relaxed him. He could hear a covey of mountain quail getting together in the trees, lightly fluttering and calling. On the stream there was the crash of bigger birds, turkeys banging against limbs as their big wings lifted them to safety. They let out an occasional yelp, calling those still on the ground to join them.

The forest had little regard for man. The fact that one had tried to kill another tonight changed nothing. Trees would continue to grow, and water would continue to flow. The animals lived and died and thought little of man.

Jack watched Jessup make his way to the bunkhouse. He was a strange man. He had dove under the table with the children instead of trying to thrust them under first or, like Quint, leaping up to close the shutters of the window. His first thoughts had been for himself and his self-preservation. *I don't know if you're involved in this,* Jack thought, *but I will find more out about you.*

His thoughts went to the shooter. Why had the man missed? The first shot had been so close. No more than an inch to the right, and Jo would no longer be alive. Jack racked his mind, but he could find nothing to explain it. Maybe the bullet had clipped an unseen twig. Maybe the sniper had pulled the trigger instead of squeezing it. Maybe the man had anticipated the shot and bucked the recoil.

He stepped off the porch and headed for the bunkhouse. *No, he thought, this man's been at this a long time. He doesn't make rookie mistakes. There had to be another reason for him missing tonight.*

The sprinkles felt cold on his hands as he walked across the yard. A sudden gust of wind made him grab for his hat, then the wind was gone. *Could that be it? Could it have been an unexpected wind gust? Maybe.* He opened the door and stepped into the bunkhouse. Quint was still dressed and pulling on a heavier coat. "You fellas putting out a watch tonight?"

Tripp nodded. "Yep. This caught us by surprise, but we can't be surprised again. We'll be standing guard every night until whoever is responsible for this is caught." He gave Jack a pointed look.

"I'm planning on getting right on it. I'll be pulling out in the morning, but I'd be glad to toss my name in the hat for tonight. That'll shorten up the watch for the rest of you."

Tripp shook his head. "Thanks, but there's four of us. None will stand watch more than two hours. We want you rested up so you can figure out who's doing this. Whoever it is needs to be stopped as soon as possible."

Jack sat on the edge of the bunk where his saddlebags and rifle were laid. He opened one side of the bag and took out four of his horse cookies. They were made of molasses, apples, oatmeal, and carrots. He had gotten the recipe from Truman Shelby, who had sold him Pepper and Thunder. The animals loved them, and so did he. He tossed one to Tripp and then to each of the cowhands. He started to throw one to Jessup, but the man had already crawled into his bunk and turned his face to the wall. Jack shrugged. *So be it.*

Quint caught his and looked at it. "Whatcha doing, lawman, giving us horse food?"

"You bet it is. That's the best-tasting horse cookies you'll ever slap a gum over. I eat them on the trail for treats."

The young puncher Blaze was the first to try. He bit off a small corner and chewed for a minute, then took a bigger bite. "If any of you boys don't want yours, just pass it my way. I know what to do with it." He nodded to Jack. "Thank you kindly. Reckon this is mighty tasty, especially since we didn't get any of Teresa's pie tonight."

Quint took a bite. After chewing for a while, he took another bite and pushed the remainder of the cookie into his coat pocket. "Humph. Passin' good. Think I'll save the rest till later." He started for the door, but stopped at Jack's bunk. Jack was pulling his boots off. He looked up at Quint and waited.

"I've been joshing you some, boy, but I've gotta tell you. You'll do to ride the river with. You saved the boss tonight, you surely did, and took a bullet for doin' it. Plus you had me beat today, but ain't lorded it over me. You ever need a pardner, you just let me know."

"Thanks, Quint. You never know, I might take you up on it. It could mean some riding."

Quint nodded. "I was born to ride. I reckon I'll die in the saddle. You call me." With those words, Quint walked out the bunkhouse door.

Monty was in the bunk next to Jack. He let out a long whistle. "You beat Quint today? I'd a never guessed it." He shook his head. "Never."

The bunkhouse was quiet as each man contemplated the goings-on of the day. They undressed down to their long johns and socks and crawled under the blankets. Blaze was closest to the lamp. He leaned over the chimney, cupped his calloused hand around it, and blew. The light snuffed out, and there was pitch darkness in the bunkhouse. Clouds covered the sky, and the patter of rain sounded on the roof.

Jack felt the warmth of the two wool blankets and stretched

his long legs as far as he could, which wasn't far enough. He listened to the rain. The bullet's track across his shoulders burned, but he had been shot worse. It wasn't so painful it would keep him awake. This had been an eventful day. What would tomorrow bring? He closed his eyes and sighed. His last thought was of Amy's fingertips caressing his shoulders and neck.

JACK AWOKE EARLY. It was still dark as pitch inside the bunkhouse. He lay still for a moment, but he wasn't one to waste his time in bed. He threw the blankets back and hit the floor with his feet. The potbellied stove sat cooling in the middle of the bunkhouse. Occasionally the metal would pop. Whoever had had the last shift had opted to not take the chance of waking the sleeping men and therefore had not stoked the fire, but he knew everyone would be getting up soon. He walked over to the stove and opened the door. It was warm. A few glowing coals remained. He picked up several chunks of wood from the adjacent pile, shoved them into the stove, and closed the door as quietly as he could. He carefully walked back to his bunk. The last thing he wanted was to drive one of those long splinters from the rough-cut floor into the balls of his feet.

Within seconds, flames began in the stove, providing enough light for him to dress quickly. He pulled on his pants, followed by his boots and hat, and then slipped a shirt on. His back was painful and stiff, but he'd work it out. Next, he leveled his hat on his head and reached for his guns. There was a hook on the edge of the bunk where he'd hung them within reach. He unhooked the belt and slung it around his waist and adjusted it until the holsters settled in exactly the right position. Next he pulled on his coat, which felt good in the chill of the morning, and grabbed his saddlebags and rifle. He looked around the bunkhouse. *This wouldn't be a bad place to work,* he thought and headed for the door.

Once outside, he looked up. Through the trees he could see a sky replete with twinkling stars. He carefully made his way to the barn, slipped through the door, and strode toward his animals. "Which one of you boys do I take today?" He rubbed the back of each as he moved along, making up his mind.

These horses meant a lot to him. If he ever settled down, he knew what he'd like to raise. Sure, he'd have cattle to bring in the bread and butter, but he'd also like to do like Truman Shelby and raise the kind of horses men would fight over to own. He patted the big gray's neck. "But that'll never happen, will it, Thunder? This is my work, and someday, somewhere, someone will be faster than me and be a straighter shooter. I just hope whoever it is likes horses as much as I do."

The big gray turned and nuzzled Jack. "I'd like to think you like me, boy, but I know you want a cookie, don't you." At the word cookie, the other two horses and the mule looked toward him. "Alright, I'm a sucker, I know." He stepped over to his saddlebags and retrieved five cookies and dropped one into his coat pocket. Reaching each horse, he allowed the big animal to take the cookie from his hand. Stonewall rubbed his head against him before taking his, and Jack scratched the mule between the ears. While Thunder was crunching his cookie, Jack saddled the gelding, slid his rifle into the scabbard, and fastened his saddlebags and bedroll.

He backed Thunder from the stall and turned him toward the door.

A sharp voice spoke from the hay pile. "I thought you might try to slip away."

6

Jack spun around to see Amy standing in the shadows. She wore a heavy robe over her light blue bed shirt. Her boots came up to well below the hem, exposing several inches of slim calves. Her blonde hair was tousled from sleep, and bright green eyes looked dark in the night. She carried a canvas sack.

Holding her robe closed, she walked to Jack, extending the canvas bag, her boots crunching lightly in the hay. "You'll need this. There's enough of Teresa's fried chicken to make a couple of meals, plus a few other things, including over a dozen of her doughnuts."

He felt his throat catch. In the darkness, this woman, this widow of his good friend, was standing close enough for him to smell the faint odor of lilacs. Her height normally gave her a stately, sophisticated appearance, even in pants and boots, but here in the barn, in the shadows of the night, she looked small and fragile, beautiful and enticing.

Though still sharp, her voice flowed smoothly, like warm honey. "You saved my life and Davy's, and to top it all off, you saved Mama Franklin's life, and you did it all in one day. Now you leave us without a word? That's mean and unkind. What kind of cold-hearted man would do such a thing?"

"I'll be around. I'm searching for the gunman, and whether I find him or not, I'll be back."

"Will you, Jack Sage? Can you promise me you'll be back?" Her hands were made into fists and pressed against her hips. Her coat gaped an inch. "Or will you be shot down on the trail like Warren and Papa Franklin?"

He gazed down at the beauty only inches away. Every fiber of his being yearned to reach out, to grasp this firebrand in his arms. Yet he would not. His friend was barely gone from this earth. Honor demanded he keep his hands to himself. He wasn't a man after romance, he was a U.S. Marshal after a killer.

Extending a long index finger, she reached until it was inches from his nose, shaking it in his face. "Promise me, Jack Sage. You won't ride off to another adventure before coming back here." The finger stopped, aimed between his gray eyes. "Promise me!"

He took a deep breath, inhaling her. "I promise."

Past the open barn door, Jack saw a kerosene lamp illuminate. The light moved from Jo's bedroom, through the parlor, and into the kitchen. He cleared his throat, bringing his mind back to business. When he spoke, his voice had taken on a stern, professional tone. "It looks like Jo's up. I'd better talk to her before I leave."

She stepped back, her voice devoid of emotion. "Yes, you should. Leave Thunder in the barn. He'll stay dry. After the rain last night, we'll have a heavy dew."

He led Thunder back to his stall, loosened his cinch, and patted him on the shoulder. "I won't be long, fella. Have a few more bites." Thunder's head had already lowered into the trough, and he was pulling out a mouthful of hay. Jack turned to address Amy. She was gone. Except for the animals and him, the barn was empty. He looked around once more, his eyes wide in the dim light, and his lips pressed together in frustration. *Yep, nowhere to be seen,* he thought. Jack shook his head, his mind still on the departed woman. *She's a pistol, for sure. Whoever she hitches up with best have a kind but firm hand.*

His long strides took him rapidly out of the barn, across the yard, and up the porch steps. He knocked softly on the front door. It opened immediately. Jo stood in the doorway, eyeing Jack, one eyebrow elevated. "Good morning, Jack. You're getting an early start. Coffee?"

"Thanks, ma'am. That'd sure hit the spot." He stepped through the door and followed her into the empty kitchen.

"Sit," she ordered, and went to the stove, grabbing a thick hot pad with which to grasp the steaming blue porcelain pot. She poured Jack's coffee, leaving plenty of room for cream and sugar.

"Thank you. Since I saw you up, I figured to speak to you before I left."

The eyebrow shot up again. "Meaning you wouldn't have bothered if you hadn't seen my lamp?"

"Ma'am, I wanted to get out and away from the ranch before daylight, find a nice place to hunker down, and do a little watching. No telling who might show themselves."

"You know, there would've been quite a few disappointed people. We knew you wanted to leave early, but had no idea you were planning on this early. Davy is going to be brokenhearted."

Jack shook his head. "Well, I don't know about that." He watched Jo's lips purse.

She straightened, her back stiffening and tone sharp. "You can take my word for it, Marshal."

Jack shook his head. "I certainly didn't believe you weren't telling the truth. It's just hard for me to believe he'd be torn up over a worn-out old saddle tramp."

"Listen to me, Jack Sage. You saved their lives yesterday. Goodness gracious, you saved mine too. You're his hero. If you leave without telling him goodbye, that's the same as telling him you don't give a cow pie for him or his feelings."

Jack started to say he figured that was a bit of an exaggeration, but saw Jo's scowl, and thought better of it. Discretion dictated he take a sip of his coffee, maybe two. "Fine coffee, ma'am. You reckon Davy might be up yet?"

"I'm sure he is. When his mother came in from the barn, *with her nightgown on*, she marched straight to his room. I imagine he'll be here shortly."

Jack frowned. *Is she insinuating something happened between us?* He had to respond. "Ma'am, she was also wearing her coat. Nothing improper went on out there."

Jack watched the frowning woman lean toward him. He pulled his head back and picked up the coffee cup, holding it in front of him like a shield. He couldn't help but think, *She looks just like a coyote when it's about to pounce on a mouse.*

"So you did see her?"

"Yes, ma'am."

"What did you say to her? She stomped back into this house. Don't you realize she has just lost her husband? She is in a very fragile state. You can't be harsh with her. She cannot take it."

Jack thought of the woman yesterday, back at the wagon. *She sure didn't look very fragile with that rifle pointing at my belly.*

"I asked you a question, Jack. What did you say to her?"

"Mrs. Franklin, I didn't say anything, just that I saw your lamp, and I needed to talk to you."

"Is that the tone you used?"

Jack's eyebrows knit in puzzlement. "Well . . . yes."

Jo leaned back, her face relaxing, and her head nodding as if she was confirming something. "How old are you, Jack?"

This is getting out of hand, he thought. *I have no idea what she's driving at.* "I'm thirty-eight, but I don't see what my age has to do with anything."

She leaned toward him again, but her posture had relaxed, along with the muscles in her face. A faint smile stretched her lips. "Jack Sage, in all your thirty-eight years, you haven't learned much about women."

Jack shook his head and took a long sip from his cup. The hot liquid not only tasted great but warmed his body as it flowed down. Grasping the cup, Jack looked into the pale gray eyes of the woman he had saved from death the day before. "Finally, something we can agree on. Jo, as I get older, I realize I know less and less about women."

"That's the first smart thing you've said this morning." She looked around at the pan of donuts.

Jack could see the stack was smaller than when he had left the night before. He knew where a bunch of them were.

"Did she bring you a lunch?"

"More than just a lunch, at least a couple of meals."

"Do you like her, Jack?"

Jack's brow drew up in a ladder of wrinkles. "What's that got to do with anything? Jo, I have a job to do, and the most important thing is to keep you and everyone here safe. It doesn't matter who I like or don't like."

Ignoring his statement, she continued, "Do you like Davy?"

"Of course I do. He's a fine boy." Jack stopped, finally figuring out what Jo was leading up to. "Now wait just a minute, ma'am. I don't have any designs on Amy or any of your daughters. Like I said, I've got a job to do."

"Really, Jack?" She leaned back in her chair, and it was her turn to pick up her coffee cup and take a long sip, her eyes locked on his. She set it down and leaned toward him again. "I just want you to be aware that you are dealing with a tough but, right now, a very fragile woman. Be considerate of her, and don't lead her on. Do you understand me?"

Jack shook his head. "Yes, ma'am, maybe. I think I do, but, again, I have no designs or plans for any female around here except keeping all of you safe." Through the windows, he noticed the sky was beginning to lighten. "I've got to be going, but there's something important I need to make sure you know. That shooter, the one who took a shot at you last night, could be back anytime. He could be here, or he could be waiting to waylay you when you go riding out. I think it would be best if you stayed in the house for the next few days. Let Tripp and the boys do all that's needed out there. They're good men."

Jo's lips pursed again. "I am not going to let some bushwhacker control my life. If I need to work cattle, I'll do it."

"I surely know how you feel, but for the good of everyone, follow my advice. Your riding out will put your hands in danger. They'll be watching out for you and not keeping an eye on what they're doing. That's a good way to end up getting stomped by one of those big longhorn bulls." He could see Jo was listening. Maybe he was getting through.

"Also, stay away from the windows. In fact, I'd shutter this place up. You never know where he might be. I'm going to hang around for a few hours, then I'm going to visit your neighbors and see if I can get a feel for them and their feelings toward you. After that, I'll be heading into town. I might be back in a week, or it might be two weeks, but if there's any trouble around here, get word to me in Laramie. The sheriff will know where I am." He heard running footsteps and looked around, raising his voice. "Now, where's that Davy boy?"

Davy burst into the kitchen. A grin spread his mouth wide. "I'm right here."

"Well, get on over here, boy, and give me a hug. I'm headed out for a while, and I didn't want to leave without seeing you." The boy dashed into his arms, and he encircled the lad. His eyes went to movement behind Davy, and he spotted Amy walking slowly into the room.

She had dressed quickly, donning a green dress that, with the flickering light of the lamps, emphasized her eyes. A faint smile touched her lips, her eyes on her happy son. Even as she stood watching her son, little hands grasped her skirt, and Jack saw Flo, still in her nightshirt, step out from behind Amy. Once clear, she released Amy's skirt and, with the backs of her hands, rubbed at sleep-filled eyes.

Jack smiled at the sleepy-eyed girl. "Would you like a hug, Flo?"

She grinned at him and nodded her head, her springy blonde hair bouncing around her shoulders. He opened one arm. She walked to him, big blue eyes watching his face. He wrapped her in with Davy and gave them both a big hug. When he released them, Flo looked around for Jo. Finding her, her tiny voice asked, "Is it breakfast yet, Mama?"

"It can be, sweetie," Jo replied.

Teresa was busy at the stove.

Jack stood. "Reckon it's time I hit the trail. It'll be daylight before long."

Amy straightened. "You could stay for breakfast."

Jack shook his head. "Can't, I need to get nearer the valley so I can keep a lookout for a while. Those doughnuts you brought me will keep me going."

Davy looked up at Jack. "Are you coming back, Marshal Sage?"

Jack knelt to bring himself near the boy's level. "I aim to, Davy. You take care of your folks while I'm gone."

"Yes, sir, I sure will."

Jack patted the boy on the shoulder and stood again. Dot and Lilly had joined them, and Jack could see light coming from the bunkhouse. He looked at Jo. "Stay safe."

She nodded. "Good luck."

He left the kitchen and, passing Amy, said, "Walk with me to the door?"

She nodded and turned to Davy and the others. "I'll be right back."

Reaching the door, he asked, "How long had you been waiting in the barn?"

"I couldn't sleep. After getting up, I packed a few things together in the kitchen and brought everything out to the barn, maybe an hour."

"I want you to know that was mighty nice of you." They stopped at the door. She didn't have a coat this time, and it was cold outside. Jack, though he would have preferred to be talking on the porch, away from prying ears, said, "I'm mighty sorry for speaking sharp in the barn. I meant no harm. Trust me. I'll be back. You take care of yourself and Davy."

Her eyes gazed deep into his. "You be careful. Come back in one piece."

He nodded and stepped out the door. Light was breaking in the east. He had used too much of the darkness.

Tripp waited next to Thunder. "You're not staying for breakfast?"

"Just had a hot cup, and morning's breaking. I need to be out in those hills before full daylight is on us." He strode to Thunder, pulled the big horse's cinch tight, and swung into the saddle. "Where do I find these other ranches?"

Tripp frowned before responding, "Closer than I'd like. The general bought the water rights along the south fork, so we're well set for water, but we're kinda cornered down here. The Polings' ranch, the Circle P, is located north of here, on the west side of the valley, same as us, only about six miles away. Just turn north when you exit the tree line. You can't miss their ranch. It's on the other side of the creek and a ways into the hills, just north of the middle fork.

"Hank Schmidt, the other rancher in the valley, has his Rocking HS up on the north fork. If I had my druthers, we'd have the whole valley, but the general said this was more than big enough for him. He liked the looks of this area. Both Poling and Schmidt got along fine with the general and Warren, but old man Poling sure don't like the idea of Josephine running this here ranch."

Thunder stamped. Jack patted him on the neck. "He's getting restless. Anything I need to know about either bunch?"

Quint walked into the barn. "You're getting an early start."

"Not early enough. Keep an eye on Jo and the family. No telling where this shooter may be."

Quint nodded. "Aim to. Where you headed?"

"Poling's and then Schmidt's place. Aim to get a better feel for the valley." He looked back down at Tripp. "Anything else I need to know?"

"Schmidt's friendly enough, but he keeps to himself. He's about your age, maybe a couple of years younger. I think he's had his eye on Amy, but I'm not sure. He's got a couple of tough riders working for him. One's left-handed and quick with a gun. He killed a guy in Laramie. They had an inquest, and it was ruled self-defense. Name's River Jordan." He paused, looked over to Quint, who remained silent, and turned back to Jack. "That's about it. We'll keep an eye on the folks around here. Watch your back. That bushwhacker could be anywhere, and keep your eyes open for Indians. You never know when the Cheyenne will come chargin' over a hill. They're kinda friendly with us, but you're a stranger."

Jack gave a nod to Tripp and Quint. "Thanks for the lowdown. I'll be heading into Laramie after I finish with them."

He walked Thunder out of the barn into the yard. Glancing toward the house, he picked up movement behind the parlor window. Davy stood inside, watching. Jack gave the boy a wave, bringing an enthusiastic return and a grin. Jack smiled back, gave Thunder his head, and the big horse immediately broke into a trot, weaving through the trees.

As horse and rider moved down the slope toward the valley, the tall ponderosa pines quickly thinned, giving way to scattered lodgepole. A ridge to their left sloped from the high mountains and cut into the valley where it tapered and then flattened. A thicket of lodgepole stood at the end of the flattened ridge. He brought Thunder to the right of the thicket and pulled him to a stop. He could see past the pines and into the valley.

A herd of elk slowly grazed their way toward the treeline, with a smattering of mule deer along their perimeter. Jack watched the herd closely. He reached into his saddlebags and pulled out his field glasses. After scanning the herd, he examined farther up the valley and traversed the glasses across to where the opposite side disappeared into darkness. Nothing, other than cattle, deer, and more elk. The bunch nearest him wasn't spooky, a good indication there were no riders near.

The rolling hills could hide a sizable war party. He watched and waited. When the herd passed him and were beginning to enter the timber, he made one additional sweep across the valley with the glasses. All clear.

He slid them back into the saddlebag and pulled his Winchester from its scabbard. He eased the lever down just far enough to open the chamber so he could see the shiny brass cartridge. Satisfied, he pulled the lever back into its up position, shoving the cartridge deep inside the chamber, ready to fire. After slipping the rifle back into its scabbard, he checked the loads in each revolver. He thought about leaving the leather thong off the hammer of each, but decided to keep them secure for now. The last thing he wanted was to bounce a revolver out of its holster in a hard ride.

Clucking, Jack moved Thunder out from behind the trees and north. He'd take his time, stay in or near the timber, and work his way toward the Poling ranch. *Who knows what I might spot*, he thought.

7

It was nearing noon when Jack crossed the middle fork. At this point, the creek was twenty or so feet wide but no more than two feet deep at the crossing. It danced around and over the rocks. Trout dashed from behind small boulders, disturbed by Thunder's intrusion. He promised himself fish for dinner.

Jack's morning had been spent traveling north, weaving in and out of the treeline. Late in the morning, he spotted smoke rising out of the tops of the pines, and shortly after, came across a road of sorts, which led him to the creek crossing, and continued along the opposite side of the creek. When Thunder had quenched his thirst, Jack moved him out of the creek and toward the smoke.

Occasionally he could hear shouts coming from the general direction of his travel. Breaking through the trees into a manmade clearing, he saw the reason for the shouting. A cowhand was on the back of an unhappy buckskin. The animal, as far as Jack could tell, was intent on getting rid of the cowpoke. He was a tall slim rider who looked equally insistent that he stay glued to the buckskin. Jack rode up to the corral, shoved his hat back, leaned a forearm on his saddle horn, and watched the show through the cloud of dust the buckskin was raising.

The cowhand's back was covered with dirt, an indication he had lost this argument to the buckskin at least once before, but now was hanging tight. Every time the bronc reached his zenith, the men watching would let out a whoop. The rider appeared to be stuck like glue to the saddle, never breaking clear when the horse topped out. Jack watched the battle between bronco and rider. The horse was giving the cowhand a tough but straightforward ride. Up and down, up and down, over and over, spine jolting but consistent. Then, of a sudden, he went up, and when he reached the top, he spun, twisting, turning, and changing direction. His new antics were enough. The tall cowhand was in the saddle one moment, but with the horse's turn, the saddle disappeared from under his airborne body, leaving the cowhand with nothing but air and ground beneath him. He crashed to the dirt.

The instant he was unseated, the horse stopped bucking and turned to look at his tormentor, who had managed to struggle to his feet. He was bent over, but had his eyes locked on the buckskin. The cowhand was gasping desperately to regain his breath. With great effort, he managed to get his lungs working and gulped in a breath. Reaching behind his neck, where his flattened hat hung by a leather string, he grasped it and pulled it forward, punched it back into shape, and slapped it onto his head.

The three men who had been watching whooped and clapped. Jack joined in the clapping, for the man had given an excellent ride, though the buckskin had proven his mettle and won this round.

At Jack's clapping, the three men, who had no idea Jack had ridden up since they had been so engrossed in the show, turned in surprise. The cowhand in the corral straightened and, keeping a cautious watch on the buckskin, walked stiffly to the corral fence. He examined Jack and turned toward the older of the three men who had been watching. "Pa, you know this here feller?"

When the three men had turned toward him, Jack spotted the older man. From under a long-tailed red wool cap, clumps of dingy gray hair erupted over his wide forehead. Through the grime, he looked twice as old as the other three, but his same gaunt features were reflected in the younger men. Scraggly sideburns extended to nearly hide his face behind an outbreak of uncontrolled gray beard, chin whiskers stained brown from dripping tobacco juice.

"No, son. I ain't got the slightest idea of who this gent is." He addressed Jack. "Who are you, feller, and what's brought you up here?"

"I'm Jack Sage, U.S. Marshal. You would be Mr. Connor Poling?"

"Yes sirree, every day of my life."

Jack noticed the buckskin was unshod, but that wasn't unusual. If he was freshly wild, the animal wouldn't yet have shoes. "Mind if I swing down?"

"Shore, Marshal, join us on the porch for a cup of coffee. We was just takin' a break here from watchin' Billy Boy show that buckskin who's boss." At his comment, Poling broke out in cackling laughter, and everyone else joined in, even Billy Boy.

"I'm obliged. I've been sitting that gray all morning. It'll be good to stretch these legs." Jack swung down and led Thunder toward the ranch house. Billy stepped in beside him, and Jack noticed the man was about his height. He carried himself like many a tall man, a little stooped, shoulders pulled together, but Jack could see the shoulders had width and thickness to them, and the younger man's wrists were thick from hard work.

"Whatcha doin' up here, Marshal?" Billy asked. "We don't get many visitors out this way."

One of the brothers, for that was who Jack figured these men were, cleared his throat, spit, and wiped his mouth on his sleeve. His voice came low, threatening. "That's the way we like it."

The older Poling spoke up. "Leave the marshal be, boys. Let him wrap himself around a cup of Liam's fine coffee."

The youngest and undoubtedly the dirtiest, besides Billy, who was still covered in dirt from the corral, shot a long stream of tobacco juice across the yard. He spoke up in a high-pitched whiny voice. "Pa, I fixed the coffee this morning. It ain't right I should have to do it all the time. I ain't no woman. Why don't you make Oscar do it? He don't ever do nothing."

Oscar, short and stocky, reached out and gave his younger brother a hard shove just as Liam was stepping on the first weather-worn step leading up to the porch. He stumbled and barely, with some fancy footwork, managed to keep his footing. He spun around, fists raised. Oscar snaked a long-bladed Arkansas toothpick from the scabbard on his gunbelt. He dropped into a crouch, grinning at his brother. "Come on, little brother, if you're feeling vinegary, jump on."

The old man's laughing eyes and wide grin disappeared in a flash. He took two quick steps, bringing him in range of Oscar, and slapped his son so hard he staggered. With his other hand, he yanked the long blade from the man's hand and shoved it behind his belt, then turned toward his youngest. "Boy, don't you back-talk me in front of guests, you hear? Now git inside and fix that coffee."

Jack kept his eyes on Oscar. The stocky man stood rubbing his cheek where his pa's wide palm had left a red imprint. *If looks could kill, Pa Poling would be dead on the ground*, Jack thought, but Oscar said nothing.

During his years in the army and enforcing the law, Jack had dealt with many men. There were basically three groups. There were the windbags, bullies who ran over weaker folks.

Others, tough, hard men, lived their lives with intent. They neither took advantage of weaker men nor stepped aside for the bullies. They came straight at an offender. A man always knew where they stood.

The old man fell into the third group, the unpredictable, volatile personality. He could change in an instant. Jack had seen men go from laughing and joking to shooting down an unsuspecting innocent whose only crime was bumping into them. Poling and possibly his sons were dangerous. They might not have killed the general and Warren, but they certainly had the capability. *Yep,* Jack thought, *these are men to keep an eye on.*

Two tired rocking chairs sat on the wide porch. Poling motioned to one. "Have a seat, Marshal. Liam will have us a mighty fine cup of coffee out here pretty quick."

Jack eased himself into the rocker. "How long you folks been running cattle here?"

Poling leaned forward so he could spit over the porch's bannister into the yard. "Reckon we been here goin' on four years. Course, I trapped these mountains long before these boys was born. There was an almighty batch of beaver in them streams back then. They're mostly gone now."

"How many head of cattle do you run?"

"Couple thousand, keeps us and the hands busy."

Jack looked around. "Hands?"

"Yep, we got four. They're out to town. Fellers need a day off occasionally. It ain't like we're a big place, not like that foreigner north of us. He's got nigh on to four thousand head."

Liam stepped out onto the porch with two cups of coffee, handing the first to Poling and the other to Jack. "He keeps adding to the herd, too, Pa."

Jack took the cup and looked into the black coffee. Fortunately, nothing floated in it. He nodded his thanks. "What about your neighbors down south?"

Billy, who had taken a seat on the steps next to his brother Oscar, turned to look at Jack. "They've got a mighty small herd. Reckon they don't have more'n a thousand."

Oscar shook his head. "You ain't never seen the like. It's run by an old woman and a bunch of girls."

Before Jack could respond, Poling spoke up. "The feller who owned it was a general in the Yankee army. Bought it about a year ago. Not a bad sort. Got himself killed a few months back. His onliest son was with him. Both shot down not too far from here." Poling took a long slurp of his coffee. "Only folks remaining, besides the hands, are women, his wife and daughters. Plus the son's wife."

Billy stood to head into the house for a cup of coffee. Passing Jack, his head bobbed in an enthusiastic nod. "That whole bunch of women are lookers, Marshal. Reckon they'll all be married off in no time."

Liam had stepped back on the porch, a cup in his hand. He gave a high-pitched laugh. "Billy's got his eye on one of 'em. She's a fine-looking woman. We need a woman around here to cook and keep this house clean."

Oscar stood, following Billy into the house. He glared at Liam as they passed. "Don't you take my spot on that step, little brother. I'd hate to have to gut you like a fish."

Liam glared back at his brother, but when he sat, it was at the far end of the steps, leaving room for both Billy and Oscar.

Poling, his head down over his coffee cup, cut his eyes toward Jack. "So why are you dropping by, Marshal? You're not from this part of the country."

Jack shook his head. "No, I'm not. I'm here investigating the deaths of General Franklin and his son, Warren."

"Yep," Poling said, "that was mighty bad. Any ideas?"

Jack shook his head. "No. I'm just riding around talking to the neighbors. Hopefully someone will have seen or heard something."

Poling leaned his head back against the support of the ladder-back rocker. "I'm wishin' we could help. Yes, sir, I surely am, but we ain't seen nor heard nothing."

His eyes on Poling, Jack said, "Someone took a couple of shots at Mrs. Franklin last night."

The three men sitting on the steps jerked around, staring at Jack.

Billy was the only one who appeared concerned. "Anybody hurt?"

Jack shook his head. "Fortunately, no one. Of course, they're a little shaken, but the shooter missed."

Poling pointed a long bony finger at Jack. "I told that Mrs. Franklin, for her own safety, she oughta sell that ranch and get out of here. This ain't no place for all them women. Plus, she don't know diddly about ranching. They need to head on back east where they come from."

From his seat on the porch step, Billy looked up at Jack. "We heard a bit of shooting going on yesterday. Sounded like it was on the road. We rode down to investigate, but by the time we got there, weren't nobody around."

Liam turned toward Jack. "Yeah, but we did find a new grave. You know what happened?"

Jack placed his almost full cup next to the rocker and stood. "Outlaws tried to ambush Warren Franklin's wife and son. I happened along. I had a little argument with one. He lost." Jack turned to Poling. "Doesn't look like Mrs. Franklin is inclined to follow your suggestion. I get the idea she's planning on making a go of it."

The boys looked at Poling. He slowly rocked, staring at the buckskin in the corral. "Danged stupid woman. I gave her good advice. She needs to be outta here. Ranchin' in this country is a man's job."

Jack stepped between Billy and Liam, making his way off the porch to Thunder. He swung into the saddle and, before turning toward the valley, nodded to Poling. "Thanks for the hospitality. I imagine you heard the fella who ambushed the Franklins was riding an unshod horse."

Poling stood and leaned on the bannister. "I heard. Also heard the sheriff blamed it on Blackfeet."

Jack held Poling's gaze. "You've been in these mountains a long time. Do you believe the sheriff?"

Through his scraggly beard, Poling flashed Jack a lopsided grin. "That sheriff wouldn't know Indian sign if they was about to scalp him, and whoever heard of a cagey Injun leaving an arrow behind? Shoot no, that weren't no Injun. My guess is a white man did the shooting, and a white man rode that unshod horse."

"I agree." Jack motioned his head toward the corral. "I noticed the buckskin is unshod."

Poling's grin widened, exposing black and broken teeth, but the grin showed no humor. "You got yourself a pair of mighty sharp eyes, Marshal. We just caught him a few days ago, but I'll tell you something afore you feel the need to go snooping around. We ride unshod horses. I figure it works for the Injuns, it'll work for us. Been doing it many a year, and before you do any more figuring, I don't shoot at women, but if'n I did, I wouldn't miss."

Jack, his face hard and solemn, held the old man's cold flinty eyes. "Good to know. Keep an eye out for anything or anyone who doesn't look right. Let me know what you find."

"I don't work for the law. If'n me or the boys find anyone snooping around, on a shod or unshod horse, we'll take care of him ourselves."

Jack held the man's gaze a moment longer, then raised a finger to his hat brim. "Much obliged for the fine coffee and hospitality." He turned Thunder and walked the big gray out of the yard and into the trees. His spine itched with apprehension until the trees blocked the view of his back from the house. He leaned forward and patted Thunder on the neck. "Boy, those are some unpredictable hombres back there, and I have a feeling we'll be heading out here again. Now let's go talk to this Hank Schmidt."

RIDERS APPROACHED as Jack neared the steep bluffs. It had taken him the remainder of the day of walking Thunder alternately through high grass at the edge of the timber and through the tall pines. Most of the cattle he had seen over the past couple of hours had carried the Rocking HS brand. It wasn't like Texas, where cattle were still almost as thick as jackrabbits, but they were definitely thicker at the north end of the valley, near Schmidt's ranch, than the south around the Franklins'.

He allowed Thunder to climb out of the creek to level ground, where he pulled up to await the approaching riders. There were five of them, three riding on ranch horses, and two on fine-looking, extra-well-fed animals. Coming out of the creek, Jack had loosed his Smith & Wessons in their holsters, and though he expected no trouble, he believed in being ready.

The five riders slowed their horses to a walk and pulled up within ten feet, all lined across in front of him.

Jack scanned each man. Three looked like cowhands, and two gunmen. "Howdy, boys. I'm looking for Hank Schmidt."

"Why?" The sharp-toned question came from a younger man riding a smooth-coated bay.

Jack figured he couldn't be more than twenty-five or twenty-six years old, and the younger man's attitude grated on his patience. "I don't figure you to be Schmidt. I was told he's a German in his thirties, and you're still wet behind the ears."

The gunman bristled. "You wanta find out how wet behind the ears I am?" The boy's left hand dropped to the butt of the revolver on his left side.

Jack gave him a cold smile. "Youngster, you better think long and hard before you go for that hogleg. You don't want your pards to miss supper 'cause they're out here digging your grave. Think about all the girls you'll never get to kiss."

The man's shoulders leaned slightly forward, and his legs tensed in the stirrups.

One of the other riders stepped his horse closer to the gunman and spoke softly. "River, don't draw that gun. I've seen this feller in action in Texas. You don't want any part of him."

The youngster, keeping his eyes on Jack, tilted his head slightly toward the speaker. "I can take him. Look at him. He's ancient."

8

Jack didn't much like the gunman's comment on his age. He smiled at the younger man. "Don't let a few years and a little gray hair fool you, boy. Relax and tell me where I can find Schmidt."

The cowhand leaned closer, his voice insistent. "I'm telling you. He's greased lightning. You'll be dead before your gun makes it out of the holster. I've seen both of you shoot, and you don't stand a chance."

Jack nodded to the other cowhand. "That's who you need to be listening to. Don't let your pride talk you into an early grave. I want no trouble. I've got nothing against you, but if you pull that iron on me, I'll have to kill you. You'll leave me no choice."

River stayed tense for an instant longer. Suddenly he relaxed and laughed. "I was just joshing with you, mister."

Jack, his hard gray eyes locked on the boy's, had seen fear slip into them when he was told Jack was faster. "I wasn't. I don't joke when my life's on the line. Now if you're through with your threats, take me to Hank Schmidt."

The gunman's grin disappeared. He wheeled his horse in the direction they had come, slamming the spurs to the fine-looking bay. The horse leaped forward, and all of the riders except the one who had spoken to River raced after him.

Jack watched them kick up a dust cloud. Thunder's day had been long, and Jack knew the big gray was tired. He clucked and started the horse walking after the disappearing riders. The man who had stayed swung in beside him.

"Howdy, name's Dallas Fisher."

Jack nodded to him and motioned his head toward the departing riders. "You're not clearing out with your friends?"

Dallas shook his head. "Not so's you'd notice. I ride for the brand, but it don't mean they're my friends." He patted the big blue roan. "Buster here's better than any of them, and we've been working most of the day. I could run him back to the ranch, but I don't reckon he needs that."

Jack examined the slick-looking roan. "It's a smart man who takes care of a good horse. Jack Sage, U.S. Marshal, but it seems you already know my name. Where from?"

"Laredo. Saw you beat Ike Jackson in the street. You were a lawman then, too. You unlimbered them hoglegs mighty fast. He never cleared leather. It's been a while back, but I don't reckon it's been long enough to slow you down much."

The two horses made their way around a tight bunch of longhorns, staying away from the wide, sharp horns. Once they passed the big animals, they rode from behind a stand of lodgepole pines, revealing the ranch in the distance.

Jack's mind drifted back to Laredo. It seemed a long time ago, but wasn't much over three years. He glanced at Fisher. "Ike Jackson. Now that's a name I haven't heard for a while."

"He was building quite a reputation until you loaded him down with lead."

"Tell me, Fisher, what brought you up to this cold country?"

"Last year I trailed a herd up from Texas and figured I'd stay, but it does get cold. Winters are miserable. I swear, for six months my feet never thawed out, but look around. This is mighty pretty country, and I ain't seen a Texas tornado around here yet, just a lot of soft snow."

"Cold weather's never been my favorite." Even as he spoke, Jack was examining the well-maintained ranch. It was the complete opposite of Poling's. There was a corral attached to a large red-painted barn. Not far from it stood a long whitewashed bunkhouse, and across the ranch yard from the bunkhouse and barn, a two-story main house of the same color. Everything was clean and crisp, with high bluffs framing the ranch house.

Nearing, Jack glanced at Fisher. "Can you tell me anything about Hank Schmidt?"

Fisher thought for a moment before he spoke. "He's a determined man. He brooks no messing around. He's fired several since I've been here, but he does pay well, and the grub's good."

"At least I'll know where he stands. How about pointing him out to me?"

"You won't have any problem recognizing him. He'll be the biggest man in the bunch. You're a big feller yourself, but he'll see you and raise you about thirty pounds, and he ain't seen fat since he was a babe."

They rode into the yard to a large welcoming committee. Jack easily picked out the huge man in front of the cowhands. Neatly dressed, blond hair trimmed close, a frown graced the Schmidt's clean-shaven face. Arms folded across a wide chest with sleeves stretched tight around his massive biceps, his shirt looked ready to burst.

Fisher wasn't kidding, except maybe he was a little too conservative, Jack thought. *I'd say he's packing at least fifty pounds on me.* River Jordan stood on Schmidt's right, while a tall, older man was on the opposite side. A respectful distance from the ranch owner, Jack pulled Thunder to a stop. "From what Dallas tells me, you must be Hank Schmidt."

"*Ja*, you are correct. Who are you?"

"I'm Jack Sage, United States Marshal."

Schmidt's frown didn't change. "You rode onto my land, uninvited, and threatened to kill one of my hands. Does being a marshal give you the right to threaten innocent people?"

Jack remained motionless. He could feel his temper stirring. "I'll tell you what right it gives me. It gives me the right to arrest anyone who threatens a U.S. Marshal, and the law of the land gives me the right to kill your gunman if he draws on me." He leaned toward Schmidt. "Is that laid out clear enough for you?"

Jack watched the big man's fists clinch. "I'll tell you what is clear, Marshal. It's clear you don't belong on my land, and it's time you turn around and take that gray nag out of my sight."

"Schmidt, your man threatened me, and your other men were there to see it. I don't know who stuck that burr under your saddle, but I don't leave until I get my questions answered. Where were you, and where were your men last night?"

Schmidt took a step toward Jack. "It is not up to me to keep up with my men. I was here at home. You've got your information. Now get off my land."

Jack shook his head. "Not quite that easy. I need to question each one of your men to find out where they were last night."

The ranch owner swung his arm toward his men. "Ask them, and then get off my land."

Jack looked around at the men. They were all tough-looking specimens, and he knew he was stymied. This was a hostile environment, and there was no way he would get anything from these men now. He'd have to wait until a better time, when he could question each man separately. He stared down at Schmidt. "Thanks for your hospitality. I'll be seeing you."

The German's face reddened. Jack knew his words had struck home. In this country no man was turned away from a ranch or a campfire, but Schmidt, his jaw set, stood his ground, feet wide and arms folded.

Jack turned his tired gray and walked him slowly toward the stand of lodgepole pine. He hated leaving Schmidt's ranch without talking to the hands, but there was nothing he could do. Even he had to recognize when he was outnumbered, and Schmidt had a right to protect his property.

He guided Thunder past the pines and around the longhorns. Before riding down the cutbank of the north fork, he pulled his horse to a stop. The sun was slipping toward the mountain peaks. He stopped in the creek again, letting Thunder drink. When he was done, they rode out and up the other side, and in the distance he could see a short ridgeline rising in the middle of the valley.

Patches of timber showed themselves around the edges, but the top was rocky and bare. He bumped Thunder into a lope. They had to cross several washes prior to reaching the ridge, but made it while there was still light. At the northern end, Jack found a beaver pond surrounded by willows and a thicket of aspen. The stream meandered away toward the creek he had crossed. Nearing the pond, he dismounted and watched as the surface of the water was broken with multiple dimples. He glanced back at the western sky. Soon darkness would cover the valley. Did he have time?

He tied Thunder to a willow and fumbled through his saddlebags till he found what he was looking for. He didn't have time to make it sporting. He was hungry, and the fried chicken Amy had given him had made a fine breakfast, with a couple of donuts, but that was hours ago.

He unwrapped twine from around a carved stick he had taken from his bag, careful to keep the hook clear. Searching in the grass, he found a small grasshopper, grabbed it, and speared it onto his hook. With only the weight of the hook and hopper, he swung the line in an ever-widening circle over his head until he had the line extended ten feet over the water. Carefully, he let it settle to the surface.

The grasshopper kicked twice on the pond's surface and disappeared. Jack felt the pull of a trout and gently set the hook.

There was no time to play it. No time for fun, he was hungry, and it was getting dark. He pulled it in as fast as he could without tearing the hook from the fish's tender mouth, unhooked him, and tossed him farther up the bank. He immediately searched for another grasshopper on the tall grass stems. Finding one, he repeated the process and had a second trout on the bank in no time.

When he had two more fish flopping on the bank, he quit. Racing against darkness, he quickly cleaned the four fish. Finding a thin willow limb, he cut it at a fork, leaving a short portion of the fork extending from the base of the limb to hold the fish. He slid them down the limb and, with his treasure, mounted Thunder. He wanted to move away from the pond so his human presence wouldn't prevent thirsty animals from getting a drink. Also he needed cover for his fire.

Riding slowly up the lightly timbered ridge, he found a shallow draw. The draw would hide his fire, and there was plenty of grass for Thunder. He stripped his saddle and gear from the animal, tossed his rope over Thunder's neck, and looked around. Spotting the perfect place, he moved him a short distance away from the campsite and staked him out in the thick grass.

Light was growing dim, but he could still see well enough to make out the dry twigs and limbs he needed for his fire. He worked rapidly, collecting what he needed for his fire, and finding a sufficiently clear area, he dropped his burden to the ground. He pulled a tin from his vest, opened it, and extracted a match. After sliding the tin back into his pocket, he snapped the match across the butt of his Smith and held the flame to the kindling. It caught. He blew lightly on it, satisfied to see it growing. He carefully stacked a few of the small twigs across the flames. He didn't want a big fire, just enough to make some coffee and cook the fish.

He laid the four fish across the green willow limbs he had cut, and while they were cooking, moved his saddle and gear thirty yards up the draw, well away from the fire. He settled on a spot with large boulders and grass, well out of the ring of light. There he set out his gear, laying his rifle next to his bedroll, and reached into his saddlebag for a cookie and a handful of oats. He moved back to the fire just in time to turn the fish, and slipped quietly to Thunder.

The big horse was busy pulling and chewing grass. Jack moved up close and draped an arm around the horse's neck, holding the hand out with the oats. He flattened his palm and felt the big lips and tongue devour the oats. Then he pulled the cookie out of his vest. "You deserve this, boy. Don't you mind what Schmidt called you, you're no nag. You'd outdo anything I saw under his men or in the corral, and you've worked hard all day." Thunder's teeth gently grasped the cookie and began crunching. "I'll be back."

Jack hurried to his saddlebags, grabbed his coffee pot and bag of coffee, and strode back to the fire and his fish. Moving the fish from the hot coals, he laid them on the grass, dropped the bag of coffee, and slipped to the stream that fed the beaver's pond. The water trickled along a rocky bed, barely deep enough for him to partially fill his coffee pot. Once he had enough, he moved back to the fire, set the pot on the coals, and opened the bag with the coffee. He extracted a partial handful of coffee and dropped it into the pot, then he grabbed two of the fish and quickly made them disappear, savoring the delicious taste.

Fish always taste best in the wild, he thought. Carefully moving the two remaining trout well clear of the coals, he eased out of the firelight's weak gleam.

Finding the perfect boulder, Jack dropped his things, picked up a blanket, and hurried back to the fire's remains. Near it, he gathered a few larger rocks, piled them about his length, and spread the blanket over the pile. He placed a small boulder at the end, for his head, and draped the edge of the blanket over it. When he was finished, he stepped back to admire his work. He had to admit, it wasn't very good. It looked like a pile of rocks with a blanket over it, but maybe when the coals burned down and the moon shadowed the area, it might be good enough to confuse a marauder. *It will have to do,* he thought and slipped back to the nicely angled boulder he'd found.

Once there, he lowered himself to the ground and relaxed his tired back against the rock face. Other than the problem with Schmidt today, he was feeling pretty fine. He sucked the tender flesh from the trout's bones and sat contentedly leaning against the big boulder. The fire was already sputtering. It had been just enough.

Rising, he grabbed his cup. He could hear the water boiling in the pot. After pouring a cupful, he moved back to his rock and reached into the bag Amy had given him this morning. After feeling around, he found what he was after and pulled out a doughnut. Before biting into it, he held it close to his nose. The aroma brought a smile to his lips. This was the life. He took a bite, allowing the sugary pastry to dissolve in his mouth. "Thank you, ladies. These are mighty fine."

He gazed up at the myriad of stars. The night was clear, and the moon was just slipping into his vision above the ridgeline. It was as white as a bride's wedding dress. Memories flowed to the surface. He remembered a moon like this in Algiers. All had been right with the world. Two young people saw nothing but happiness ahead. A wolf howled, and another. The spell was broken. *It's hard to believe Algiers was almost twenty years ago,* Jack thought. *So many things have happened since then. Life has happened. Life and death.*

Jack closed the bag and carried it back to his saddle and gear. From here he had a good view of what remained of the campfire, his fake bed, which wasn't too bad, and Thunder. Past the scattered trees lay open range to the west until reaching the base of the mountains and Schmidt's ranch. In the faint moonlight, he could see no near movement. He spread his blankets, leaving one to pull over him, and stretched out. Slipping a revolver from his right holster, he rested it across his hip. The glint of his Winchester was visible next to him within reach. He felt his body relaxing.

It's funny, he thought, allowing his head to drift back against his saddle. *I've been alone for so long, this solitary life has grown on me. There's something about being out here, alone under the stars, listening to the wolves, feeling the deep solitude, the peace. I don't know if I could find this kind of contentment with another person, a family. It might be too late for me to adapt to such a thing.* His eyes grew heavy, and his body relaxed. He drifted away to the low moan of the wind through the trees, the rattle of the cattails, and the comforting sound of Thunder chewing.

Jack's eyes popped open. He immediately noticed the waxing moon had moved past its zenith and was arcing toward the west. The steady wind had ceased, and there was quiet across the prairie. Jack lay still, listening. Something had awakened him. Beneath the blanket, his right thumb rested on the hammer of his Smith & Wesson.

Silence. A heavy silence, and there was the problem. He should be hearing a great horned owl hooting or a coyote howling, perhaps a wolf lifting its cry to the moon, possibly even the sound of a pack rat scurrying across the rocky landscape, but there was nothing. The animals were as still and alert as he.

In the moon's pale light, Thunder stood still, silent. There was no grass cropping or chewing, only a big gray head erect, ears forward, staring into the pale darkness. *Whatever's out there doesn't belong,* Jack thought, *but what?* A stray breeze caressed his forehead, bringing the faintest sweet acrid smell of tobacco. The transient puff had reached him from the direction of his fake camp. He slowly began to move his head, looking to both sides. For him to check behind, he would have to roll forward and raise his head. Even the slightest noise would be heard in this quiet. *No, better I remain still than give away my position.*

He waited. A rock grated against the leather of a boot, and whispering drifted to him. Then he saw, emerging from the trees, two men. They were no more than ten feet from his decoy bed. In the dim light of the moon, he could see their outstretched arms pointed toward the blanket-covered rocks. Steel glinted in their hands. Jack had seen this before. He closed his eyes, barely in time to protect his night vision. Two guns roared, each firing multiple shots, and even with his eyes closed, he could see the flashes through his eyelids. Though it dimmed his night vision, upon opening his eyes, he could see the men's outlines, and they were close enough for him to hear them clearly.

Their words were preceded by a bark of laughter. "He ain't budged, River. That there is one dead lawman."

Jack recognized the second voice. "I could've beat him in a draw."

"Sure you could, River, boy. Sure you could, but why take the chance?" The two killers advanced toward their dead quarry. Reaching Jack's blanket, one drew back and gave the boulders a hard kick. The man let out a yelp, bent over, and yanked the blanket clear of the rocks.

9

Jack thumbed the hammer back on the Smith & Wesson .44. The metallic sound of the hammer going to full cock jerked the men erect. They swung their handguns left and then right, unsure of the location of the frightening sound.

Jack had remained on the ground, his blanket covering his body. Lying among the boulders, he provided no silhouette for the gunmen to see. "Throw down your guns, boys. Marshal Sage, here. I'd prefer not to shoot you, even though you did interrupt a mighty fine sleep."

The two guns lowered, and the gunmen's heads swiveled like an owl's, searching for the threat.

This time, Jack's voice was hard. "Time's up. Drop your guns or die."

Jack heard one gun clatter to the rocks, and Jack recognized the laugher's voice. "I dropped my gun, Marshal. Don't shoot."

"I need to hear more than one gun hit the ground. Jordan, drop your gun."

The second gun dropped.

Jack threw his blanket back and stood. He still had the boulders behind him, breaking up his outline, but he knew he presented a big target. "Hands up, boys. High, so I can see them. And step apart."

The laugher threw his hands up so hard, Jack chuckled. The fella might've dislocated his shoulders. The two men had started separating when the flame from a muzzle blast ripped through the night, instantly followed by the roar. The slap of a chunk of led slamming into a boulder behind Jack was immediately followed by the fading whine of a ricochet. He fired instinctively and cursed himself. River Jordan was left-handed, and he had automatically fired assuming a right-hand hold. He saw a man fall, but knew it wasn't the shooter.

"I'm shot, Marshal," the laugher cried. "I dropped my gun. I ain't done nothin'."

River's tense voice cursed his partner and said, "Shut up, Cain, or I'll shoot you myself."

Cain let out a long high-pitched moan. "River, I'm hurtin' bad."

The gunman followed his threat with another shot at Jack. The bullet missed flesh but tugged at his left sleeve just below his shoulder. *Remember, he's left-handed,* Jack reminded himself. This time he corrected his aim to the left of the muzzle blast and fired twice. The reports of his revolver were immediately rewarded with a cry of surprise and pain and the rattle of a weapon hitting the rocks. Jack squatted down next to his gear and quickly reloaded.

He removed the empty casings, pulled fresh rounds from his belt, dropped them into the waiting cylinder, and snapped his weapon shut. Following the click of the mechanism locking, River Jordan spoke. His young voice no longer sounded threatening but pleading. "Marshal, I'm shot. Help me. I'm hurtin' powerful bad."

"Not tonight, Jordan. You brought this on yourself. You two

might try to help each other. If you last, I'll check on you at daylight, not before."

Cain added his voice to Jordan's. "Marshal, we might die afore daylight. You've got to help us."

Jack pulled the bag Amy had given him close. Reaching inside, he found another doughnut. He chewed on it in the moonlight, watching the location where the two men had fallen. *The last thing I'm going to do,* he thought, *is walk up on two gunmen in the dark. I can't think of a faster way to get a belly full of lead. No, I'll sit here until daylight or until Schmidt sends riders out from the ranch. I know they heard the gunshots.*

Thunder had gone back to cropping grass. An owl hooted from the darkness.

Cain moaned again. "Marshal, I swear I'm dying. I need help bad."

Jack took another bite of doughnut, chewed, and swallowed. "How about if I help you the way you boys were set on helping me."

"Marshal, you cain't be holdin' a grudge. We was afeared you might come after us. It was crazy, I know, but you know how fear works on a man. Ohhh, Marshal, I'm hurtin' real bad."

Jack was on his third doughnut when Thunder's head lifted and turned toward the ranch. A couple of heartbeats later, Jack heard horses' hooves walking, more than one. He shoved his revolver into its holster and picked up his rifle. Raising his voice to ensure he was heard, Jack called, "You boys best ride in cautious like. There's a couple of wounded coyotes on the ground. No telling whether or not they might start throwing lead at you."

Someone in the group called, "Is that you, Marshal Sage?"

"Yep."

River Jordan spoke up, his voice weak. "Dallas?"

"Yep. Marshal, mind if we ride in? No matter what they've

done, those are our men. We'd like to pick them up and get them back to the ranch."

"Sure, but stay clear of me. After your boys tried to ambush me, my finger's a little itchy. I'll ride in at daylight."

"We brought some torches. Mind if we light them?"

"Go right ahead. Just keep all your men together over there. I'd hate to see someone else pick up a bullet tonight."

Torches lit. In the light, Jack could make out four men, but he kept his eyes moving, making sure there was no one trying to slip in from behind him. *I don't think Dallas would try something like that,* he thought, *but I didn't get this old by taking chances.*

As if reading his mind, Dallas called, "We'll stay over here, Marshal."

Cain moaned. "Right here, Dallas. Hurry, I'm almighty bad, so's River."

Jack could see the riders pull up. In the rocks, he was protected from their light, but he was able to watch as they dismounted and went to work on the two men. One of the riders led the gunmen's horses to where they lay. Jack saw Dallas pick up the bullet-riddled blanket. He held it up to one of the torches.

He must be checking for bullet holes, Jack thought.

"Marshal, you mind if I take this blanket back to the ranch? I'd like to show Mr. Schmidt."

"You best not. It's evidence. When daylight rolls around, I'll pick it up and ride by. Schmidt can see it then."

"Alright."

Jack watched Dallas Fisher lay the blanket next to the pile of rocks and turn to the wounded men. The other hands were getting them as ready as possible. "You boys sure played hob tonight. What the blue blazes got into you?"

River Jordan said nothing. He had been quiet for a while.

Cain spoke up. "Get me back to the ranch, Dallas. I'm hurt bad."

The cowhand looked down at the prone figure. "You're lucky

you ain't dead, or unlucky. Your little ambush will get you a date with the hangman for sure."

Cain gave a low moan and was silent.

"We're gonna take them now, Marshal."

"Go ahead. I'll be in at daylight."

The men loaded River Jordan in front of one of the cowhands and helped Cain to his feet. "Oh, it hurts. Cain't you fellers get a wagon out here? I don't know if I can ride."

"The ranch ain't far. You can ride or stay till daylight. Your choice."

Jack chuckled at Dallas Fisher's response. He was a hard, impatient man and was saying what Jack might have said.

They shoved Cain into the saddle, and Jack watch Dallas swing up.

"We're gone, Marshal. Much obliged. Come on in when you're ready. There'll at least be coffee, I'll promise you that, and I think this'll straighten out Mr. Schmidt's thinking as far as River's concerned."

"At daylight, then." Jack watched the hands ride slowly away from the ridge and toward the ranch. When they were gone, he lay back down, pulled his blanket up, and was fast asleep.

A bright blue sky awoke him. He checked Thunder, who was chewing and staring at him. Throwing the blanket aside, he rose and stretched. It was cold, but there would be no fire this morning. The thought of possible fresh coffee at the ranch, no matter how unwelcome he might be, kept him moving. He picked up his brass casings from the night before and dropped them into his saddlebags. Next he rolled his bed, tied it, and laid it across the rest of his gear. First thing was to get Thunder to water. He strode to the big horse, untied the rope from the stake, and coiled it. Reaching the animal, he patted him on the neck and led him to the tinkling stream. When the horse was finished drinking, he led him back and began gathering his equipment.

Jack saved the blanket for last. He had saddled and loaded the big gray, and now he bent to check River Jordan and Cain's handiwork. His rock pile had been real enough to fool them. Grabbing the blanket, he held it high. His would-be killers had managed to put five bullet holes through the wool blanket. He found it funny that there were only five holes. They had shot at least eight times, maybe more, and only hit five out of eight. Jack shook his head. They had been almost on top of the bed.

He folded the blanket and looked back toward where he had been in the rocks and boulders, and congratulated himself. He had been pretty well hidden, yet as big as he was, he was lucky Jordan hadn't hit him. At the thought, he fingered the bullet tear in his upper left sleeve. Close.

Grasping the riddled blanket, he swung into the saddle. After stopping at Schmidt's to find out how his two would-be attackers were, he'd head into Laramie.

From his camp to the ranch was a short ride, and a different Schmidt greeted him from the tall porch. "It is good you came back, Marshal. It gives a hard-headed German an opportunity to apologize. Step down and come in."

Jack swung down from his saddle. He loosened the cinch on Thunder, tucked the blanket under his arm, and looped the reins over the hitching rail in front of the house. Schmidt met him at the bottom step, his big hand extended. "I am sorry, Marshal Sage. To my discredit, I believed River Jordan."

Jack shook the extended hand. "Think nothing of it. Some folks can be mighty sly."

"*Ja*, now how about something to eat?"

Jack nodded. "Well, sir, I sure wouldn't say no to that idea."

The two men walked up the steps to the porch. Schmidt rubbed his hands together. "It is a cold morning. You would think it would be warmer. This is much like our Bavarian alps, cold mornings, nice days."

"Mr. Schmidt, I need to check on Jordan and Cain first."

"*Ja, ja*, of course." He opened the door and led Jack into the big warm house. A fire roared in the massive fireplace, which filled the right side of the parlor, fronted by a long green upholstered divan with wide wooden arms. A low coffee table, blonde wood glistening, ran the length of the divan. Across from the table sat two oversized cowhide leather chairs.

"This way."

Jack followed the German across the parlor and past the wide entrance to the kitchen, through which poured aromas that immediately kicked Jack's salivary glands into a full gallop. He followed the ranch owner down a hall. Halfway to the end, Schmidt stopped and opened a door to the left. There were two single beds sitting side by side. One held the man Jack suspected was Cain. It was impossible to tell whom the other bed held, for the sheet had been pulled over the person's face. Jack stepped to the dead man's bedside and pulled the sheet back to see a very pale, very dead River Jordan. He covered the man's face and turned to Cain.

He wasn't looking much better, but his red eyes were fastened on Jack. "I think you killed me too, Marshal."

Jack stepped to Cain's bedside. The stench of a punctured gut was strong. "Who hired you?"

Cain's eyes widened, and he gave a feeble shake of his head. "Ain't no one hired us. We had a bottle in the bunkhouse. After a few drinks, River got a wild hair and decided to go after you. I went with him." Pain racked his body, causing his legs to pull toward his chest. He was rigid for a few moments, then slowly relaxed. "I shoulda stayed here."

Schmidt looked at Jack and gave a faint shake of his head.

Cain caught the look and movement. His hand pushed from under the sheet and grasped Schmidt's arm. "I'm dyin', ain't I? Tell me the truth, boss. I got a right to know."

"*Ja*, Cain, you are dying. There's nothing anyone can do for you besides making you as comfortable as possible."

"Could I have some whiskey, boss?"

Schmidt nodded. "*Ja*, though it sounds like demon drink is exactly what got you into this. I'll have a bottle and glass brought in."

Cain grimaced again. "Soon, boss. It hurts somethin' fierce."

"I'll see to it right now." He left the room.

Moments later a square-faced, heavyset young woman walked in with a bottle of whiskey and a glass on a tray. "Good morning, sir."

Jack nodded. "Ma'am."

She placed the glass on the small table next to the bed, uncorked the bottle, and poured until the glass was half full. Looking at Cain, she said, "Do you need help?"

Beads of perspiration covered his forehead. "Ma'am, I'd sure be grateful if you would."

She grasped the glass and slid her other hand behind his head. She lifted slowly, raising his head while placing the glass at his lips. He took three large swallows and relaxed his head. She allowed his head to sink to the pillow and removed her hand. Turning to the table, she picked up the bottle and repeated her pour, then placed the bottle on the table and looked at Jack. "If there's anything else, sir, please call."

"Thanks," Jack said. His eyes locked on Cain. He heard the door open and close.

"So the only reason you two came out to my camp is that Jordan wanted to dry gulch me, and you went along?"

"That's about the size of it, Marshal. It was a wild hair on his part. Me, I was just stupid."

"But if you had succeeded, you would've thought you were really smart."

Cain wouldn't meet his eyes. "I reckon you've got me there. I been following the wrong people my whole life. I finally get a chance here, and I blow it." Tears welled up in the man's eyes.

Jack watched the man prepare for his demise. *He's young,* he thought, *can't be over twenty-three or four.* "What's your name, Cain?"

Cain looked up, a tear leaking from his left eye. "The name my ma gave me is Cain Thomas Walker. Guess that'll be the name I'll go out with."

The gunman looked across at his trousers. The maid had folded them over a ladder-back chair. "Marshal, there's a twenty-dollar gold piece in my pants pocket. I'd be obliged if you'd send it to my folks. They're in Danbury, Connecticut. My pa's name is Abraham Jonas Walker." He coughed and grimaced. "You'd never think a Connecticut boy would end his life like this."

For several minutes his moans were louder, then gradually decreased in volume. He gazed up at Jack. "I don't blame you, Marshal. I knew River had that other gun. I should've moved farther away. You did what you had to do."

Hank Schmidt cracked the door. "Marshal Sage, you have a minute?"

Jack walked to the door, stopped, and looked back. He felt sorry for the man, but he also knew when they had arrived at his camp, River and Cain had been set on killing him. He released a long sigh and stepped through the door. "What can I do for you, Hank?"

"You hungry?"

"I am."

"The men have eaten, and the kitchen is free. We can eat and talk. The only person who will be in there is Olga, a fine cook. My mother wouldn't come to the states unless we brought Olga. Thankfully, she wanted to come."

"Thanks, I'd like that."

Entering the large kitchen, Schmidt pointed to a chair and took one across the table from him.

There was more food than he could devour in a week. Olga fried him six eggs and placed a huge platter of bacon and another of biscuits on the table. He made the eggs disappear along with a large portion of the bacon and several biscuits. "Olga, that was mighty fine, thank you."

"*Ja*, is my pleasure, Marshal."

He took a long sip of coffee. "Are you planning on burying the two bodies?"

Schmidt nodded. "If that's alright with the law. We've got a graveyard of sorts. One of the hands was a preacher. He handles whatever ceremonies we need."

"That'll be fine. The government will pay you."

"No need. Now, what did you ride out here for? I feel sure there was something before all of this craziness started."

"Yep. Someone tried to kill Josephine Franklin a couple of nights ago."

Schmidt jerked erect, eyes wide with surprise, and began speaking in rapid German. He stopped, took a deep breath, and began again in English. "Was she hurt?"

"No, she's fine."

"How about the girls and David?"

"They're all fine. Whoever made the attempt missed. It was close, but she was lucky. You heard the killer of General Franklin and his son rode an unshod horse. Have you or your men seen anyone riding such an animal?"

Schmidt nodded. His mouth curled in disgust. "All the time. Most of the Poling bunch ride shoeless stock. He is hard on his animals and doesn't take care of his ranch." His eyes focused on the fireplace in the parlor. After a few moments, he looked back at Jack. "I don't think much of that bunch, but ambushing and backshooting doesn't sound like Poling. He strikes me as the type who comes straight at you, though I don't know about the boys."

Jack nodded. "My thoughts exactly. I think they are all dangerous, but I'm guessing the boys are much like the old man." When he had entered the kitchen, he had laid the folded blanket on the table. Now, he slid his chair back, took another sip of coffee, and rose. Picking up the blanket, he let it fall open, exposing the holes puncturing the woolen fabric. "Just wanted you to see for yourself. Those two slipped up within ten feet of where they thought I was sleeping and cut loose. They shot eight times."

Schmidt shook his head. "I'm mighty sorry my men would do such a thing. I am an honest rancher and never expected anything like that from them. I was growing mighty fond of River. It just shows how a man can be fooled."

"When did you hire them?"

"Couple of months back. Only I didn't hire them. Brock Stewart, my foreman, hired both River and Cain at the same time. He said they were good men."

"Is that the older fella who was standing with you when I rode in yesterday?"

"That's him, Brockman Stewart. He goes by Brock. He's been with me since I started this ranch. He's a good man and knows cattle like a swamper knows his spittoons."

Jack took another sip of coffee. "River and Cain came in together?"

"*Ja*, that is a fact."

"And Stewart said they were good men." Jack spoke this last sentence softly, almost to himself.

He folded up the blanket and placed it on the table. "I need to talk to Stewart."

Through the window, a cowhand could be seen walking by the kitchen. Schmidt rose and walked to the kitchen door. Opening it, he called to the hand, "Tell Brock to meet me in the kitchen. I need to talk to him."

10

The kitchen door swung open, and Stewart stepped in. "You wanted to see me, boss?"

"*Ja*. The marshal has a few questions for you."

The man removed his leather gloves and shoved them into the pockets of his coat, then slipped it off. "How's Cain doing?"

Jack shook his head. "That young fella will be dead before night." He pointed to a chair across the table. "Have a seat."

Brock Stewart dropped his coat across the back of the chair and sat. Olga placed a full cup of steaming black coffee in front of him. He gave her a relaxed but sad smile. "Thank you, Olga."

She returned the smile. "My pleasure, Mr. Stewart."

Jack took his seat again and sat evaluating the foreman. He was probably mid-forties, graying black hair, and straightforward gray eyes. He had the wrinkles of a man who had spent most of his life battling the elements, staring into the distance, looking for cattle, rustlers, or Indians. He carried himself with the confidence that would be expected of a foreman of a ranch like this, wide shoulders, thick forearms and biceps, though he didn't compare in size to his boss. Jack figured he was a couple of inches under six feet. He sat quietly sipping his coffee, accepting Jack's examination with aplomb.

Jack began. "You hired River Jordan and Cain?"

Stewart turned slightly in his chair to face Schmidt. "Figured they might be what this was about. Boss, I shoulda been straight with you. When I finish explaining, I'll be moving on. I know you won't have a dishonest man workin' for you." He turned back to Jack.

"River was my nephew, my sister's boy. You should've seen him when he was a tyke." He stared out the window as if he were looking into the past. "He was the kind of towheaded kid any man would be happy to have for a son." His eyes found Jack's again. "But his pa was a no-good drunk who wasn't happy unless he was beating on something weaker or smaller than himself. They'd come as far as St. Louis. He didn't have the gumption to come any farther. They settled on a small dry-land farm that barely produced enough to keep them alive, and then he drank up what he made. River was their oldest, and he took the brunt."

Jack stopped the man. "We've got the picture, Stewart. It's a sad thing, but there's a lot of boys who are beaten and don't grow up to be killers."

"You're right, Marshal. But he was my kin. Don't get me wrong. You did what you had to do. I hold nothing against you. The boy and Cain crossed way over the line." He turned again to Schmidt. "But he was finding his way. He was a hard worker. It looked like he might make it. If it just hadn't been for love of the bottle and his temper."

Schmidt's jaws were set and brow wrinkled. "You should have told me, Brock. I trusted your judgment. I would have been more than willing to take him on."

Brock Stewart said nothing, but turned back to Jack. "I wanted to give him a chance. I figured I could keep an eye on him and maybe hogtie any wild ideas he might have."

Jack watched Stewart's eyes as he made his next statement.

"Someone shot at Josephine Franklin night before last. She was almost killed. You have any ideas who might have pulled that off?"

Brock's gray eyes opened wide. "Why would anyone shoot at Mrs. Franklin? She wouldn't harm a soul."

"Stewart, I'm asking you."

The foreman shook his head. "Shoot no, I don't have the slightest idea who would do such a thing. I've been racking my mind trying to figure out who killed General Franklin and his boy. None of it makes any sense. There's been way too much killing in this valley, if you ask me."

Jack leaned toward Stewart. "Amy Franklin and her son, Davy, were attacked the same day."

The big German leaped to his feet. "What are you saying? You said everyone was alright."

"Relax, Hank. Everyone is fine. Sit down, and I'll tell you about it."

Schmidt hesitated and then eased back into his chair. Jack told them everything about the broken wheel and the gang from Laramie. When he was done, Schmidt was aghast. "What is going on? Who could want to harm the Franklins?" He turned to Brock. "Get men together. Leave enough here to run the ranch. We're going down to help them."

Stewart was startled. "I still work here?"

"*Ja*, you're a good man who knows cattle. I'd be a fool to fire you over one mistake. I'm thinking you won't be keeping anything else from me."

Brock Stewart got to his feet and grabbed his coat. "You're thinking right, boss." He glanced at Jack. "You have any more questions for me?"

Jack shook his head.

"Then I'm gonna check on Cain, and I'll get the crew together."

He circled the table, and his boots and spurs could be heard going down the hallway.

Jack shoved his chair back and stood. "I'll be heading for Laramie. I think it's a good idea to head down and give your neighbors a hand. I know Tripp and the boys are trying to keep a watch on Jo and the others while working the ranch. They've got to be a little thin." He picked up the blanket. "Thanks for your hospitality." He grinned. "I mean it this time."

Schmidt rose. "You are welcome anytime, Marshal. I wish you good hunting."

Jack was opening the door when he heard the steps of Stewart returning from Cain. With his hand on the door, he waited.

The foreman strode out of the hallway. "He's gone." He glanced at Schmidt. "I'll get the boys working on another hole next to River's. If it's alright with you, before we leave, I'll have Lester say a few words over them."

"That'll be fine."

Jack pulled the door open and stepped back, allowing Stewart to step outside. He followed him to Thunder, while Schmidt stopped at the low fence, staring at Stewart's back as he strode toward the bunkhouse. "You think I'm right in keeping him? After all, he did lie to me."

"All I can tell you is what I've seen. He appears to be a dependable, competent man, who made the mistake of hiding his relative's flaws. Reckon that could happen to any of us." Jack tightened Thunder's cinch, securing the loose end, dropped his stirrup, and stepped into the saddle. "I'm obliged for your help."

"Haven't been much. Good luck to you."

Jack raised an index finger to his hat in salute and turned Thunder toward the valley and Laramie.

∼

It had been a long ride. His old leg wound was acting up. When he swung down, it almost gave way. He hung onto the saddle, flexed and swung the leg until it would hold his weight. Then he let Thunder drink. They had reached the Laramie River, just north of the town of Laramie. Smoke rose from the rail yards, and even from here, the clang of hammers against steel assaulted his ears. Trains brought civilization, but they brought so much more to the west he could do without, including civilization. When Thunder had drunk his fill, Jack tightened the cinch and climbed aboard.

It was time to see what Laramie was all about. When he had passed through before, he had been set on reaching the ranch. Was it only the day before yesterday? So much had happened in the last two days. His last stop here had netted him no information. Of course, he hadn't known what he knew today. He wanted to find out about this Bowden Jessup and anything else that might pertain to the D Bar J and the death of the Franklin men. He had a wheelwright who ranked high on his list, but he would ask a few questions before he broke one of Toler's hammers over his head. Just the thought of the man intentionally putting a bad wheel on Amy's wagon started Jack's blood percolating.

He guided Thunder past Toler's place, a general store, a gun shop, five saloons, two law offices, two hotels, a shipping office, and a barbershop next door to Otto's Livery. "Looks like here's a chance for you to rest up, fella." He swung down in front of the wide door and led Thunder into the stable. From inside, he could hear someone whistling "Yankee Doodle Dandy." At the clump of Thunder's hooves, the whistling stopped. A blocky man of about forty years, with huge forearms, stepped from a stall, rake in hand.

"Morning, mister. Looking to put your horse up?"

"Howdy. I'd like that. You Otto?"

"In the flesh, I be. Best livery this side of Denver."

"Thunder's mighty glad to hear it."

Otto laughed. "Most animals are. They tend to like it around here. He might not want to leave."

Jack gave the man a wry grin. "Being a horse, as much as I like him, he's not gonna get much of a say."

"Yep, I can understand that. It'll be two bits a day, and I'll take good care of Thunder. Looks like he'd appreciate a good rubdown and some oats." The man pointed to a stall just past the one he was cleaning. "If you want to leave your gear in the tack room, it'll be safe until you call for it."

"Much obliged." Jack stripped his gear from Thunder and carried it to the tack room. When all was secured, he stepped out with his rifle and saddlebags.

Otto had already given Thunder oats and hay, had a stiff brush in hand, and was working on the big horse. The livery door faced west. Jack glanced at the lowering sun. "Where's a good place to eat and stay? I'm looking for food, rest, and information."

"I can definitely help you with the first two. The best place to eat is the Laramie Eatery. It's run by a crotchety old railroad cook who can make magic with food. I will tell you though, don't complain about anything, or, even as big as you are, he'll run you out of his establishment with his ten-gauge shotgun."

"Duly warned. I have no argument with a man if he's a good cook."

"That's the reason he's survived all these years. Everyone would miss his cooking if anything happened to him."

"So where is it?"

Otto had been brushing Thunder's flank. He straightened and held the brush up at Jack. "Hold on, don't be in such a hurry. It will all come together. Now one of the things you'll have to contend with is train noise, plus all the noise coming from the Union Pacific Machine Shops. Seems they're banging those hammers into the night almost every night, but a man gets used to it. Anyway, the best hotel is the Gleason. The buildings in town are new, no more than three or four years old, since the railroad came through, but the Gleason is a little more expensive. Enough so, most of the folks who stay there like to take baths. Meaning no bedbugs. Cleanest place in town. The downside is it's the closest to the train station and the machine shops, so it's gonna be a little noisier. Somehow, Mrs. Gleason managed to coax old man Farnsworth into her establishment. So the Laramie Eatery is in the Gleason Hotel, and the hotel is closest to the train depot, which you can't miss. So there you've got it all."

Otto had gone back to work on Thunder.

"All except information."

The liveryman didn't miss a stroke. "Barbershop right next door. That's my brother. Nicest fella in the world, but if there's anything going on within a hundred miles of Laramie, he'll know about it."

Jack rubbed his stubble, which was longer now that another day was almost over. "I could use a barber and a bath before I eat."

"If you hurry, he can take care of both. He closes around five thirty."

Jack took out a silver dollar. "Otto."

He looked up, and Jack flipped it to him. His big hand snagged it out of the air. "Four days?"

Jack shrugged. "Maybe. Thanks for the info."

The man waved, and Jack turned for the door and the barbershop next door. He needed a good washing and shave. He stepped around the corner of the livery and headed toward the barbershop. He was reaching for the door when it was jerked open, and a big man charged out, slamming into Jack.

Jack's weight was spread nicely when the man hit him, and with his bulk, it was almost like running into a tree. The big man bounced off Jack, slammed back into the door facing, stumbled, and sat down hard on the boardwalk. Jack felt bad about knocking the man down, and reached his empty right hand out to give him a lift. "Sorry—"

The well-dressed bruiser slapped his hand away and lunged to his feet, straightening his frock coat. "You should be sorry. You cow nurses are all over the place. For two cents I'd teach you a lesson you'd not soon forget."

Jack stepped back and braced himself, still feeling a bit guilty about knocking the man down. "Friend, tell me your name, and after I get cleaned up, I'll buy you a drink at whatever establishment you prefer."

The man looked him over, taking in the two days' growth of beard, red eyes from being on the trail, and trail dust. "I'd drink nowhere a saddle bum like you could afford."

Jack could feel his temper beginning to rise. This altercation was kinda his fault, and he was the law, but this blustering windbag was getting on his nerves. "Mister, I've tried to apologize, but it seems you care nothing about anything but insulting people. It strikes me you must be too full of yourself. The offer of a drink still goes, but if you feel your small amount of dignity has been insulted, I'll be glad to give you whatever satisfaction you desire. I need to get cleaned up, but a tiny bit more sweat from taking care of you won't make any difference." *Great,* Jack thought, *that's defusing the situation. The last thing you want is to make a scene in this town, and you a United States Marshal.*

The man's little pig-eye pupils tightened. "You listen to me, saddle tramp. I don't take insults from the likes of you. I chew your kind up and spit them out for snacks before breakfast."

Jack shook his head. *This guy is going to talk me to death,* he thought. He reached for the barbershop's door handle and pushed. "Have a nice d—"

He never saw the blow coming. The massive fist caught him behind his left ear and dropped him like a sack of rocks.

The next thing he knew, he was stretched out in the doctor's office. His eyes blinked open to see a gray-haired man standing over him with a stethoscope hanging around his neck, holding Jack's wrist. He looked up at the man. "Doc?"

Relief flooded the doctor's face. "Ahh, good. I was concerned about you. I saw where you'd been struck before in the back of the head and hoped this blow didn't exacerbate the old injury. How are you feeling?"

"Wobbly as all get out. What happened?"

"It seems that you got into an argument with the wrong man."

"All we did was bump into each other, and this fella goes crazy. I was trying to get away from him because I have a lot to do. I reached for the barbershop door, and that's the last I remember until now."

"Yes, well, unfortunately the gentleman you had the disagreement with is Lewis McClain. He's the western manager of the Union Pacific. I know little about him except he worked his way to his current position from a track layer, and he's a hard, unforgiving man. He said you attacked him."

Jack pushed the doctor away and swung his legs over the side. He was woozy for a few moments, then the room stabilized. "Well, if that means I accidentally ran into him when he came charging out of the barbershop, then he would be right. But that is a funny thing for a man to say who sucker punches another." Jack could feel his anger beginning to rise. The train executive had hit him completely unaware. The act of a bully. He looked around for his coat, vest, hat, and guns. They were laid out neatly on a divan in the examination room. He stood and found he was stable. Evidently the effects of the blow had worn off.

The first thing he did was pick up his guns, swing them around his waist, and fasten the buckle. He checked their positions were proper, and released the leather loops that kept the revolvers in their holsters. Then he picked up his vest and swung it on. As he was putting on his coat, the doctor spoke.

"I guess he didn't know you were a U.S. Marshal." A small grin played at the corners of the doctor's lips. "I imagine he'll be a little surprised."

Jack shook his head as he pulled on his coat. "The man I talked to wouldn't have cared. This was the most self-centered individual I have met, other than the ones I've put behind bars."

"How much do I owe you, Doc? And I don't even know your name."

"I'm Jeff Tilson. How about four bits?"

Jack pulled out a fifty-cent piece and handed it to the doctor. "I'm obliged. Where will I find this Lewis McClain?"

"What are you going to do, Marshal?"

"I'm going to arrest him and throw him in jail. It'll do him some good to cool his heels in the lockup for a while. Maybe there's some cowhands in there. He'll like that." Jack stopped. "Where's the jail?"

"Across the street toward the train station. You can't miss it. Sheriff Wright may be there, then again he may not. He spends a lot of time fishing."

"And where is McClain's office?"

"By the train station. You can't miss it. There's a big Union Pacific Offices sign above the door."

"Thanks, Doc. I appreciate your help."

"Good luck to you."

Jack grinned. "Doc, I'm always lucky."

He stepped out the door onto the landing and heard a train whistle blow. He marched down the stairs and turned left toward the depot. On the way he crossed the street to stop at the sheriff's office. Pushing through the door, he stepped inside to see a young man, his feet propped on the desk, a cup of coffee in one hand, and a dime novel in the other. The young fella looked up. His hat, both sides of the brim bent up and folded against the crown, was pushed to the back of his head, balancing precariously. "Can I help you?"

"Looking for the sheriff."

Feet still on the desk, the young man shook his head. The hat wobbled. "Not here. Gone fishing. Good fishing up the Laramie a ways."

"Need a set of wrist irons."

At the request, the deputy looked closer at Jack. "Who are you, and what do you need wrist irons for?"

"Look, I don't have time to play question and answer here." He pulled his coat back so the deputy could see his U.S. Marshal badge.

The deputy's eyes bugged, his feet hit the floor, and his hat followed, hitting the floor and lying on its side. He spun around, grabbed his hat, slapped it onto his head, reached into a drawer below the rifle rack, and pulled out a well-cared-for set of wrist irons.

"Key?"

The boy took a key from the sheriff's desk and handed it to Jack. He shoved it into a vest pocket and handed the deputy his saddlebags. "Hang onto these, will you?"

"Sure." The deputy took them and leaned them against the back side of the desk.

Jack pointed his chin toward the jail. "Get it ready. I'll be bringing in one man. Put him in a cell by himself. He'll be a little upset."

"Anybody I know?"

"Maybe." Jack picked up the irons with his left hand, which was also holding his Winchester. "I'll be right back."

"Need some help?" The deputy rose as he was asking the question.

"Nope, this won't take long." Jack was out the door. He walked down the boardwalk, rifle in one hand and irons hanging from the other, until reaching the big Union Pacific Offices sign. Opening the door, he strode toward the clerk standing behind the counter. "Where's Lewis McClain's office?" Before the clerk could answer, Jack recognized the loud voice coming from a large office to his right. "Never mind." He turned and headed for the door.

"Sir," the clerk called. Then seeing Jack wasn't stopping, he called again, more insistent, "Sir, Mr. McClain is in a meeting. He can't be disturbed."

Jack walked up to the door and, without stopping, drove a booted foot through the latch. The etched-glass section with McClain's name engraved across it shattered, and the door flew open. McClain sat behind a large desk, one of his big hands grasping a tumbler of liquor, the other caught in the air pointing at one of the men, the laugh frozen on his face. The other two men in the room were dressed much like McClain, executives of some type.

Jack continued across the room to halt next to McClain's chair. "Mind if I join the party?"

McClain slammed his drink on his desk, liquor splashing across scattered papers. "You broke my door. You can't come in here. I'm Lewis McClain."

Jack dropped the heavy wrist irons on the desk, gouging the polished wood. "Thanks for identifying yourself. Recognize me? You're under arrest for assaulting a United States Marshal. Put those wrist irons on."

The other men were on their feet.

McClain's lower jaw shot out. He yelled to anyone within the sound of his voice, "Get the detectives in here, and throw this yahoo out."

One of the other men in McClain's office shouted, "You're making a big mistake, Marshal."

Jack swung the rifle around the room, holding it like a sixgun. "You gents take a seat and shut up." He turned back to McClain. "Last chance, big boy. Walk to jail or be carried, your choice."

McClain glared at Jack through hard blue eyes. "You can go to H—"

Jack hit him in the back of the head with the Winchester's

butt. It wasn't hard enough to kill him, just enough to jostle his brains a bit. McClain dropped into his plush leather chair.

"Now put those bracelets on like I said."

McClain reached for the irons as two big men, sixguns in hand, charged into the room.

11

Loud enough for the two men to hear him, but in a conversational tone, Jack said, "United States Marshal, boys. I recommend you lower your weapons and let the law take care of its business." Jack pulled his coat back, exposing the U.S. Marshal badge.

One of the men began to step forward, but the other man put his hand out to stop him. It was the second man who said, "What's the charge?"

McClain had dropped the wrist irons when the detectives rushed in. Jack nudged him with the muzzle of the Winchester. "Get on with it."

Still woozy, he picked up the first one and slipped it on his wrist. As soon as it was pressed together, Jack pulled the key from his vest, inserted and turned it. "Now the other."

McClain slowly picked up the other wristband, slipped his thick wrist in, and pulled it together. Jack locked the second one.

He moved slightly so he could more directly address the detectives and keep his eyes on McClain. "The charge is assaulting a United States Marshal."

The detective's eyes grew big, as if he couldn't believe what he was hearing. "You're the man he coldcocked at the barbershop?"

Jack nodded. "One and only." He prodded McClain in the ribs with the rifle's muzzle. "Get up."

McClain slowly stood, glaring at the detectives. "Aren't you two going to stop him?"

The one who had been talking shook his head. "No, we're not. You slugged the wrong person this time, Mr. McClain. You don't pay me enough to tangle with the marshals."

McClain turned to one of the suits in the room. "You're a lawyer. Do something."

The man held up shaking hands. "Nothing I can do, Lew. He's a federal lawman. The judge isn't due through here from Cheyenne for another week. You'll spend at least that long there unless you can work something out with the marshal."

McClain's voice rose. "You're telling me I'll have to spend a week in that pest-ridden jail? Do something now!"

Jack poked the rifle barrel in McClain's ribs. "The best part, you'll probably have some of those filthy cowhands you like so much in there with you. Now move. I don't have all day. I still need a bath and a shave."

McClain turned his big head toward Jack, the new lump behind his left ear standing tall. "I'll have your job, lawman. You'll never work for anyone again."

The muzzle of the Winchester prodded again, harder. "Don't make me give you another tap."

A string of oaths poured from the man's mouth, but he started for the door. The two detectives moved out of their way, allowing both McClain and Jack to pass.

Stepping by the detective who had stopped the other from moving on Jack, McClain spoke two words. "You're fired."

The man dropped his gun into his holster, turned, and led them toward the front door. By now, a crowd had gathered in the lobby and could be seen outside around the office's entrance. McClain looked up to Jack and spoke, almost in a whisper. "Marshal, don't make me go out there with these irons on. My kids might be outside. They don't need to see me like this."

The man didn't know it, but with those words he had hit Jack in a softer spot than when he'd sucker punched him. "Hold up."

McClain stopped.

"Are you telling me the truth, or is this just a ruse to keep from having to walk to jail in irons in front of your neighbors?"

"Gospel truth, Marshal. I've got four kids. They could be out there or their friends could. I'll give you my word, I'll walk to jail and give you no problem. Just let me do it without these irons on."

"I'll make you a deal. You rehire the detective you just fired, right now."

McClain looked at the man and nodded. "That's not hard. I'd a probably done that anyway, but you're hired back."

The man nodded to Jack.

Jack reached into his vest pocket and pulled out the key. "Understand, you're still going to jail, but we'll walk together, side by side, no irons."

"I'm good with that."

"Hold out your hands."

McClain followed orders, and Jack unlocked the wrist irons. Once they were off, and while McClain rubbed his thick wrists, Jack handed the irons to the rehired detective. "You mind bringing those around to the jail later?"

"Be glad to, Marshal."

Jack nodded. "Let's go, McClain."

The two men walked outside. They were met with a crowd flowing into the street.

A cute little girl with a turned-up nose and red hair came running up to McClain. "Are you alright, Papa?"

He knelt and picked her up in his thick arms, continuing

down the boardwalk. "Of course I am, my darlin'. I'm as fine as a frog's hair." Jack strode alongside them.

The little girl didn't crack a smile, but eyed him cautiously. "Who's the big man?"

"He's a United States Marshal, honey. Would you like to see his badge?"

She nodded, and McClain looked up at Jack.

Jack pulled his coat aside, exposing the badge for her to see.

She reached out, and Jack leaned over, letting her touch it. "It's really shiny."

McClain said, "It sure is, honey." He stopped, gave her a kiss on her plump cheek, and set her down. "Now go tell your mama I might not be home tonight, but I'm all right."

She kissed his cheek in return. "Bye, Papa." She dashed off, her fat little legs almost a blur.

They continued to walk.

"This don't mean I'm not gonna beat you to a pulp, *Marshal*." The last word was spoken in contempt. "I don't let anyone treat me like this. I've beaten people so bad their own mother wouldn't recognize them, and when I'm finished with you . . ."

"You sure talk a lot, McClain, and sucker punch folks."

They reached the jail and left the crowd outside. When Jack stepped in behind McClain, he was greeted by a man about his age. Shorter and slimmer, but wearing a sheriff's badge and smelling like fish. Jack ignored him. He shoved McClain toward the door leading to the cells and said to the deputy, "Lock him up."

The deputy opened the door and stepped through to the back. Jack shoved McClain toward the last cell.

The man turned. "Don't push me, Marshal."

Jack leveled the rifle at the man's belly. "I don't have time for you now, McClain. Get moving."

The railroad man grudgingly turned and followed the deputy to the empty cell. There were three jail cells. The other two were occupied, one with drunken cowhands and the other with drunken railroad hands. The railroad hands stared, their mouths open, as McClain walked past to the last cell. When it was locked, Jack nodded to the deputy and exited the jail. He was immediately confronted by the sheriff.

"Can you explain to me why you've jailed Mr. McClain? He's an important railroad executive in this town."

The sheriff had a pointed nose, and his chin seemed to disappear under his bottom lip with his head tilted up while he glared at Jack. His eyes were narrow, with a perpetual squint, but Jack had learned you can't judge a man by his looks.

"Howdy, Sheriff Wright, I'm United States Marshal Jack Sage."

"I don't care if you're President Grant. I wanta know why you've arrested Mr. McClain."

"Sheriff, I haven't arrested him, I've jailed him. I'm releasing him in the morning. I've jailed him because he is a rude and inconsiderate man, and he assaulted me at the barbershop."

"He assaulted you?"

"Yeah. He sucker punched me in the back of the head as I was entering the barbershop, knocked me cold as a poleaxed steer. If I wanted to push it, I could wait and take him before a federal judge, but that's too petty. I just want him to think before he goes off on some innocent citizen who can't defend himself."

The sheriff stared up at Jack. "I could release him as soon as you leave."

"You could, Sheriff, but you'll have the entire Marshal Service down on you. Hold him until in the morning after he's had his breakfast with the rest of the drunks. Then if I haven't made it back, turn him loose." Jack's gaze stiffened. "But don't you release him before then for anyone."

Jack nodded to the deputy as he picked up his saddlebags. "Thanks, Deputy." He glanced toward the sheriff. "If you need me, I'll be at the barbershop and then the Gleason Hotel."

The sheriff pulled out his pocket watch, stared at it, and

dropped it back into its pocket. "Barbershop's closed. He locks up at five thirty on the dot. You'll be getting that shave tomorrow unless you do it yourself."

It was Jack's turn to glare at the sheriff. He jerked his head toward the jail. "So he not only sucker punched me, but he cost me a shave and a bath. I should drag him out of there and give him the beating he deserves."

The deputy spoke up. "Better bring a lunch, Marshal. You got you one mean hombre in there. The sheriff's almost arrested him several times for assaultin' folks." He grinned at the sheriff. "But he didn't."

The sheriff frowned at the insinuation. "Johnny, it's time for your rounds. Get 'em done."

Johnny hung the jail keys back on the wall and sauntered out the door, whistling.

Wright watched him go. "The son of my sister. He needed a job."

Jack watched the young fella through the office window. "In a town like this, that's the kind of favor that could get him killed."

Wright shook his head. "Johnny's pretty good with a gun, and he's smart. He's doing fine."

"Pretty good will get you killed, too, but it's none of my business. You know where I'll be. Stop by, and I'll buy you supper."

The sheriff perked up. "Sure thing. When?"

"About an hour." Jack walked out the door and headed for the barbershop. He had no desire to eat with Sheriff Wright, but he had questions, and over supper might be a good time to get them answered.

Reaching the barbershop, he clasped the latch and tried it. Locked. In the large picture window, on the other side of the red, white, and blue barber pole, hung a closed sign. Jack looked through the glass. Inside, he could see a man in a long white apron sweeping. He knocked gently on the window's glass. The man looked up, saw Jack, and started to shake his head. Jack could see him look closer, lean his broom against the shelf behind the barber's chair, and walk to the door. It took him a moment, but he unlocked the door and swung it open.

"Yes?"

"I'm mighty sorry to bother you this late, but I sorely need a shave, haircut, and a bath. I know it's late, but it'd be worth a five-dollar gold piece to me." While he was talking, Jack examined the man. A little taller than average, probably in his late forties, thick, coarse, black hair going to gray, a well-trimmed mustache, and an honest-looking face. Jack liked him even before he spoke.

"You're the man McClain sucker punched."

"That's me. Caught me like an unsuspecting babe."

"You're a U.S. Marshal?"

"I am."

"Well, don't just stand there, come on in. I'll be glad to take care of any man who throws that loud-mouthed bully in jail."

Jack walked in, and the barber locked the door behind him. "Gotta keep it locked. There'll be others see you come in, and they'll be pounding on the door any minute, though they know I close at five thirty sharp. I like to have supper with my family." He pointed at the chair as he walked through the building, heading for the back. "Have a seat. I'll be right back, gonna get the fire going under the water pot so's you'll have some hot water for your bath."

Jack sat down in the barber's chair. The front door was to his right and the back door his left. He thought about it for a moment and drew his left Smith & Wesson, laying it across his lap. He could hear the barber in the back raise his voice with a call.

"Grant, come down here, son, and give me a hand."

From upstairs, Jack heard, "Right now, Papa? It's almost suppertime."

"We'll be a little late tonight. I have a customer who needs a bath."

Moments later Jack heard boots racing down the stairs. Voices continued, but now too low to understand. He looked around the shop. There were two barber chairs, and facing them were eight chairs for waiting customers. Above the customers' chairs was a long rectangular mirror that allowed Jack to see the room to his side, behind him, and through the back door. Above the mirror were bottles of different concoctions, and above them hung the green felt mounted antlers of a mule deer, a white tail, and a nice six-point bull elk. The ceiling was tall, allowing plenty of room for the elk's massive spread. In the mirror, Jack could see the shelf behind him, with scissors, combs, brushes, and more bottles of sweet-smelling mixes. The shop itself had the sweet astringent smell of a well-kept barbershop. On a couple of the chairs, assorted newspapers and magazines lay for the waiting customers.

Jack removed his pocket watch, a gift from his dead wife. It had an emerald, shaped like an exploding grenade, set in the cover. His thumb rubbed over it. He never failed to think of Yasmina when he checked his watch. In fact, often, he would reach into his pocket to caress the green stone. While he was checking the time, it was ten minutes till six, the barber came back in, moving behind Jack and taking a chair cloth from a hanger behind Jack's chair. He snapped it a couple of times and slung it around and over Jack's lap, covering the watch and the revolver, quickly fastening it behind his neck.

The instant he had, there was a knock at the door. Two men stood, looking through the glass.

"We're closed," the barber called.

One of the men spoke up, shouting through the door, "Need a haircut, Wilkins. I know it's past five thirty, but you're working. A couple more won't make any difference."

"Closed!"

The barber turned back to Jack. The man who had been talking grabbed the door handle and shook the door.

The barber opened a drawer and took out a club about two feet long. It was shaped with a knob on the small end for a handle and was polished smooth. The opposite end was quite a bit larger than the handle. A hole had been burned through the small end, large enough to allow a leather cord through to form a loop. The club held a strong resemblance to the billy clubs the San Francisco police had carried when Jack was out there.

The barber walked to the door and brandished the club. "I said I'm closed. I'll be glad to cut your hair tomorrow."

Both men stepped back from the door, held their hands up in defense, and walked off. The barber laughed as he dropped the billy club back into the drawer. "They're alright. They'll be back tomorrow."

While he had the drawer open, Jack saw, by way of the mirror, he also had a Remington Pocket Pistol in the drawer. He joined the barber in a laugh. "Guess you don't often have problems."

"Not many. Sometimes a stranger might get belligerent, but they seem to settle down pretty quick. I couldn't help but see your watch. Mighty fine instrument. Looked like the emerald was cut by a person of experience. Were you in the Foreign Legion?"

Jack was surprised the man recognized the emblem. "A long time ago. It's unusual for someone to recognize the cut of the stone." Jack looked at the man again. Though his hair was graying, his face showed fewer wrinkles than Jack, but along his hairline there was a lengthy scar. "What's your name?"

"Brad Wilkins." He walked to the back and returned with a dripping, steaming towel. He laid it around Jack's face, leaving his eyes uncovered, and removed his bandanna. The barber stopped.

"Not very pretty, huh?"

Brad Wilkins hesitated for only a moment. "No, it isn't, and it also isn't very old, within a few months."

Jack nodded. "Yep. A bunch of killers I was trailing caught me with my guard down and almost did me in."

Brad laid the bandanna on Jack's shoulder. "I imagine they weren't too happy to see you when you caught up with them."

Jack shook his head. "Not much."

His muscles relaxed under the heat of the towel. He felt the warmth moving into his neck and body. It had been a long day. A drop of water ran down his neck and across his scar, tickling. He reached around with his right hand and trapped it. "I'm Jack Sage. How are you familiar with the Legion?"

"I spent a short time there, in my wilder days. I was lucky. I managed to get wounded early. They sent me to France to recover and discharge me. That's where I met my wife, Margot."

"In that case, Brad, I'd say it was a fortunate wound. Looks like the sword came close to scalping you."

"Yep, I thought he was going to cut off my head, but my bayonet caught him first. I bled a lot, but you know how head wounds are." He rubbed his chin with his right hand and repeated Jack's name. "Jack Sage. You were several years before me. I remember your name being mentioned."

Brad removed the towel, stropped his straight razor, and began on Jack's beard. He worked quickly and efficiently, carefully shaving around the scar. When he was finished, he swapped towels and cleaned Jack's face. He nodded to the scar on Jack's right temple. "You get that over there, too?"

Jack laughed. "No, back here chasing bad guys. Funny thing, as long as I was in the military, I was never wounded, but since becoming a lawman, I've been cut, shot, beaten, and hanged. Makes me think I should have stayed in the army."

Brad gave a single laugh. "Sounds like you should try another line of work." He began cutting Jack's hair.

"Brad, do you know the owners of the D Bar J ranch, the Franklins?"

12

The scissors never paused in their clicking. "I do. That's a real shame. Both the general and Warren were in here for haircuts and shaves almost monthly. Fine men. I would have gladly served under either one. It would take a real lowlife to murder those two. I love this country, but it doesn't always attract good folks."

Jack started to nod, but Brad grabbed his head.

"Sorry, don't want to cut off an ear. Sheriff Wright said it was Blackfeet Indians."

Jack started to shake his head and stopped. "Doesn't sound like it."

"Yeah, I didn't think it was when I heard about it. There's something going on. I can't put my finger on it, but there's something fishy around here besides the sheriff."

"He likes to fish?"

"Way too much. He seems to be fishing whenever a lawman is needed. His deputy, Johnny Johnson, ends up having to take care of most of it."

"He have any other deputies? With such a big county, I'd figure he'd need several."

"Yeah, he's got three more scattered around the county. They're seldom seen here unless a judge is in town and they're needed as a witness."

Brad pushed Jack's head forward to cut the hair on the back of his head and neck.

"You see many strangers come through here?"

"Of course. We have cattle buyers, buffalo hunters, skinners, gamblers. You name it, we see them."

"Any one you could put a finger on who might have pulled the trigger on the Franklins?"

Brad stopped cutting, moved to Jack's front, and stood silent. "No one in particular comes to mind. Most any of those buffalo hunters could've done it, but I don't know of any who would. Let me think about it. I see a lot of shady people, but ones who might have ambushed the Franklins?" He stood shaking his head slowly. "I can't think of anyone offhand, but like I said, let me think on it." He moved back to Jack's opposite side from the front door.

Jack checked his watch again. He was going to have to hurry if he wanted to meet Wright for supper.

"Why don't you stay for supper? Margot will be thrilled to meet another legionnaire. Don't know what she's cooking, but I know it'll be good."

"Brad, I wish I could, but I've already invited the sheriff to supper at the Laramie Eatery. Figure to try to get some information out of him."

"Understand. Maybe some other time."

"I'd like that."

Brad stepped back. "Alright, looks like we're done here, and I bet Grant has gotten your bath ready." He brushed the hair from Jack's face and neck and yanked the chair cloth clear.

Jack stood, sliding his Smith back into its holster. He had hung his hat and coat on the rack and removed them now, following Brad out the back door to a small detached bathhouse. Inside was a tub full of steaming water, and a bench with a washcloth, soap, and towels next to it. On the wall was a mirror and a shelf with a comb, brush, and a bottle of hair tonic.

"I'll be in the shop when you're finished."

"Thanks." Jack dropped on the bench and pulled off his boots. He was anxious to climb into the hot water and get rid of the trail dust he'd been collecting. Hopefully, the clean clothes he was carrying in his saddlebags weren't too dusty.

Twenty minutes later, washed up and slicked down, Jack walked back into the barbershop. He felt like a new man, though the days on the trail were catching up with him. *I hope I don't fall asleep in my food,* he thought.

Brad was sitting in the barber chair, reading a newspaper. He closed it when Jack walked in, stood, folded the paper, and tossed it on the pile. "You look like a different man. It's amazing what a shave, haircut, and a bath can do."

"Yes, sir." Jack pulled out a five-dollar gold piece and a silver dollar. "Thanks for opening and passing along your information. If you would, you can also give your boy my thanks and this silver dollar." He dropped the two coins in Brad's hand.

"I'm obliged. It's good to meet a fellow legionnaire. I'll keep thinking and watching. If I come up with anything, how do I let you know?"

"I'll either be at the Gleason or the Franklin ranch." He extended his hand. "Thanks for opening. I needed your services."

Brad took his hand. "Be careful. McClain has a long memory and no honor. He'd just as soon have a bunch of his toughs jump you and then finish you off himself."

"Thanks for the warning, and tell your wife I'm sorry I missed the opportunity to meet her. Hopefully it will happen before I leave."

Brad unlocked the door, opened it, and locked it behind Jack.

With rifle and saddlebags in hand, he headed for the Gleason Hotel.

"You've got to tell me how you did that."

Jack looked to his right and saw the sheriff approaching. "I just asked. He recognized me, and I guess he felt bad because I had shown up earlier and didn't get the haircut I was hoping for."

"That was mighty decent of him. He don't usually open that door for anyone. Why, I've gotten there right after he closed, and he's sent me away. Reckon you must be special."

Jack ignored the comment and entered the hotel. It was a lot more active than he expected. There were several divans and wingback chairs around the waiting area, turning the space into a welcoming parlor. Two stands had different publications to read, including a stack of newspapers. To the left was an entryway, about the size of two double doors, and over the top was a neatly lettered sign, The Laramie Eatery. Noting the restaurant, he walked straight to the sign-in desk at the back.

The desk clerk was a neatly dressed older man, wearing a green visor, his bare dome shining above his white eyebrows. The man looked up from the register and slid it across to Jack. "Good evening, sir. If you'll sign in, I'd appreciate it. One dollar a night to share a room. Two dollars for a private room."

Jack signed in as U.S. Marshal Jack Sage. "I'll take a private room." He extracted a double eagle. "Don't know how long I'll be staying."

The desk clerk nodded. He reached for the coin, pulled out a drawer, and dropped it in with other coins and paper money. "Yes, sir, Marshal Sage, that'll cover you for ten days." He pulled a key from a board on the back of the front desk and handed it across to Jack. "You're in 204, top of the stairs, third door on the right."

Jack handed the man his rifle and saddlebags. "Would you take care of these? I plan on eating before going up."

"Of course, sir," the man said as he took the rifle and bags. "Thank you, and have a good evening."

Jack nodded to him and turned to Wright, who had been standing silently watching. "You hungry?"

"Ain't eaten since I went fishin' this morning."

"Sounds like a yes." Jack stepped inside the restaurant, looked around, and started toward an open table at the back of the room. A rough-looking gent with an apron on came through the door at the back of the dining room.

"Where you headed?"

Jack pointed to the empty table.

"We seat our guests."

Jack looked at the man, guessing this might be the crusty owner. "Sorry, I'm new here. I didn't see anyone around and saw this table empty. I feel a little more secure with my back against the wall."

The man eyed him for a second. "You the feller what throwed McClain in jail?"

Railroad man, cook, Jack thought. *I'm about to get us thrown out of here.* "Guilty as charged."

"Well, mister, I'll say that any man who slaps McClain upside the head with a rifle butt and throws him in jail can sit anywhere he wants to in my restaurant. I can't stand the man. He's not allowed to set foot in here." He waved his hand toward the table. "Help yourself. There'll be a menu out in just a second, but I personally recommend the chicken marsala with mashed potatoes and green peas." He spun around and charged back into the kitchen. Moments later, a young man hurried out with two menus, arriving before they had a chance to sit.

Jack shook his head. "I think I'll pass on the menu. Let me have the chicken marsala with all the trimmings."

The sheriff took the menu as they sat. "I'm mighty hungry. That may not be enough for me. You said you're buyin'?"

Jack nodded and lowered himself into the chair facing the door and front windows. The other guests had turned to watch, and several were smiling and nodding at him. "I gather McClain isn't the most liked man in this town."

"He ain't, that's for sure, but he is one of the most powerful. He's been here nigh on to a year. Seems the train executives figure every word out of his mouth is gospel, but he does run roughshod over other folks. He's crippled several men. He just don't have no control over that temper."

"I'm surprised someone hasn't shot him."

"Funny you should mention that. One man tried, but McClain's bodyguard killed the fella. Shot him dead in his office. It was pretty cut and dried. The man came in with a gun, and they carried him out on a door. McClain ain't nobody to mess with." The sheriff looked knowingly at Jack. "You're in mighty deep trouble, Marshal. It don't make no never mind to McClain if you have a badge or not. You made a fool of him, and he wants to hurt you."

The waiter came back and looked at Wright. "Are you ready to order, Sheriff?"

"I sure am. Let me have that big T-bone with plenty of mashed potatoes."

The man nodded and walked back to the kitchen.

"They make a fine steak here. Can't afford to eat one very often. I'm in your debt."

"My pleasure. I'm sure you won't mind helping me."

The sheriff eyed him warily. "What've you got in mind?"

"You familiar with the Franklins?"

The sheriff nodded slowly. "Yep, them are some mighty unlucky folks. It's too bad the general and the boy got murdered like that, but them Blackfeet, when they get their blood up, can be murderous Injuns."

"Why do you think it was Blackfeet?"

"Shoot, feller, I seen the spot where they was shot from, and I seen the horse tracks. That horse's hooves were slick as a baby's bottom. Them feet ain't never seen a shoe. Plus they messed up and dropped one of their arrows. That clinches it. I'd recognize a Blackfeet arrow anywhere."

The waiter showed up with Jack's chicken marsala and Wright's T-bone. Each was on a large, completely filled plate.

Jack put a bite of the chicken in his mouth—delicious. The rest of his questions for Wright could wait until he had finished eating. It looked like Wright felt the same way. He was busy stuffing steak and potatoes down his gullet.

Jack finished before Wright and sat waiting for the sheriff. He was eating every bite of his steak. It didn't matter if it was meat, gristle, or fat, it was going on his fork. Finally, the bone clean, and the mashed potatoes gone, he looked up. "That was mighty good."

"How about dessert?"

"Don't mind if I do."

Jack motioned to the waiter. "What do you have for dessert?"

"We have a choice of pies. Apple, peach, cherry, and berry."

Jack raised his eyebrows at Wright.

"I'll have a piece of apple. Do you have any sweet cream?"

"Yes, we do, Sheriff."

"If you could send that along, I'd be obliged."

"I certainly can. Marshal?"

"I haven't had cherry pie in a long time. That would be fine. A little cream would also be nice."

"Yes, sir. It'll be right out."

Before Jack could begin questioning Wright further, the waiter returned and placed a huge piece of cherry pie in front of Jack with a small pitcher of cream. Wright received his apple pie along with his own pitcher of cream. "Enjoy your desserts, gentlemen." The waiter moved to another couple who had just entered and were waiting to be seated.

Jack poured cream over his pie and sliced a large bite. He

could see heat rising from between the crust. He slid the hot piece of pie into his mouth. A smile drifted across his face. It was the perfect combination of tart and sweet, with the crust melting in his mouth. His plate was soon clean. He leaned back and sighed. "Now, that was a delicious meal, and that pie was the best I've tasted." He glanced over to see the chef standing in the kitchen entry, smiling. The man walked to their table.

"I take it you enjoyed your meal?"

Jack looked up and smiled. "I'm sorry, I don't know your name."

"I am Roland Farnsworth."

"Mr. Farnsworth, I am Jack Sage, and I don't think I have ever eaten chicken marsala as delicious as what you just prepared, and the potatoes were the smoothest I've ever tasted. You used such wonderful seasonings on the peas, and I cannot say enough about your cherry pie. I've eaten cherry pie in Paris, in Washington, D.C., and New Orleans. I have never eaten any as delicious as yours. This has been an eventful day, but I can think of no better way to end it."

Farnsworth was beaming at Jack's over-the-top compliments on his dishes. He turned to Wright.

"That steak was mighty good, Farnsworth."

The smile disappeared, and the man sighed, then turned back to Jack. "You are welcome in my establishment any time, Marshal Sage. I will look forward to seeing you again." He gave a small bow and turned back to the kitchen.

As soon as Farnsworth had departed, the waiter arrived. "Gentlemen, that will be a total of three dollars and fifty cents."

Jack pulled out a five-dollar gold piece and dropped it in the man's hand. "Keep the change."

"Yes, sir, thank you, sir. Can I get you anything else?"

Jack glanced at Wright, whose eyes were wide as saucers, staring at the five-dollar gold piece. Finally he cleared his throat. "Sheriff, would you like some coffee?"

The sheriff nodded, and Jack told the waiter, "Two coffees. We might tie up your table a little longer. Is that all right?"

"Oh yes, sir. Take your time, and I'll have your coffee out in just a moment."

As soon as the waiter turned away, Wright leaned forward. "You way overpaid that feller."

"It's only money, right, Ned?"

The sheriff looked at Jack like he'd lost his mind.

The waiter brought the coffee with a cream pitcher and a bowl of sugar. Jack fixed his coffee just the way he liked it, took a sip, and asked, "Did you ever consider the bushwhacker could have been a white man setting the scene up to blame the Indians?"

Wright frowned. "Fake Indian? No way, I know what I saw."

"Maybe you saw what he wanted you to see. Has there been anyone through Laramie riding or leading an unshod horse? Maybe one of the buffalo hunters?"

"Shoot, no. I know what I saw."

Jack was getting fed up with this closed-minded sheriff. "Do you adhere to the thought that Indians do not attack at night?"

"Well, yeah. Everybody knows they're afraid of their spirits wandering in darkness forever if they should be killed."

"In that case, what would you say if I were to tell you that someone took two shots at Mrs. Josephine Franklin two nights ago."

The sheriff stared at Jack like he was trying to figure out if he was pulling his leg. "Are you funnin' me?"

"No, I am not."

"Did you find any tracks?"

"No, it rained almost all night. All the tracks were washed away."

"Well then, it could've been anyone."

"Are you saying there's more than one person out to kill the Franklins?"

"Well, no. I'm not. It could've been the same person."

I don't know how you were elected in a booming town like this, Jack thought, *but you're in way over your head.*

The sheriff burst out, "Dang it, Sage. I don't know if it's one, two or ten. You understand me? Their ranch is so far out there, I don't know how I could protect them."

"Get one of your deputies to stay out there until the killer or killers are caught. Give those ladies at least a little protection. One man's not enough, but it's better than no men. The way it is right now, except for their own men, who will need rest soon, they're unprotected. That's what you're supposed to do, protect your citizens." Jack decided to say nothing to the sheriff about Schmidt taking his men to help the Franklins. There needed to be a lawman out there, besides himself, and the deputy was a good choice.

The sheriff took a long sip of his coffee. "Who do I send? My other men are scattered all over the county."

"That's easy, Sheriff, send Johnny. You say he's a good man. Let him prove it. I'll even go out there with him."

The sheriff scratched his head and took another sip. "That might work, but it'd leave me short-handed here."

"It would help Tripp and the other boys keep a lookout on the women, plus the voters would see you doing something. That counts for a lot."

The sheriff nodded, making up his mind. "That's what I'll do. Thanks, Marshal Sage, I appreciate your help."

"Glad to help, Marshal. What say Johnny and I ride out there day after tomorrow? That'll give me some time to look around here."

Jack stood, followed by the sheriff. The two of them walked out to the lobby.

"See you tomorrow, Marshal."

"Sheriff." Jack watched the sheriff for only a moment and turned to the desk.

The clerk handed him his rifle and saddlebags. "Have a good night, Marshal."

"You too." Jack headed for the stairs. He couldn't wait to get a good night's sleep, though it wasn't going to be in his bed. He took the steps two at a time, found his room, unlocked it, and went in. He closed his door, but didn't lock it, nor did he put a chair under the door handle. He walked over to the window and opened it, letting the cool breeze billow the curtains and freshen the room. Moving to the armoire, he took out all of the extra bedding and carried it to the floor on the opposite side of the bed from the door and window. Folding the bedding double, except for the blanket, he spread it on the floor.

Jack was tired, but he trusted his senses. He knew, no matter how tired he was, he'd awaken at the slightest sound, though he missed Thunder. That horse was as good a watchdog as Smokey or Pepper and almost as good as Stonewall.

Keeping the room dark, he positioned everything where he could reach it fast. At last, his bed on the floor made, he took the remaining pillow and pulled the cover in the bed over it to make it look like a body. When he was finished, he positioned his hat over where his head should be. *I hope I'm wrong*, he thought. *I sure don't want this hat to get shot up. It fits really well, and anyway, who would expect this to happen two nights in a row?* Finished, he moved to the other side of the bed, took off his gunbelt, and removed both guns, placing them on the floor next to him with his rifle. He pulled his boots off and wiggled his toes. It felt good to be clean and wearing clean socks. After three days, the other pair were getting a little ripe. At last, he stretched out on his pallet, let out a long sigh, and thought of Amy Franklin.

Was what I thought she felt just my imagination, wishful thinking? Shoot, was what I felt just plain old loneliness? It's difficult for a man to know his mind sometimes. His last thought was of the blonde in the barn who had taken the time to fill a sack for him. It had been a while since he'd had such special attention. He was usually the one taking care of others. *Maybe that's it. Maybe she was just feeling grateful for my saving her and her son.* A low, short laugh escaped him. *That's it. Gratitude was what she was feeling, and she was his friend's wife.* He drifted off with a confused mind, trying to solve the unsolvable problem.

13

This time, it was the blast of the gunfire and the flash of burning powder that yanked him from a sound sleep. Fully awake instantly, he saw the door open and the top of a hat, over the edge of the bed. The gunman fired again.

Jack's hand flew to one of his revolvers. While it was coming up, his thumb was cocking the hammer. At the movement and noise, his assailant gasped and threw a wild shot across the bed at him. It smashed the lamp, dumping whale oil over the side table. Jack's .44-caliber bullet followed, tracking along the same path as the attacker's previous shot. The shooter, disappearing behind the open door, gasped, as if he might've been hit.

Jack was on his feet. He could hear the man's running steps down the hallway. He jumped into the hall and had a perfect target of the man's back. Just as he began to apply pressure to the trigger, a woman dashed screaming in front of the Smith & Wesson's muzzle. He jerked his finger from the trigger and raised the barrel toward the ceiling. The woman stood in the middle of the hallway, waving her arms and screaming at the top of her voice. A man stepped into the hall, wrapped his arm around her, and glanced toward Jack. Seeing the drawn gun, he jerked the woman toward the room, where they disappeared, the door slamming behind them.

Doors were opening, and Jack could hear steps pounding up the stairs. "It's all right, folks," he called. "The excitement's over. Go back to bed." As people turned and stepped back into their rooms, Jack could hear their murmuring about the wild west and no law in Laramie. Moments later the clerk from downstairs eased his head high enough above the steps to see Jack.

"It's safe. The shooter's gone."

The man jogged to the top of the stairs and stopped when he reached Jack. "I'm a little cautious. Knew another clerk who dashed up them stairs and got a bullet for his reward."

"Smart to take it easy. You sure don't want to run into a gunfight."

The man stretched his neck to look around Jack and into his room. "What happened?"

"Seems someone doesn't much care for me being here."

The clerk looked at the lock. "He didn't break the lock."

"I didn't lock my door."

The man motioned toward Jack's room. "You mind?"

"Go ahead." Jack followed him in and pushed the door closed.

The clerk started to go around the bed to light the lamp, then saw the shattered remains and smelled the oil. Puzzled, he asked, "What went on here, Marshal?" He pointed to the pallet Jack had made on the floor. "It looks like you were expecting something like this."

The clerk reached for the remaining lamp on the dresser, and Jack shook his head. "No light. With that window open, I'm a little light shy right now."

"Oh, yes. I understand."

"You think the sheriff will be up?"

The clerk chuckled. "If he is, I'll be surprised. We may see him in the morning, but not tonight. His deputy could come by, depending on where he is, but it won't be the sheriff." The clerk looked at the pallet again. "So you were expecting this to happen?"

"Not expecting, exactly, more like preparing for it. I've upset a few people, so I figured it would be smart to exercise a little caution."

"But you didn't lock your door?"

Jack gave a slight smile. "No, I didn't."

In the moonlight through the open window, Jack could see the man ponder the unlocked door, and then his head nodded. "I see. You were setting a trap."

"I wouldn't go quite so far to call it a trap, maybe just a precaution."

The clerk headed for the door. "A blamed good one, it looks to me, but I'd say, if you want any sleep, lock the door and the window. There's somebody around here who don't like you even a little bit." He pulled the door open and stepped through. "Have a nice night, Marshal, what's left."

The clerk shut the door, and Jack locked it. This time, he shoved a chair back under the handle. They'd have a tough time getting through there, and by the time they did, whoever was trying wouldn't enjoy his welcome. Jack strode to the window, pulled it down, locked it, and drew the drapes. He walked to the other side of the bed, picked up his gunbelt, dropped his other revolver in its holster, and grabbed his Winchester. He moved them to the opposite side of the bed, removed his unharmed hat, for which he was greatly relieved, and stretched out. *Even with two holes in the mattress, it still feels mighty good,* he thought. Jack opened the revolver he had fired, withdrew the single empty casing, and replaced it with a fresh round. After closing the action, he laid it across his belly and was fast asleep.

The knock awoke him. Light was streaming around the edges of the window drapes. He reached for his watch on the side table. The knock came again, louder, more insistent.

Jack yelled, "Hold your horses," and picked up his pocket

watch, admiring the carved emerald bursting bomb on the top, and flipped it open—seven thirty. He'd gotten a good night's sleep even after all the commotion. Gently, he placed the watch back on the table and, holding his revolver in his right hand, swung his feet to the floor. Erect, he spread his arms wide, stretched, filling his thick chest, and blew out the air. He felt good. Moving to the door, he opened it to find Deputy Johnny Johnson grinning at him.

"What've you got to grin at? Did you get an uninterrupted sleep last night?"

Johnny's grin got wider. "More'n you. I didn't find out about your shooting until I got up this morning. I slept at home. The sheriff decided he'd stand guard at the jail last night. Not only did I get a good night's sleep, I got a good breakfast. My ma fixed it. She's a mighty fine cook. When I stopped by the office, the sheriff told me to check on the hotel shooting. Said it took place last night. So I'm here checking. By the way, we had one unhappy guest in our jail. Seems them cowhands ragged him and those railroad folks just about all night, until the sheriff threatened to hang 'em all. McClain is fit to be tied. The sheriff let him out this morning, so you best walk softly. He's like a bear with a thorn."

Jack sat on the bed to pull his boots on. "You're just full of all sorts of good news. I should have you waking me every day."

Johnny's grin couldn't get any wider, so he laughed. "I'm available. You can hire me anytime. Course, good work is expensive nowadays."

Jack stood and slung and buckled his gunbelt around his waist. At the washbasin, which sat on top of the dresser, he poured water into it from the pitcher and washed his face. He tilted his head. Sometimes, he could see the corner of the deep indentation at the back of his head where DeWitt, the man whom he had thought was a friend, had smashed him with the butt of his Spencer. He had another small scar, maybe an inch long, from an attacker's rock, over his temple. He was lucky he had turned his head. It was one of the few times he had ever been caught on the ground. The prisoner had straddled him and brought that rock down so hard it would have splattered his brains all over that creek bed if he hadn't gotten his head turned. Now, the scar was so faint it could hardly be seen except for the outline of white hair. He yanked his bandanna from around his neck to wash the dust from his neck, and Johnny gave a long whistle.

"Looks like somebody gave you a necktie party. I'd say you're mighty lucky to be alive. Are they?"

Ignoring the question, Jack washed his neck and dried it with the hotel towel. The scar circled his neck. It was actually beginning to look better, he thought. Though, in spots the flesh was still bunched where the rope had pulled and ripped the skin, making dime-sized lumps. He flipped his bandanna back on and tied it. With wet hands he combed his fingers through his thick brown hair. Jack had to flex his knees to see his hair and the back of his head in the small mirror, especially with his boots on. Being almost four inches over six feet was handy most of the time, but sometimes it presented problems. He strode to his clean shirt hanging over the back of the empty chair. Johnny had dropped into the other. Jack slid it over his head, tucked the tail into his waistband, and looked around. "I think that's it."

"You leavin' your stuff here?"

"Yeah, I'll be here at least through tonight. Has the sheriff said anything to you about going out to the Franklin ranch?"

Johnny's grin disappeared. "He sure did. I was glad to hear Mrs. Franklin wasn't injured. She was sure lucky."

"You're right. She was lucky she wasn't hit, but not very lucky the general and her son were killed."

Johnny shook his head. "No, not lucky about that at all. That's a hard thing. I liked Warren. He seemed like a mighty fine feller."

"He was. I knew him in the war. He has a nice family."

Johnny cut his eyes toward Jack. "You know his wife, too?"

"I met Amy back during the war. Didn't really know her. Come on, I'm hungry."

"Me too."

Jack frowned at the deputy. "I thought you said you'd eaten breakfast."

"I did, but that's been at least an hour ago. I'm still growing, and from what the sheriff said, you don't mind buying."

Jack shook his head and opened the door. "Why do I feel like you're going to be expensive?"

Johnny grinned again. "Must be that marshal instinct."

THE TWO LAWMEN stepped out the front door of the Gleason Hotel. Johnny rubbed his belly and belched. "Now that was about the best food I've slapped my lips around in an eating joint."

Jack shook his head. "I've never seen anyone your size keep up with me eating. Are both of your legs hollow?"

"A man's got to take advantage when the opportunity arises. I woulda eaten more if Ma hadn't fed me this morning. It's a good thing I don't eat like that all the time, or my horse would refuse to carry me. Thanks, Marshal. I ain't never eaten at the Laramie Eatery. It's way too expensive for a deputy like me." He belched again.

Jack smiled at the young deputy. It had actually been entertaining to see just how much the young fella could put away. It appeared Roland Farnsworth was also surprised. He had looked at Jack several times for confirmation of the boy's orders, and Jack kept nodding. Jack was pleased that Johnny had looked a little sheepish when he found out how much all the food had cost. There was hope for him yet. Jack had enjoyed Roland Farnsworth's food himself, but now it was time to get to business.

It looked to be a hectic morning in Laramie. The streets were full of wagons and riders. Men getting supplies for their ranches, wagons bringing ore for loading on the train cars, and people trying to safely dodge the traffic while crossing the street. *The town's growing fast,* Jack thought, *and where there's rapid growth, there's graft and corruption.* He looked down main street. Along with the businesses, he could see five saloons with two more going up. "The town looks like it's booming. Did the railroad do this?"

Johnny followed his gaze. "Yep, ranching is growing, and the gold strikes seem to be everywhere. We're not far from the edge of Colorado Territory south of here. They've found gold down there. Laramie's the closest railroad. Plus the other strikes around. Folks are prospecting in all the mountains. Shoot, it wouldn't surprise me to see prospectors panning in the Laramie." He nodded toward the Laramie River, which coursed along the western side of town.

Jack momentarily thought about his gold strike near Silver City, New Mexico, then put it out of his mind. He glanced toward Otto's Livery, but Thunder could wait. He needed to find Toler. "You know where Toler's place is?"

"You mean the wheelwright?"

"That's the one."

"Sure, follow me."

Jack fell in beside Johnny as he turned and headed in the direction of the jail. "What kind of reputation does this Toler have?"

"Kinda mixed. There's been a few complaints about him gouging folks, especially since the town started booming, but not enough to run him out of town."

"There has been now."

Johnny looked up at Jack. "What do you mean?"

"I know he was willing to put a bad wheel on Amy Franklin's wagon and send her on back to the ranch to break down in the middle of nowhere. I hope he's not the only wheelwright in town, because I'm about to send him packing, if I don't throw him in jail first."

The two lawmen walked in silence. Their step had changed from casual to determined. They passed the sheriff's office, Jessup's law office, and the general store. On the far side of the store, a sign hung above a wide double door, Toler's Wheelwright. With both doors open, there was space enough to drive a large ore wagon into the building, but this morning the doors were closed.

Jack grabbed one of the handles to swing it open. Locked. "What time does he usually open?"

"He's normally open by daylight. Wagons break down all the time, night or day. He opens early and stays open late. He lives here, too. Has him a small place above the wagon barn."

Jack grasped the handle on each of the doors and shook them.

Johnny called, "Toler, open up. It's Johnny Johnson."

A man wearing a long apron stepped out of the saloon across the street. "Hey, Johnny, you looking for Toler?"

Johnny turned at the call. "Yeah, Ben, you seen him?"

"Nope. I ain't seen him for two days. Figured he was sick or hungover. You know how he gets occasionally."

Johnny waved and looked up at Jack and shrugged.

Jack took a new grip on the two handles, took a step back, and pulled. The doors creaked and groaned. For a few moments it looked as if the doors would win, but Jack took another step back. The muscles in his back and shoulders bulged. There was a single crack, and then a splintering, ripping sound came from the inside of the doors, and they swung open. Flies promptly filled the open entry.

Johnny jumped back. "What the blazes?"

Each man took a door and yanked it wide, fastening it to the ties on the side posts. Jack palmed a revolver.

Johnny followed suit. "This ain't lookin' good."

Jack nodded. "Hopefully, he left his dinner out."

Light flooded into the building. There was no movement except the churning and constant buzzing of the flies. Tools were scattered across workbenches. It looked as if the man never put a tool back in its place. Jack walked around the building, examining every corner, the storage bins, behind the anvils, nothing. There was a long straight stairway on the far side of the building. "I'm guessing that goes up to his apartment."

Johnny nodded.

"Have you ever been up there?"

The deputy shook his head. "I've got a bad feeling, Marshal."

"Trust it. I do too. Stay alert and ready. Just don't shoot me."

The stairs squeaked as they made their way up. The mass of flies thickened as they buzzed out the open door at the top of the stairs. From the apartment came the stench of human waste. Jack stepped inside. It was a single room. A bed, pushed tight against one wall, had a pair of homespun trousers lying on it. Only a few feet from the bed was a small rectangular pine armoire. Next to it, seeming the culprit of the smell and the flies, sat an open half-full chamber pot. The flies buzzed in and out of it like a seething tornado. Against the opposite wall ran a counter that had obviously been built by Toler. It had a loaf of bread partially covered by a bread cloth, the only portion that wasn't covered with flies. A dish of butter, next to the loaf of bread, also provided a landing area for its share of the buzzing little beasts.

Jack recognized the additional stomach-turning smell. Yes, the chamber pot was bad, but there was more to the smell than just human waste. He was familiar with the smell of dead bodies from the wars he had fought. He didn't think of himself as hardened to death, because the loss of life still affected him, but he was more tolerant of it. He moved to the armoire and pulled the rough-hewn pine door open. Toler's bloody body rolled out. At least he figured it was Toler. It was definitely a body. He turned to Johnny. "Is that Toler?"

Johnny had been holding back. Now he walked forward, looked at the dead man, nodded, and gagged.

"Why don't you go on downstairs and fetch the undertaker. The town pays him to deal with these kinds of things. I'll be down in a minute."

Johnny was barely able to murmur, "Thanks." He spun around and strode to the door. His boots hammered out a staccato tattoo down the stairs. The crunching in the dirt stopped, and Jack could hear the young man's retching. The thought slipped through his mind, *Two good breakfasts, what a waste.*

Toler's face was completely disfigured. Jack looked further inside the armoire and found a blacksmith's hammer. The wheelwright's skull had been crushed with the first blow, and then his face had been beaten to a misshapen pulp. Whoever had done this was strong and vicious. The only man he could think of with both the strength and the absolute disregard for his fellow man was McClain, but, as far as Jack knew, he would have no reason to do such a thing. He continued to look around the apartment, finding nothing that might be of any help. After a time, he figured he had seen all of this he either wanted to or needed to, and started down the stairs. Reaching the bottom, he turned right and began to go over every inch of the work area. On one of the benches, he found several cards and receipts. He picked them up and shoved them all into an inside vest pocket and continued searching. Nothing.

Finished, he turned and strode to the front door, where a crowd of gawkers had gathered. Jack realized, after his little run-in with McClain, people were beginning to know him. A woman called out, "Marshal Sage, is Mr. Toler really dead?"

14

Jack knew that rumors would grow like wildfire if he didn't answer some of these folks' questions. "Yes, ma'am. He surely is. It looks like he was murdered, maybe a day or so ago. Did any of you folks see anyone go in or out of Mr. Toler's place of business over the last two days?"

One of the men spoke up. "He's been closed for at least two days." He looked around for confirmation from the people around him. A couple of them nodded. Ben, from the saloon across the street and still wearing his apron, said, "Two days, Marshal. He closed up the other night, and then never opened up again. I just figured he was on another bender or had maybe gone fishing, but I never heard any shots."

Jack shook his head. "He wasn't shot. Someone beat him to death with what looks like one of his own hammers."

There were a couple of gasps from the crowd, and then they began buzzing with gossip, almost drowning out the flies.

Jack held up his hands. "Folks, hold up. Do any of you know anyone who might have been upset with Mr. Toler?"

There were several short laughs and snorts from the crowd.

Ben chimed in again, "Marshal, he wasn't the friendliest sort or the most well-liked. His work wasn't the best, either. In fact, most folks have started going up the street, 'specially the womenfolk."

One of the ladies, a rather round, jovial, and well-dressed lady, her face now stern, spoke, her words clipped. "He wasn't a nice man, Marshal. He'd sit in front of his place, leaning his chair back against his door, and leer at the women who passed."

Johnny came jogging back, his face still chalky white. "Undertaker's on the way, Marshal."

The woman who had been speaking gave Johnny an icy glare. "I own the dress shop across the street, and I've seen how bad Mr. Toler's gotten. I know several women who have reported him to the sheriff." Her eyes locked on Johnny. "He hasn't done a thing."

Johnny ducked his head to the woman. "Miss Maybelle, the sheriff spoke to him a couple of times."

"Humph, spoke to him, you say. That never did a bit of good, Johnny Johnson, and you know it. He should've been run out of town a long time ago."

Jack figured Johnny had taken enough heat for his employer's slack and cleared his throat, drawing the crowd's attention. "Miss Maybelle, if I may, Mr. Toler won't be bothering anyone else from now on. Thank you for your information."

The woman beamed a warm, wide smile at Jack. When she spoke, her voice had softened. "Why, thank you, Marshal. You certainly may. It is a sad thing for any of God's children to pass on, but I fear Mr. Toler will not be greatly missed. By the way, should you have a lady friend, I have some lovely new apparel that just arrived on the train from St. Louis." With her last statement, her eyes traveled over the crowd.

Jack saw several of the women in the crowd begin to edge away. "Thanks for your information, folks. If you'll go on back to what you were doing, we'll take care of this situation."

The crowd dispersed slowly except for three ladies who joined Miss Maybelle. She held up her substantial hand to a muleskinner driving an approaching ore wagon, who had to jerk his team to a halt. She smiled, waved to the driver, and led her entourage across the street and into her store.

Johnny leaned toward Jack and in a soft voice said, "I think you've gotten yourself a girlfriend, Marshal."

Jack looked down at the young deputy, who was still pale from his run-in with the corpse upstairs. "You ready for dinner?"

The deputy's grin faded, and twice he swallowed, but not to be outdone even in his discomfort, he forced his grin back. "You buying?"

Jack shook his head in mock disgust. "First I want to go over a few things. Let's go back to the hotel and grab a cup of coffee. You look like you could use it. Will the undertaker take care of cleaning up?"

As he asked the question, Brad Wilkins, driving a wagon, pulled up to the entry of Toler's place.

"You the undertaker, too?"

Brad grinned at Jack. "A man's gotta make a living. Most of the town's burials are pretty straightforward." He glanced at the flies around the door. "This one may make me earn my money."

Jack looked at the entrance, where the flies seemed to have multiplied. "Yep. I reckon it just might. Once the body's gone and you get the place cleaned out, throw a chain on the doors. I want to keep people out of there until I've had a chance to go over it at least one more time."

"Will do," Brad said, pulling a bandanna from his pocket and tying it around his face, just below his eyes.

"That ain't gonna help much," Johnny said.

Brad nodded. "No, I expect not, but it'll make me feel better."

Jack started to head to the hotel and stopped. "If you're up to it, have a look around. If you find anything, let me know. By the way, you're gonna need some help with the body. I don't think even I could handle that much dead weight."

Brad climbed down and tied the team. "I've got Otto coming

to help. He didn't want to, but my brother always responds well to the click of coins."

Jack waved and took off with a long step toward the hotel.

Johnny swung in beside him, hurrying to keep up. Jack glanced down at the deputy. The young fella was looking better. Death was pleasant to no one. He remembered the first dead body he had seen. At sixteen, he had gone ashore in Montego Bay, in charge of a small crew of sailors, to find one of their men. Preparing to sail, the sailor had not reported for muster, and the first mate had sent him in search of the man.

They found him dead in an alley. His throat was cut, and his belly had been violently slashed, dumping his organs on the ground. The other sailors stared at their young officer, waiting. *I'm sure*, Jack thought, *they expected me to lose my lunch, but fortunately, several quick swallows saved the day.* The sailors wanted to tear the adjacent bar apart, but Jack persuaded them, at sixteen he was nearing six feet and husky, to pick up their mate and follow him back to the ship. Once at sea, they gave him a proper burial. Jack had several sleepless nights after the man's death, but the rigorous demands of the ship and men took his mind from the gore. Soon it was just an incident in his past.

They entered the Gleason and headed for the restaurant. Jack swung by the reception desk. "Any messages for me? Jack Sage."

"Mr. Sage, your room is cleaned. The bed and lamp have been replaced."

Jack saw a piece of paper in the cubbyhole where his key was kept. "Thank you, messages?"

"Sir? Oh, yes, sir." The clerk turned, pulled the message from the slot, and handed it to Jack. "This gentleman was here earlier this morning. He said he would return this evening, and you should plan on dinner."

Jack took the note. "Thank you." He continued toward the Eatery.

At the sound of boots, a voice called from the kitchen, where dishes and pots could be heard. "Seat yourself. Someone will be right out."

Recognizing Roland Farnsworth's voice, Jack responded, "Good morning, Roland. Jack Sage and Johnny Johnson here. Thought we might be able to talk you out of a cup of your delicious coffee." He strode to the table where he had sat the night before. It provided cover for his back and side and allowed him to see out the front window and cover the main door. He removed his hat, pulled out the chair to his right, and placed his hat on it.

Jack lowered himself into his chair as Farnsworth stepped through the kitchen door. "Good morning, Marshal Sage. It would be my pleasure. I made a coffeecake this morning. Would you care for a slice to accompany your coffee?"

"You're making my day, Roland." He held up two fingers to the man, who nodded.

Jack turned back to Johnny. "You do feel like eating, don't you?"

The young man lit his perpetual grin. "Never felt better. Don't know what happened this morning. Must have picked up a bug."

Jack couldn't help but toss a smirk at the younger man. "I think it was more like a fly, or a bunch of them."

The deputy held up his hands, palms toward Jack. His belly growled. "I give up. Let's not talk about Toler or his flies anymore."

Jack shook his head. "Can't promise that. We've got to figure out who killed the man, unless you think the sheriff will beat us to it."

Johnny shook his head. "I'll be surprised if he gets near the place, much less looks at the body."

Jack reached inside his vest and pulled out the stack of receipts and cards he had taken from the dead man's workbench. While he looked through them, he questioned Johnny. "Ben said something about Toler that got me thinking. Did he drink a lot?"

Johnny shoved his hat to the back of his head. The front brim had been bent down over the deputy's eyes. Jack motioned to the hat. Johnny frowned at him. "What?"

"Your mama didn't teach you to shed your hat at the table?"

"Oh." He grabbed the front brim with his left hand and jerked the hat from his head. "I forget."

"If you want to associate with anyone other than your running buddies, you better remember. Good folks require a modicum of politeness."

Roland brought out a ceramic coffeepot, two cups, a sugar bowl, and a small creamer pitcher, along with two forks and two saucers, each containing a large slice of coffeecake. He placed the cups in front of each man and poured the coffee, filling the cups half-full. Next, he served the coffeecake to each man and laid the fork by the saucer.

Jack smiled. "It looks and smells delicious, Roland. How did we warrant such personal service?"

"Any man who enjoys good cooking warrants good service." He smiled. "Enjoy. If you need anything, let me know."

Eyes wide, Johnny stared at Roland's retreating back and then at Jack. "I've never seen him like that. Usually he's growling and griping at his customers. Why, he's run people out of here with his shotgun on several occasions."

Jack shrugged and concentrated on doctoring his coffee. "I guess the man likes to have his work complimented." When he had finished with the cream and sugar, the cup was almost full. He took a sip and smiled. "Now that's a good cup of coffee."

Johnny picked his cup up and tasted it. "It is good, but I don't see how you could tell, what with all that cream and sugar you put in it."

"You know, your mouth is going to overload your rear sometime if you're not careful."

Johnny grinned at him. "Yeah, my mama tells me that all the time."

"We were talking about Toler. You were going to tell me about his drinking habits."

Johnny braced his elbow on the table and took a sip of coffee. "He wasn't a constant drunk. He'd go on binges once or twice a month. When that happened, he'd be out for a couple of days. Then the doors of his place would open, and he'd be back at work like nothing happened."

"Did he have a favorite hangout where he went to drink?"

"Yep, he always went to the Last Chance Saloon. Never drank anywhere else. A person knew, when he was seen heading north, he'd be out of business for a couple of days."

Jack watched an ore wagon roll past the window on its way to the depot. When it was clear, he glanced back to Johnny. "What about a bank, where he ate, friends? Did you notice where and who they were?"

Johnny shook his head. "I don't think I've ever seen him inside a bank. Always figured he didn't have any money. He just seemed to drink it up when he got it, and I don't think I ever seen him eating in a restaurant." He paused. "Wait a minute. There's a little Mexican place down by the depot. I remember seeing him there on occasion. Not often, but he did eat there every once in a while."

Jack nodded, finished his coffee, poured another cup, and continued with the questions. "What about friends? You ever see him with anyone?"

"Not often. Once in a while, he'd play cards with Slim Deeds, Holt Maize, and Beau Clark. That was always over at the Last Chance."

Interesting, Jack thought. *He played cards with three of the same bunch who ambushed Amy and Davy. We can't be talking coincidence here.* He looked further through the receipts and cards and stopped. A card for attorney Bowden Jessup was in the stack. Also interesting. "Does Bowden Jessup frequent the Last Chance Saloon?"

Johnny's head rose from his coffeecake, eyes focused on Jack. "How'd you know that?"

"I didn't. Just asking."

"Yeah, he does. In fact, I've seen him playing cards with those fellas you were asking about."

Jack stared out the front window and slid the batch of papers into his vest pocket. He felt the note the desk clerk had given him. He pulled it out, read it, and returned it to his pocket, another interesting development. He finished his coffeecake and coffee and watched Johnny take his final bite. Placing two silver dollars on the table, Jack stood. "You want to take me to the Last Chance? I want to look around. No telling who or what we might see."

Johnny stood. "Sure." He turned and headed for the hotel front door.

Jack called to the back, "Thanks, Roland, delicious as usual. I'll see you for dinner."

The owner stepped from the kitchen, drying his hands on a dishcloth. "See you tonight, Marshal."

Reaching the Last Chance Saloon, Jack followed Johnny into the dark interior. The smell of sweat, sawdust, stale beer, and cigars filled the room. To the left, a scratched, much-abused bar extended for twenty feet toward the back. Past it on the same side were a couple of round tables. Opposite the bar on the right side of the room, five round and two rectangular tables crowded together. This time of day there were only eight customers, three at the bar and the others scattered at the tables.

It took a minute for Jack's eyes to adjust to the darkness of the saloon. The standard raucous piano was being hammered in the back of the saloon. Jack didn't spend a lot of time in saloons because of the pianos. He had learned, when he was a child, he was tone deaf, and he particularly could not stand the constant clattering of a piano. He strode to the player banging on the keys, and dropped a gold quarter eagle into his cup. The man stopped, looked into the cup, and straightened. "Yes, sir. What can I play for you?"

"Nothing."

Puzzled, the man frowned. "Nothing?"

"That's right. I'm only going to be in here for a few minutes. For that time I'd like no sound to come from your piano." Jack stabbed a finger at the instrument. "Is that possible?"

The piano player shrugged. "I don't think I've ever been paid not to play, but sure. I'll have a drink." The man stood and headed for the bar.

One of the patrons yelled at the player, "Hey, don't stop. I like the music."

Jack stopped next to the man's table, towering over him. "I paid him not to play. Is that alright with you?"

The man's eyes started at about Jack's waist and slowly traveled up to his face. When he reached it, his head was tilted back so far his hat almost fell off. It took him only a moment to respond, "Yes sirree. If you're willing to pay him not to play, I'm willing to listen."

"Thanks." Jack continued to the bar. He motioned toward the piano player. "Give the man whatever he wants as long as I'm in here. I'll have a glass of buttermilk when you're through, and some questions answered."

The bartender gave the piano player a shot of rye. He tossed it back and slid the glass across the bar to the bartender. He filled it again and slowly slid it across to the musician. "Go easy. I pay you to play, not drink. When he leaves, I want you sober enough to play the rest of the day."

"Sure, boss," the man said, nodded, and took a tiny sip of his drink. The bartender stopped at a small jug on a stand in the corner and poured buttermilk into a glass. He then moved down to Jack and Johnny and slid the buttermilk in front of Jack. "Now, what questions do you have, Marshal?"

"You know me?"

The man shook his head. "Only from watching you march Lew McClain to the jail. I also saw him coldcock you. You went out like a snuffed lamp."

Jack nodded. "I did that. You work here, or you own the place?"

"Both. I tend the bar in the mornings. My regular man will be coming on shortly."

"You heard Toler is dead?"

"I did. In fact, I saw Bob and Otto haul him out of his shop." He shook his head. "That was one banged-up wheelwright. Can't say he didn't have it coming, what with some of the comments he made to the ladies who passed his place. If one of them had been my wife, I woulda killed him a long time ago."

Jack looked the man over. He was average height, wide shoulders, thick forearms, and hard brown eyes. *He could probably do the damage I saw on Toler,* Jack thought. "You married?"

The bartender gave a derisive laugh. "No, not now. Tried three times, and they all left me. I guess you could say I've got a roving eye. I didn't kill him, Marshal, but I don't blame the man who did."

"You have any idea who did, Mister . . . ?"

The bartender paused the wiping of a beer mug and looked up at Jack. "Conor O'Brien, pleased I am to meet you, and no, I don't know who killed him."

Jack lifted his glass of buttermilk in salute. "Are all saloon owners Irish?"

O'Brien gave him a devilish grin. "Only the good ones, Marshal. Only the good ones."

"I'll have to remember that. How's business?"

"A bit slow at the moment, but it'll pick up as the day goes by. We'll be getting an assortment of thirsty men later in the evening." He shot Jack a conspiratorial smirk. "The ladies will be coming to work about three o'clock. You might like to stop back by then."

Jack kept his eyes on O'Brien. The realization floated through his mind. *I don't think I like you, O'Brien. Though you're smiling at me, I feel like I'm being stared at by a snake.* "What can you tell me about Toler?"

15

O'Brien's expression didn't change. He nodded at Johnny. "Not much more than Johnny boy has probably told you. He didn't come in here often."

"Anyone he hung out with?"

O'Brien's eyes narrowed in thought. His hands moved the towel slowly over the beer mug. "You've got to understand we get a lot of folks in here."

Jack said nothing. Keeping his eyes on the bartender, he took another sip of buttermilk. He liked a glass occasionally. This was pretty good. He waited.

Finally O'Brien nodded. "Aye, now I remember. Once in a while, mind you, he would play cards with Slim Deeds and Maize Holt. Both fine upstanding Laramie citizens." His last sentence was dripping in sarcasm.

"You don't think much of Deeds and Holt?"

O'Brien shot a look at the piano player, who had just tilted his glass high above his mouth to let the last drop of rye fall between his lips. Jack saw the man catch O'Brien's glance, set the empty glass on the bar, upside down, turn around, and lean his elbows against the bar's edge, waiting for his departure.

The bartender returned his attention to Jack. "It's truth I must tell you. I care for them little. Theirs is not the type a fine city like Laramie requires for growth."

Jack kept his eyes on the man. "Did anyone else spend any time with him?"

"What is your meaning, Marshal? He talked to a lot of people. When he was on a bender, he'd buy any stranger a drink. He'd talk to them like they were long-lost family. So, no, I can't think of anyone in particular. Everyone knew he was good for at least one drink, so he became the friend of all these dregs." O'Brien swung the hand holding the towel across the room, indicating his patrons.

"You don't seem to think much of your customers, either."

O'Brien leaned on the bar. "It's a sad business I'm in, Marshal, though I know it well. Most of my life has been involved with beer and those who drink it, and I'm sorry to say, it doesn't attract the very best of men. I'm not saying everyone is a loser, but a sizable number are. They come in here to forget something someone did to them, or what they did to someone else, never realizing the answers don't lie at the bottom of a bottle."

Jack nodded, a touch of sarcasm slipping into his words. "You impress me, O'Brien, a philosopher behind a bar."

The man's eyes hardened. "Like I said, Marshal, I know this business and the people who patronize my establishment. I see things the way they are. I am not the wearer of rose-colored spectacles."

Jack tilted his head back, drained his buttermilk, and placed the glass back on the bar. "Any particular girl Toler liked to buy drinks for?" He thought he caught a momentary narrowing of the corners of O'Brien's eyes, but it was so quick he wasn't sure.

"Aye, Nancy, the redhead. Like I said, the girls will be on at three."

Jack straightened. "Much obliged. I'll see you later." He nodded to the piano player and glanced at Johnny. "Let's go."

When Jack's foot hit the boardwalk, the piano started.

Johnny laughed. "He must've been watching your feet. Those piano players like to play. So where to now?"

"I've got to make a couple of stops, and then I'm heading back to my room. I've got a few things to go over. I'd suggest you go by the sheriff's office. He may have something for you. Meet me at Otto's, packed and ready to head out to the Franklin ranch in the morning, say about seven. I appreciate your help, thanks."

He watched Johnny's grin widen. "I'll be there with bells on. See you, Marshal."

Jack lifted his index finger to his hat brim, turned, and headed down the street. Reaching the barbershop, he opened the door and stepped in. Surprised, he had been expecting the stench from Toler's dead body, but he was greeted with the clean smell of the barbershop. He closed the door and could hear racing feet coming down the stairs. Grant, the barber's son, burst into the room.

"Hi, Marshal. You looking for Pa?"

"I am. Is he around?"

"He's out back in the dead man's shed. That's what he calls it. It's where he fixes up the corpses before burying." Grant motioned him through the shop. "You can come through here. It's shorter."

Jack followed the boy past where he had taken his bath, to a shed.

"He's in there, but it stinks mighty bad. You might wanta wait or knock on the door. He'll come out." The boy turned and raced back upstairs. Jack grinned. *Reckon he must be twelve or thirteen. I can remember being that age. I never walked anywhere.* He raised his hand and gave three hard knocks. The smell had made it past the walls and doors of the shed. It wasn't as bad as it had been in Toler's apartment, but it wasn't pleasant.

The door opened. Brad Wilkins wore a full-length apron, once white but now covered with brown stains, and a pair of long black gloves. Sweat dripped from a wrinkled brow onto impatient pursed lips. Seeing it was Jack, his features relaxed. The smell poured from the door, surrounding the barber.

Jack took a step back. "He's mighty ripe."

"Normally a man doesn't get this bad in two days, but the smell of death had the opportunity to combine with that of an almost full chamber pot. Plus yesterday was unusually warm. Not a pleasant combination. You want to take a look?"

Jack took another step back to increase his range from the stink. "I think I've seen all I need to, thanks. Did you have time to search his place?"

Brad shook his head. "I gave it a cursory check. It was just too ripe in there to spend much time. I've locked all the doors and posted No Entry signs, so it should be fine. With it closed and locked, it'll take a while for the smell to disappear. In fact, I think the smell will do more to keep the curious out than the locks."

Jack rubbed the stubble on his cheek. "I know you're busy, but do you have time for a quick shave?"

"You bet I do. I want to get Toler in the ground today, but right now, I could use a break."

Jack drew a weapon, sat, and Brad threw the sheet over him, walked to the back, and came back with a hot towel.

"Leave the eyes clear."

Brad nodded and wrapped Jack's face with the towel. The hot, moist towel felt good on his dry skin. *For two cents I could go to sleep right here,* he thought. But he knew that wouldn't be smart. "You have much to do with Bowden Jessup?"

"The attorney?"

"That's the one."

Brad removed the towel and, using the shaving brush, spread the soap from the cup across Jack's face. He picked up the razor, stropped it a few times on the leather strap, and began. "I give him a shave every morning. In fact, he was here almost as soon as I opened this morning. He had the beginning of a thick beard.

He'd gone several days without a shave." He worked as he talked, pulling the skin taut before sliding the sharp edge across Jack's cheek.

"He'd been gone?"

"Yeah, he said his services were needed at the Franklin Ranch. Seems Mrs. Franklin is getting his assistance with drawing up a will of her own. Said he's been spending quite a bit of time out there. Personally, I think he's sweet on one of the daughters, and he's using the will for an excuse."

"He do much work around town?"

"Don't talk for a second." He pushed Jack's head up and began to shave his throat. The sharp razor sliced into the stubble. "Yeah, he seems to stay busy. I know he's talked about doing work for the railroad. Don't have any idea what that may be."

"People like him?"

Brad stopped, turned to the wide front window, and stared out at the traffic. After a bit he returned to Jack's whiskers. "I wouldn't say people like him. He's not the most likable person I've ever met, but he seems to know the law. All the comments I've heard from folks who have used him have been positive—about his work." He stropped the razor a couple more times and stepped to Jack's opposite side. "Aloof, that's how I'd describe him, but he's got steady business." Brad finished with the shave and retrieved another warm towel. He cleaned Jack's face and reached for a bottle of aftershave.

Jack waved him away. "Cheyenne will smell me a mile away with that stuff."

Brad nodded. "Suit yourself." He yanked the sheet from Jack's lap and began folding. "Twenty-five cents."

Jack dropped the revolver into its holster and took out four bits, flipping it to the barber. "Nice shave. Good luck with your customer in the shed."

Brad turned to his change drawer.

"Keep the change."

"Thanks."

"Don't mention it. I like to have the man wielding a blade around my throat friendly. Does the sheriff pay you for Toler?"

"Yeah. I'll have to send him a bill, but he's pretty prompt. He knows if he isn't, I might drop the bodies on his front porch."

Jack laughed. "Yeah, that'd make me pay up for sure."

He grabbed his hat off the rack, waved to Brad, and stepped outside. After leveling his hat on his head, Jack stretched his long legs across the street to Jessup's office. He had a feeling about the attorney. The name was familiar from somewhere in his past, but he couldn't place it. It was like he'd heard something a long time ago, the war, before, but he couldn't put his finger on it. Whatever it was, he couldn't shake it. Plus, the man rubbed him the wrong way. He was surprised the Franklins dealt with him.

He weaved between the riders and clattering wagons, feeling a certain satisfaction for making it safely to the other side. Reaching for the front door, it was yanked open, and Lewis McClain, head down, charged out. This time, Jack saw him coming and stepped back.

McClain realized there was someone near and looked up. His perpetual frown deepened, and the muscles in his jaws tightened. "You. You trying to get yourself knocked out again?"

Jack smiled at the man. Seeing it immediately angered the railroad executive. "You trying to get yourself slapped upside the head with a Winchester and thrown in jail again?"

If McClain had been one of his steam engines, steam would have been pouring from his nose and ears. "I told you, I'll have your job. You're nothing but a broke saddle tramp with a badge. You'll never carry a badge again when I'm through with you. I have friends in Washington."

Jack couldn't help it. He laughed. He could picture President Grant having some politician telling him what he had to do. That wouldn't go well at all. His laugh infuriated the big man in front of him.

"You'll regret laughing at me, Sage. If you'd shed those guns, I'd make you beg for mercy."

"You'd probably hit me when I wasn't looking. I understand that's your calling card, McClain. While you're standing here threatening me, let me give you one little warning. If I hear of you beating or bullying anyone around here while I'm in this country, I'm coming to get you, and I'll see you spend more than one night in jail." Jack looked around. People had started to gather, and Jessup was standing in his office door. "Move along, McClain. You're holding up traffic. I don't want to have to arrest you for disturbing the peace."

"You'll get yours, Sage, and I just might be the one delivering it." The big railroad man spun around and marched toward his offices.

Jack smiled at the people who had gathered to witness the altercation. "You folks move along, too. Nothing's happening here." He turned to Jessup, his voice growing hard. "I need to talk to you."

Jessup frowned and stepped back into his office, leaving the door open. He walked past the front desk, where a young man wearing spectacles sat, and strode through a door into his office.

Jack nodded to the young man. "Howdy." The man returned the nod and went quickly back to work.

The office wasn't large, but it was plush. There was one desk near the entry door. One end of the desk extended into the walkway far enough to make Jack take a step to his left to walk around it. On most of both walls and the back wall were bookcases stacked with thick books. In the remaining wall space were plaques and diplomas belonging to Bowden Chesley Jessup.

A door in the back wall allowed entry into a private office. Stepping inside the office behind Jessup, Jack glanced around the room. It was a fairly large room, holding a divan and two comfortable-appearing, black upholstered wingback chairs. The chairs faced a large desk. *Looks like mahogany,* Jack thought. Behind the desk was an expensive, brown leather reclining chair, similar to the one in McClain's office. Jessup sat in it. Jack moved to the wingback with papers lying on the seat. He picked them up and tossed them on the divan against the wall and lowered himself into the chair. *I was right,* he thought, *mighty comfortable.* He left his hat on and stared at Jessup. He didn't like him, and he wasn't going to pretend he did.

At last, Jessup spoke. "You know you almost started a brawl outside my office. Mr. McClain is a very important railroad executive."

Jack held the lawyer's stare. "What's your dealings with the Franklins?"

The direct question caught Jessup by surprise. "Well, uh, that's private between a citizen and her attorney."

"I'm a United States Marshal, commissioned by President Grant. Nothing's private. I asked you a question, and I expect an answer."

Jessup regained his composure. "Mrs. Franklin has employed me to draw up her will. That is between a client and her attorney. You can't come charging in here demanding to see private documents. You need court orders, which I assume you do not have."

Jack's stare didn't waver. "What's your dealings with Abraham Toler?"

Jessup blinked several times. "I knew him only slightly. Why would you ask me about him?"

"I'm asking the questions, Jessup. Did you have any business dealings with Toler?"

"Of course not. What kind of dealings would *I* have with that man? It was bad enough to hear his constant hammering and clanging. The town should never have allowed such a business in the middle of Laramie. He needed to be on the outskirts, and he was terribly obnoxious, especially to female passersby. No, I had no dealings with the likes of Toler."

Jack didn't know why, but another question popped into his

mind. "The railroad is well north of the Franklin ranch. What kind of dealings would they have with each other?"

Again, Jack could see surprise in the attorney's pale eyes. "I don't think I'm aware of why you would be asking such a question."

Jack watched Jessup pull himself together.

"Certainly, I don't know what you're talking about, and even if I did, this does not fall under the purview of your jurisdiction. Now if you have no more questions." Jessup began to stand.

Jack didn't move. "I'm not finished."

Jessup sighed his impatience and slowly lowered himself into the soft leather chair.

"How do you know the Franklins?"

"Marshal Sage, I cannot understand why you insist on asking personal questions, which have no bearing on anything. Are you just trying to upset me?"

"It's all about you, isn't it, Jessup? I don't give a dried cow pie for you. I care about the Franklins. Now you can either tell me how you know them, or since I'm going out there tomorrow, I'll ask them myself."

Jessup sighed again. "Alright, if you must be so nosy. General Franklin and Josephine are friends of my parents, Colonel Abraham Jessup and my mother, Adeline. I was also a good friend of Warren."

That's it, Jack thought. *I remember Warren saying something about the Jessups and, in particular, Bowden Jessup. What was it?* He tried to recall the conversation, but it wouldn't appear. Since he had been hit in the head and the rock splinter had penetrated his skull, it was difficult to remember some things. "I remember Colonel Jessup. How is he?"

"Not well. They have struck upon hard financial times, and I'm sorry to say my mother is very ill. I was thinking about going back to Washington to see them." The man looked genuinely concerned for a moment. "One never knows."

Jack stood. "I wish your folks well. If you think of anything that would help with the Toler murder or the Franklins, let me know." Without another word, he walked from the office and turned for the hotel. He needed to get a few supplies before leaving tomorrow, but first he'd stop by his hotel room and change clothes. He'd noticed people looking at him funny. The smell of Toler's apartment must have penetrated his clothes.

Reaching his room, he slid his key in the door. It was unlocked. Drawing a revolver, he threw the door open and charged into the room.

16

Jack slid to a stop. Carter Schofield, his liaison with the president, was sitting in one of his chairs, the back leaning against the wall and his feet stretched across the bed.

"You look almighty fierce." He took a whiff and snorted. "And you smell that way, too. Is that stink from the murder victim you found this morning?"

Jack holstered his weapon and shut the door. "What are you doing here, and who let you into my room?"

The man shrugged. "I was a spy, remember. These old locks are easy as pie to open. I hear you're stirring up trouble. The president's hearing the same thing and is having second thoughts about his decision to hire you."

"What are you talking about?"

"You know, the president. The man who hired you. First name Ulysses."

Jack unfastened his gunbelt and dropped it on the bed. "He couldn't have already heard about the little altercation between me and Lewis McClain."

"You mean the railroad executive Mr. Lewis McClain? The

one who has senators lapping at his feed trough? Is that the Lewis McClain you're talking about?"

Jack yanked off his bandanna, followed by his pants and socks and then his long johns, dropping everything in a pile. He opened his saddlebags and pulled out a change of clothes, including clean long johns, and laid them out on the bed. "Alright, you can stop with the humor. How'd he find out so quick? And no, I don't believe the president is even a little bit upset."

Schofield let out a long low whistle as he scanned the scars on Jack's bare body. "Big fella, you've been shot up a bit, and I know your service record. You were never wounded in the war."

Jack walked to the washbasin and poured some water from the pitcher. He picked up the soap and a washcloth and lathered the cloth, then went about washing away the smell of death. "Every one of these little mementos came after the war. I'm beginning to think this being a lawman is a dangerous thing."

When he had finished washing, he raised his window, checked outside, and tossed out the soapy water. After pouring more water into the basin, he rinsed off and then dried himself with the towel. "Now tell me, how did the president find out so fast?"

"The telegraph, ole son. McClain must have lit up that telegraph the moment you let him out of jail. I was sent over from Cheyenne. He wants to know what's going on."

"First off, I didn't let him out of jail. The sheriff did. Also, I know the president's not angry at me or even upset."

"No, he's not mad. In fact, I think you made his day. Three senators and two congressmen showed up at his door, and he sent them all packing. Every one of them wanted your badge. You really kicked over a hornet's nest. So tell me what's going on."

Jack had pulled on his long johns and, sitting on the edge of the bed, was slipping on his socks. He began the explanation as he dressed, covering every detail of the past few days.

He stomped into his boots and held a forearm up to his nose, better. Jack sat on the edge of the bed and finished his tale. "That's about it. I'm suspicious of a few things, but I still have no idea who murdered General Franklin and Warren. I'm suspicious of Jessup, but it might also be as simple as the fact I don't like him. You can tell the president I may have kicked over a hornet's nest, but it looks like, so far, the only one getting stung is me."

Carter Schofield let his chair come forward. "You're going back out to the ranch?"

"Yeah, tomorrow, I don't like being gone. Tripp, the foreman, seems to be a good man, but he has only three hands. They can't keep an eye on Jo, the rest of the family, and work the cattle all at the same time. I'll be taking a sheriff's deputy with me and leaving him out there to watch over her. She's not going to like it, but he seems like a good kid, and I think he'll bring her around. I'll check him out more on the way to the ranch. Also, when I left Schmidt's ranch, he was getting a crew ready to ride over and give Tripp a hand, so that'll help."

Carter leaned forward. "Good. President Grant wouldn't be a bit happy if General Franklin's wife got shot."

Jack looked askance at Schofield. "I wouldn't either. You think I'm doing this so the president will be happy? The Franklins are my friends. I don't want anything to happen to any of them."

Carter Schofield held his hands up. "Easy, Jack. I know you care. We're all concerned about the Franklins."

Mollified, Jack nodded. "Yeah, I know. I do need you to do something for me."

"Sure, you name it."

"I want you to find out everything you can about the Jessups, the parents, but primarily Bowden Chesley Jessup, the son. There's something about that pompous lawyer that sets me on edge. I remember Warren was interested in him, during the war, but I don't know what about. Get the information as quickly as you can. Like I said, I'm headed out to the ranch in the morning, but once I get the deputy settled in and I look around a mite, I'll be heading back here. You can leave it for me here. In fact, I know just the man you can leave it with. You'll be meeting him at supper."

Jack looked through the window. Evening was approaching, but he didn't need to look outside to know the lateness of the hour. His stomach was reminding him. Standing, he said, "You hungry?"

"Thought you'd never ask."

"I've got a surprise for you. You'd never expect to get the food you'll be tasting in just a bit. You're in for a real treat." Jack had made it to the door and was about to open it. Carter Schofield came up behind him, and Jack turned, holding out his hand, catching the man in the chest. "But here's a warning. If you like his food, be complimentary of it. He's been known to run customers out of his establishment with a shotgun."

"Guess I better like it, then. Let's go."

JACK WAS SADDLING Thunder when Johnny rode into the livery from the dark street.

"Morning, Marshal."

Jack nodded and glanced at the Winchester in Johnny's scabbard. "You know how to shoot that thing?"

The deputy grinned. "I've been known to hit what I'm shooting at occasionally. Why?"

Jack pulled the cinch tight around Thunder and tied it off, dropping the stirrup. He ran his hand over his equipment, taking one last mental inventory, and swung into the saddle. "You might need it."

Otto stood by his office door, watching. "You fellers be careful out there. These old bones are aching something fierce. We could have a storm coming. We're due some rain."

"Thanks, Otto, we'll keep it in mind." Jack touched the brim of his Stetson in salute to the liveryman and clucked to Thunder. The big gray walked toward the wide-open door.

Johnny waved. "See you, Mr. Wilkins. I'd appreciate it if you'd look in on my ma while I'm gone."

"Don't you worry none, boy. I'll make sure she's alright. You take care of yourself."

Jack relaxed into the saddle as Thunder stepped into the fading darkness. The wind had been blowing all night, but with dawn approaching, it had died to a light breeze. He pulled his coat tight. *It may be nearing summer,* he thought, *but this far north makes for some chilly mornings.*

Once in the street, Thunder strained at the reins. Jack could feel the gray's muscles ripple beneath his legs. "I know you want to run, boy, but we're gonna wait until we get outside of town. There might still be a few folks sleeping." The early morning creak and rattle of wagons on their way to the depot was already filling the air, along with the hammering at the train yard.

Johnny, hearing Jack, chimed in, "I don't see how there's a soul around who could be sleeping with all this town noise. I swear, railroads ain't all they're cracked up to be. This used to be a nice quiet little cattle town, and listen to it now."

"Progress, my boy. You're listening to the irritating sounds of progress, but fortunately, we'll be away from it shortly."

In no time they were outside of town, and daylight had brought the road they were traveling into bright relief.

"Johnny, is that animal of yours up to a short run? Thunder's dying to stretch his legs."

The deputy's reply was a yell, and the smaller buckskin leaped ahead. Jack grinned at the younger man's back. "Come on, Thunder, let's show that boy what running is all about." The big horse was more than ready. He leaped forward. Jack was surprised at the smaller horse's speed, but in a short distance Thunder had caught them. Jack eased his gray to where they were racing side by side and let the animals run for what he figured was about a quarter of a mile, then pulled the big horse back to a lope. He couldn't keep the grin from his face. The short race, along with the rising sun on his back, had warmed him. It felt good to be back on the trail.

Two hours later they were soaking in a steady, cold rain. The clouds had moved in from the south. Once the sun had disappeared, the chill returned with the gusty winds. The rain only served to drop the temperature more. Jack figured, since he had come from a much warmer climate, he would be more affected by the colder temperatures, but Johnny couldn't stop complaining.

"I'm telling you, it ain't supposed to rain like this. The sun oughta be out, and it oughta be a lot warmer. I can't stand cold weather when it's supposed to be warm."

Thunder, his head down, slogged along in the rain. To Jack, it was like sitting in a wet rocking chair. It could've been better, but it could sure be a lot worse.

"Boy, if you don't stop your bellyaching, I'm liable to put you out of my misery. I swear, I've never heard a body complain as much as you have since it got cloudy."

Johnny cut his eyes toward Jack from under the wide dripping rim of his hat. "I don't know why you're so cheery. It's raining on you, too."

Through the light rain, Jack could see the line of mountains ahead. There was a wide pass where the road cut through, hills on both sides, and then they'd be back onto the grassland. He stood in the saddle, his eyes searching around them. Nothing in sight but a few buffalo. Though his vision was hampered by the drizzle, he was satisfied they were alone. He pulled his neck in and lowered his head. Thunder plodded west.

The rain picked up, growing heavier as they reached the pass. Jack contemplated finding a dry spot and waiting it out, but with the rain falling so long and heavy, dry spots would be scarce. He glanced ahead to see nothing but huge continuous raindrops.

Visibility had dropped to a few yards. He patted Thunder on the neck and was settling back in when Johnny yelled.

"Look out." He jerked up as the buckskin slammed into Thunder, causing Jack to almost loose his seat. A gun roared, and he saw the outline of a man on horseback no more than thirty feet in front of them. He ripped his slicker open, but before he could bring a weapon to bear, the apparition was gone.

Johnny leaped the buckskin forward, and Jack yelled, "Hold up!" but the young deputy disappeared into the rain behind the shooter. Nothing could be heard except the sound of rain rattling on his hat and slicker. He pulled Thunder to the side of the road, held his Smith & Wesson under his coat, and waited.

Crazy kid, he thought. *He's running around out there with absolutely no idea of who or what he's looking for.* He heard the faint pop of a shot, muffled in the heavy rain. His head was on a swivel. Whoever the shooter was, he must know this country. He could easily circle and come in behind them. The rain quit abruptly.

A rider sat a scrawny bay horse, his rifle to his shoulder, the muzzle pointing straight at Jack.

He threw himself from Thunder as the rifle bloomed smoke and the blast roared over him. He hit the ground rolling. Through the grass, he could see the rider work the lever and stretch high in his saddle, searching. Jack shoved his .44 through the grass, took aim, and fired. The man flinched, spun his horse around, and raced south, into the mountains. Jack tracked him with the front sight, leading about the length of the horse's neck. He pulled the trigger. The only indication he had fired was the man's heels slamming more viciously into the bay's flanks. Before he could get off another shot, the horse and rider disappeared into the pines. Jack watched him go. He badly wanted to follow, but just before he saw the killer, he had seen Johnny's buckskin farther along the trail.

Jack looked back to see the buckskin still there. He was held by a tight rein. Either Johnny had tied it to something, or he was lying in the grass, holding the reins. Jack took one last look at where the shooter had disappeared into the forest, swung back into the saddle, and urged Thunder forward. As he neared the buckskin, he could make out a body lying in the high grass.

Reaching Johnny, he leaped from Thunder and ran to the boy's side, dropping to his knee. As he knelt, he felt the muzzle of the deputy's .44 Colt against his ribs. The boy's eyes opened.

Recognizing Jack, Johnny immediately pulled the Colt away. "Sorry, I thought you might have been the shooter. I shouldn't have chased him."

"You hurt?"

"He winged me."

Jack saw no blood. "Where?"

"Left arm. It ain't bad. I figured I was safer down here than up on that saddle with that guy around, so when he shot, I leaped off."

Jack unbuttoned the boy's slicker and then his coat and helped him sit up.

"I'm alright, Marshal." Johnny pushed up with his good arm and stood.

Jack pulled the slicker and coat from the deputy's left shoulder. He could see the bullet punctures and the blood. "You got lucky, boy. He could've killed you."

Johnny gave an emphatic nod. "Yeah, and he could've killed you, too."

"That's a fact. Thanks. If you hadn't hit Thunder, I reckon I would be staring up at those clouds right now. Let me take a look at that wound."

The bullet had entered the shoulder just beneath the top, making it a puncture and not a graze. It appeared the slug had passed through high enough to damage no bones or tendons. There was some messed-up muscle, but that would mend if it didn't get infected.

Thankful the rain had stopped, Jack opened his saddlebags

and pulled out a cleaning rod he used for his revolvers. It was long enough to completely pass through Johnny's shoulder.

The deputy looked at the rod. "I don't think I like the idea of what you have planned."

"I'll be the first to say this won't be any fun, but it has to be done. You don't want your wound to get infected. It could kill you." Jack pointed at a rock. "Sit down." He removed a package wrapped in newspaper from the saddlebags. After untying the twine holding the package closed, he took out two pieces of white cloth. Each looked to be a foot square. Jack also removed a whiskey bottle from his bag.

"You come prepared. Planning on tying one on?"

"You might need to." He handed the deputy the bottle. "Take a couple of swigs."

Johnny took the bottle by the neck and tilted it high. After the second pull, he jerked it down, coughing and gagging. "That's some strong stuff. I think it must have burned out my throat." He coughed again and handed the bottle back to Jack.

While he had been drinking, Jack had torn one of the squares in four pieces. Retrieving the bottle, he poured whiskey over the unripped cloth. Using the whiskey-laden larger cloth, he cleaned both the entry and exit wounds, which, along with the shoulder around the wound, was already turning a deep purple. Johnny gritted his teeth as Jack cleaned. "How are you doing?"

Johnny nodded. "I can honestly say I've been better."

Jack soaked one of the smaller rags with the whiskey and wrapped it around the cleaning rod. "Alright, boy, I can't lie to you. This is gonna hurt like the dickens. You feel like yelling, turn it loose. Ain't nobody out here but you and me and that no-account bushwhacker, so you can just let it go."

Johnny eyed the cleaning rod as it neared the hole in his shoulder. "Make it quick, Marshal. I don't know how much of this I can take."

"Will do." With his last words, Jack shoved the rod and

whiskey-soaked rag through Johnny's shoulder. The boy didn't utter a sound, but his jaw muscles quivered, and his eyes floated in tears. The end of the rod was protruding from the boy's back. Several pieces of bloody shirt were stuck on the end of the rod. *At least those are out of the wound*, Jack thought. He removed the cloth and debris and retracted the cleaning rod. Johnny relaxed, but immediately tensed up again when he saw Jack wrapping another piece of the cloth around the rod.

"You doing it again?"

"Gotta make sure it's clean. You don't want anything inside there."

Johnny's face turned grim. "Alright, do it quick."

Jack nodded and shoved the rod through Johnny's shoulder. The deputy stiffened, his lips formed a straight line, and his jaw muscles bulged. His hands were drawn into tight fists, and he swayed on the boulder. Jack gripped his opposite shoulder, holding him erect. He released it long enough to pick another piece of debris from the end of the rod sticking out of Jack's shoulder. After removing the second cloth, he yanked the rod out. He held Johnny's shoulder tight, keeping him from falling off the rock.

"It's done, boy. You can relax." Blood trickled from both the entry and exit wounds. Jack wiped the wound clean, ripped Johnny's sleeve from his shirt, and tied it around the wounds. Once it was secure, he helped the deputy slip on his long johns top, shirt, coat, and slicker. "How are you feeling?"

"I've been better, but I'll make it. Help me on my horse."

The marshal held the boy steady for a few moments longer. "You sure you're ready to ride."

Johnny looked up at Jack and shot him a feeble grin. "I danged sure ain't gonna get any better sitting here."

"Now that's a fact." Jack released his shoulder and retrieved the buckskin. He led the horse close to the rock. Johnny stood and managed to get his left foot into the stirrup. Jack lifted the young fellow up and into the saddle. He walked to Thunder and checked the surrounding area before swinging into the saddle. He wanted to check the bushwhacker's tracks before they continued to the ranch. "Hold on, Johnny. I'll be right back."

He rode over to where he'd last seen the shooter. The horse's hooves had left clear imprints in the mud. The animal wore no shoes. Jack looked toward the trees where the rider had disappeared. *Who are you?* Jack thought. *What do you have to gain by killing me or Johnny? What are you trying to keep us from finding?*

17

The clouds had separated, and sunshine was drying the soaked lawmen. Jack watched the three riders approaching from the herd ahead. He could tell Tripp was in the lead, riding with two men Jack didn't recognize. The three men pulled their horses to a halt, and Tripp shoved his hat to the back of his head. "What happened to you, Johnny? You ain't lookin' too fine."

Johnny had the reins in his left hand and was gripping the saddle horn with the other. The deputy lifted his head to stare at Tripp. "We had a little run-in with the mysterious bushwhacker." His head dropped forward, and he swayed in the saddle. Jack guided Thunder closer to the deputy, in case he started to fall. "Let's get him on up to the house. The past three hours have been tough on him."

Tripp nodded. "You boys take the cattle on to the point, then come in. I'll ride with the marshal and Johnny."

The riders peeled away toward the cattle, and Tripp fell in on the opposite side of Johnny.

"Anything happened while I've been gone?"

"All quiet. Nobody's been shot at or seen anything. A couple of days after you left, Schmidt rode in with five of his men. They've been here since. Jo acted upset with all the attention, but I think she was secretly relieved, not for herself but for the kids and the other women. It's impossible to keep her around the ranch house. She and the others have been out working cattle like nothing's happened. She is one hard-headed woman."

Jack felt relief flood his body. He hadn't dwelled on what could be happening while he was gone, but he knew the worry had been there. It was why he had gotten so upset with Carter when he mentioned the president would be aggrieved should anything happen to Jo. He was glad to hear she, Amy and Davy, and all the others were unharmed. "Good. I'm glad to hear it. Have you found any sign of the shooter? Anything that might indicate he's been around or who he might be?"

Tripp shook his head. "Nope, nary a thing. No tracks, nothing. It's like he fired at Jo the other night and left the country." Tripp motioned toward Johnny with his head. "Course, it looks like he's still around."

Jack eyed Johnny sway in the saddle as they neared the point before turning into the timber toward the house. "More than you know." It appeared the boy was riding in a stupor. His body swung back and forth with the gait of his buckskin. "This young fella saved my life."

Tripp's head turned toward Jack. "He saved you?"

"He did. It was raining like Noah's flood, and this owlhoot appeared right in front of us. I had just pulled my head in like a turtle, hat hiding everything. Johnny saw him and jumped his buckskin into Thunder. Moved me just enough. The fella missed."

"So he hit Johnny?"

Thunder started up the hill toward the house. Jack leaned a bit forward in the saddle and checked on Johnny, who seemed to be hanging on. He shook his head. "Nope, the fool kid took off after the bushwhacker in that heavy rain. I tried to stop him but wasn't fast enough. He disappeared in the rain, and shortly I heard a shot. When the rain let up, I found him with a bullet hole in his shoulder."

Tripp shook his head. "Young'uns have to learn by experience. All you can do is try to teach 'em and hope they survive."

"Yep," Jack said, but his mind was no longer on what they were saying. The house was in sight, and folks had started coming out of it. He saw Jo, Lilly, and Dot step from the front door, but that wasn't what had his attention. Davy and Flo had dashed out of the kitchen. Schmidt was right behind, holding the door for Amy, who came out laughing. He felt a twinge of anger and immediately put it away. She had every right to like whomever she wanted.

Davy dashed down the steps and met them as they pulled up. "Hi, Marshal Sage, what's wrong with Johnny? Is he sick?"

"You might say that, boy. Right now I need to get him into the house." Ignoring Amy, who, with Flo's hand in hers, was right behind her son, he said, "Hold that gate, Davy." Jack swung down from Thunder and tossed his reins to Tripp. Johnny's last bit of strength ran out. He fell toward Jack, who caught him gently and finished lifting him from the saddle. Tripp grabbed the buckskin's reins and led both horses toward the barn. Jack lifted the boy in his arms and looked at Jo, eyebrows raised.

"Bring him in the house, Jack." She turned and marched up the steps, Jack following close behind.

Lilly hovered near Jack. "What happened?"

"He's been shot. It's his left shoulder." Jack turned sideways so he could ease Johnny through the front door, which was being held by Dot.

Once he was through, Lilly moved ahead of Jack. "This way. You can take him to my room." She hurried in front, opened her door, and moved to the bed, yanking the blanket down. "Here."

Jack laid him on the bed and removed Johnny's hat, hanging it on the bedpost.

Jo stepped forward, lifting the deputy's leg and grabbing a boot. "We can take it from here, Jack. Go to the kitchen. Teresa has made a fresh pot of coffee. I'm sure you could use a cup."

Jack looked at the boy's inert body on the bed. "You sure you don't need my help?"

"We don't need your help, Jack. He has nothing we haven't already seen. Now go on."

Jack shrugged and turned for the kitchen, to come face-to-face with Amy, who stepped quickly aside. "I'll help, Mama Jo."

Jo nodded. "Dot, get some hot water, liniment, and linen. We'll clean this up."

Monty had stepped into the bedroom as Jack was trying to get through the crowd of women.

Jo looked at her cowhand. "Monty, tell Tripp to send someone to Laramie for the doctor. This boy looks a lot worse than he should with a simple shoulder wound."

Jack, still in the room, stepped aside and watched as the women efficiently began to strip the boy. First his boots, then his gunbelt, coat, shirt and pants, leaving him with only his long johns and socks on, which Dot was working to get off his feet.

Jo continued, "Whoever Tripp sends, tell them to stop by his ma's place and tell her. If she wants to come out with the doc, she'd be welcome." She looked at Jack. "What are you still doing in here? Go on and get some coffee. You look like you need it."

Jack shook his head. There was no sense arguing with this woman. If anything, she'd gotten stronger since the general died, and she had been plenty strong before then. "Yes, ma'am." He turned again to exit the bedroom door and came face-to-face with Schmidt. Jack nodded and pushed by him on his way to the kitchen. He felt something yank on his coat and looked down. It was Davy, Flo by his side. Both of the small faces were turned up to him.

Davy, eyes wide, said, "Is Deputy Johnny going to be alright, Marshal?"

Jack grinned at the two kids. "You bet he is. He's just feeling a little puny right now. Why don't you two come with me, and you can tell me what you've been up to."

The concern disappeared from their little faces, replaced by excitement and wide grins. They both started to talk at the same time. Jack's entourage made it to the kitchen. Teresa smiled at him. "It is good to see you again, Marshal. Have a seat." She had already filled a cup half-full with coffee and placed the sugar bowl and creamer next to it. Jack sat, and the kids pulled a chair up next to him. They both wiggled onto the same seat.

Flo started, "We saw a big porcupine."

Davy gave Flo support by spreading his arms wide to indicate the size of the animal.

Flo sent Davy a grin and continued, "It was all fluffed up, its quills sticking out like knitting needles. Davy wanted to poke it."

Davy frowned. "I did not."

"You did too. I saw you."

Amy and Schmidt walked into the kitchen together. Jack noticed.

Amy placed one hand on each child's shoulder and pushed them from the chair, guiding them to the kitchen door. "Have you checked the chickens for eggs?"

Davy frowned. "We already got the eggs this morning."

Amy picked up the basket by the kitchen door and gave it to Flo. "Then check again. You can't check too often. Now go along."

Davy turned to Jack. "We'll tell you later, Marshal Sage, and I didn't want to poke the porcupine."

Flo banged out the door, running ahead of Davy, and yelled, "Did too!"

Jack couldn't help but smile. It was nice to be around kids. At least for a while. His smile disappeared when Schmidt pulled out a chair and sat beside him. "What happened?"

"Ambush." Jack concentrated on doctoring his coffee. On the way here, he had been thinking about Teresa's coffee. All he wanted was to relax a few minutes, drink his coffee, and be left alone.

From the edge of his vision, he caught Schmidt's glance at Amy and then back to him. He poured cream into his cup, stirred, leaned back in his chair, and took a long sip. It was just as good as he remembered. He took another sip. The warmth relaxed him. Amy walked back from the kitchen door, down the opposite side of the table, behind Teresa, around the end, and pulled out a chair on the other side of Jack. *Great,* he thought, *I can't even relax with a cup of coffee by myself.* He knew he wasn't in a good mood, and wasn't too sure he cared.

Amy leaned toward him. "Jack, did you get a look at the man?"

Jack was about to answer when Lilly entered the kitchen.

"We need to make some chicken soup for Johnny."

He watched Teresa pull a large pot from a cabinet. She started to speak, and Lilly held up her hand. "Excuse me, Teresa." Lilly turned to Jack. "Mama wants to see you. She said to bring your coffee."

Hallelujah, Jack thought. He nodded to Lilly, pushed his chair far enough back where he could get up between the huge Schmidt and petite Amy, and without a word, strode to the bedroom. The door opened with his arrival.

"Let's go for a ride. I want to check the cattle Tripp was moving." Jo pulled the door closed behind her and headed for the front door. Passing the kitchen, she called, "Lilly, Jack and I are leaving for a while. Would you sit with Johnny until I get back?"

The soft voice of Lilly replied, "Yes, Mama. Teresa is making him chicken soup. I have a pitcher of water to take him."

"That'll be fine." She looked up at Jack. "Leave your cup on the table." She nodded toward a small table next to the door.

Jack took another sip of his coffee. With the cream and sugar, it had cooled down sufficiently, so he drank down the remainder

Five Women And The Star

and placed the cup on the table. He pulled the door open, and the older woman grabbed her brown hat as she walked by the hat tree. Jack closed the door behind them and was surprised to see Smokey, saddled and ready to go, tied next to Jo's palomino. She had brought the horse from their farm back east. The general had always said she loved the palomino more than him, but everyone knew he was joking. He watched as the beautiful animal stretched her head toward Jo.

He heard her say, "Good morning, Jewel," but his attention was taken by Smokey, his big grulla. He hadn't seen the horse in almost a week, and the horse acted like he had missed him, with his neck also stretching toward him. Jack rubbed the grulla's dusty gray neck. "How are you doing, fella? I've missed you too." He took a moment to scratch the horse behind his black-tipped ears before stepping into the saddle.

Jo glanced at him and nudged the palomino. The golden mare stepped toward the prairie, partially visible through the scattered pines. Jack eased Smokey to Jo's side. "So what's on your mind? You obviously wanted me out of the house to talk."

She motioned down the trail. "Later, let's ride. Jewel, go."

The palomino broke into a lope, and Jack fell in behind them. He pulled alongside when they broke out of the trees. The clouds had disappeared, leaving the late afternoon warming from the bright sun. Smells of wet earth and tall grass filled Jack's nostrils.

Jo urged Jewel into a run, and Jack could feel Smokey's delight in stretching his long legs after being cooped up in the barn and corral for a week. He scanned across the plains, watching for anything out of place, while they raced through the tall grass. He felt the anger and stress falling away. This was the life. *I need to get back to Texas. There's a ranch down there that could probably use my help.* He filled his lungs with the fresh wild air. His hat flew off. The leather string held it around his neck. He could feel the wind blowing through his hair. A grin widened his mouth. He glanced at Jo, who was alongside. Sitting atop the racing golden palomino in the afternoon sun, she returned the grin. Her face looked fifteen years younger. She slowed Jewel, and Jack followed suit with Smokey.

"Feeling better?"

Jack reached back with his left hand, caught his hat brim, and pulled his hat into place. "Best I've felt in a while. The ride was a good idea."

"I'm glad to hear it. When you rode up, you looked like a mountain storm about to rain on everyone."

Jack gave a short laugh. "That's a good description of how I felt."

The two horses had slowed to a walk. Jo's head turned as she gazed across the backs of her cattle. "I noticed you saw Amy come out of the house with Hank."

"Humph," Jack said, unwilling to commit.

"You don't have to admit it, but I've been on this earth long enough to recognize a jealous man."

"I've no right to be jealous, Jo. I hardly know her."

"You're exactly right. Though I don't know what went on in the barn—"

"I told you what happened, nothing."

"Look, Jack, I saw her when she came in the house. She was upset. A stranger couldn't have caused her to be upset in that manner. I'm thinking she may have given you some signals that, at that moment, you may have been receptive to."

Jack pulled Smokey to a halt and turned to Jo. "Mrs. Franklin, I'm not discussing my personal life. I've got work to do around here, and when it's done, I'll be going my way. It's that simple."

"Is it?" She held his gaze until he was forced to look away. "Jack, I know about your wife and child." When Jack's mouth tightened and his jaw set, Jo held up a gloved hand. "Warren told me, not to gossip, but because he was concerned about you being alone."

Jack's face relaxed. He had told Warren in confidence, but he could see the man talking it over with his mother, especially if he had been concerned about him. "We were good friends."

"I know, which is the reason he told me. I am so sorry, Jack. Until recently, I couldn't know how sorry." She bumped Jewel, and Jack clucked to Smokey. The grulla stepped forward, staying with the palomino.

"Amy has been lost since Warren was murdered. She's had a difficult time, and so has Davy. You came along and saved the two of them. They will forever be in your debt. That morning, and immediately after you left, I think she tried to make it into something more. Then you were gone, and Henry Schmidt was here. He likes Davy, and Davy likes him. Most importantly, it seems Amy is forming a healthy bond with him, not one built on gratitude and dependency."

Jack squirmed in the saddle. He had never liked talking to a third party about personal things. These types of conversations had always been disturbing to him. He was used to attacking problems head-on.

"Am I making sense, Jack?"

He had to admit, as uncomfortable as the conversation was, the older woman was making sense. "Yeah, Jo, you're making sense. I get the picture. Now, can we drop it?"

Josephine Franklin looked at the big, uncomfortable man and smiled. "I know you don't like to talk about such things. General Franklin didn't like it either, but there are times we must do uncomfortable things."

So who originated that phrase? Jack thought. *I've also heard it from the general. My money's on Jo.*

"She likes you and would like to keep you as a friend, Jack. I know this because I know my girls, and I think of Amy as one of my girls. I know what you're thinking. No, she didn't ask me to talk to you. It needed to be done, and I'm the person to do it. Do you have any questions?"

Jack rode along in silence. Jo, too, was silent. It was a lovely afternoon. The fresh rain smell filled the air. A few of the cattle were grazing, but most had bedded down and were chewing their cuds. In the distance a herd of elk traversed the high grass plains, occasionally stopping to keep an eye on a pair of wolves trotting nonchalantly through the tall grass. They were completely hidden in the thick grass only to be visible when they broke out into open strips. Two eagles circled overhead, their sharp eyes searching for prey.

Do I have any questions? "I do. You think they're serious?"

He watched the older woman contemplate his question as the horses' hooves thudded softly against the wet dirt. "Yes, I think so. Actually, I hope so. I've met Henry Schmidt's mother, and she is quite a nice person, and if they should marry, Davy will have a fine father and the chance for a wonderful education."

Jack gave a slow nod. "That's good. I wish her and Davy the best."

Jo smiled at Jack. "She may try to talk to you. If you can, let her explain. It'll be good for you both. As you probably know, women like to talk. Sometimes it helps."

Jack nodded again. "I can do that, but you know, I can't stay around here. I need to make sure you and your family are safe, but once I solve this puzzle, I'll be gone, probably back to Texas. This country is way too cold for a lowland fella like me."

This time when she turned her head toward Jack, she wore a sad smile. "I am so sorry for your losses. I wish this had been the answer for you, because I have always felt an attachment to you, even as Warren and his father did. Both Dot and Lilly would make wonderful wives for you. In fact, I think that's what Warren hoped for when he brought you home, but Lilly was too young, and, well, it just didn't work out then, and it doesn't look like it will work this time. I am sorry, Jack. You've done so much for our family. You deserve a good life for yourself, surrounded with a happy family."

Jack could see the woman's usually hard gray eyes were soft

and gentle, floating almost in tears. He had liked her when first he met her, and he still liked her. The thought drifted through his mind, *That's why you're here, to keep Warren's mother, sisters, and wife alive.* He jerked from his reverie and scanned the plains. In the distance, too far to distinguish who they were, he could see riders, a bunch of them, and they looked like they were riding toward them. "Jo, we've got a group of riders coming our way fast. It could be Indians. Head for the ranch."

18

"I'm sure you have field glasses. Use them."

Of course, he thought, digging into his saddlebags. He pulled out his glasses and jerked them to his eyes. Every second counted. He made a couple of minute adjustments. "Indians."

"Let me see." He handed them to Jo. She stood in her stirrups and said, "Cheyenne," and handed the glasses back to him.

He put them up to his eyes. "We head back to the ranch?"

"No, we'd never make it. They're friendly. I know the one in the lead."

"Looks like there are eight of them."

Having drawn closer, Jack could tell they only had their horses at a lope, which was less threatening, he hoped. No longer needing the glasses, he dropped them into the saddlebags and fastened the buckle. Next, he flipped the loops from his Smith & Wessons. If need be, he might get two, maybe three, before they got him. He rested both hands on his saddle horn and waited.

Jo looked over at him. "Relax, Jack, they're friendly."

"Yeah, there's a lot of folks who could be buried with that as their epitaph. 'They were friendly.'"

"I know them. I helped them this past winter."

"Good." He waited. These were the situations he did not like, when you knew a lot less than you thought you did.

The Indians pulled up and circled them. Even worse. Now it would be impossible for Jack to bring his gun to bear on the ones behind him. *This day has really gone downhill,* he thought.

The leader made the sign of friend to Jo. She returned it to him. He said something in what Jack figured was Cheyenne, and Jo replied, speaking slower and using more signs with her hands. She turned to Jack. "Chief Mantotohpa, it means Four Bears, says they were in the mountains where you were attacked. They followed the man you shot."

"Is he dead?"

Using her sign language and speaking slowly, she asked the chief Jack's question. He answered, speaking for several moments in speech and sign language. Jo nodded and turned to Jack. "No, he's wounded. If I'm understanding him correctly, you hit the man twice. The first shot only grazed his arm, but the second shot hit him in his right elbow. You messed it up pretty badly."

Jack nodded to the chief. "That's good. Tell him the man is probably the one who shot the general and Warren."

Jack could see the chief's eyes narrow as Jo explained. He answered rapidly and started to turn his horse. Jo shouted no and waved her hands. The chief stopped and said something else while pointing at Jack.

Jo nodded and turned again to Jack, who immediately asked, "What was that all about?"

"When I told him the man was probably David and Warren's murderer, he was ready to go back and kill him. I had to stop him. I assume you'd like to question the man."

"Danged right. Can they take me there now, before he gets away?"

The chief and Jo had another long conversation. Finally she explained to Jack, "Chief Mantotohpa said the man wouldn't be going anywhere, he is very sick, and he never saw the Cheyenne. He also said they are far from their people, scouting for buffalo, and are on their way back. If you want them to show you, they will, but they must leave now."

Jack looked directly at the chief, nodded his head, and said, "Yes."

The chief said a few words to Jo, pointed at Jack, and motioned him to join him.

Jack suddenly held up a hand. "Wait."

All eyes of the Cheyenne braves turned to Jack. "Ask him how they happened to ride all the way here to tell us about finding this fella. They couldn't have connected me to you, or the bushwhacker to you."

Jo's head turned a bit to the side. Jack could almost see the thought working its way through her mind. She turned to the chief and began slowly speaking, her hands moving as words formed. She first pointed to the chief and then to herself. The chief listened, his broad face concentrating on what she was asking. Then his eyebrows rose. He turned and pointed a large finger solemnly toward one of the braves and began to speak slowly. It was obvious to Jack, who knew not a word of what they were saying, the chief wanted to be sure Jo understood his every word. The large, impressive man slowly moved his arm, describing an arc that took in all of the prairie and mountains. He brought both hands to his chest, pointed again at the brave, and then Jack. Lastly he pointed at Jo and stopped.

Jack was almost bursting with curiosity.

Jo turned to him. He could see her concentrating, striving to interpret to him what she had understood.

"This is quite amazing, Jack. The brave's name, who Chief Mantotohpa pointed to, is Heammawihio. It translates to Wise One Above. He is their shaman. He travels with the chief wherever he goes. They have been friends since they were boys. Chief Mantotohpa says Heammawihio is a very wise and spiritual man whom he trusts with his life. They followed the bushwhacker on Heammawihio's direction. Once they found his camp, they were about to move in and either help or kill the man, I'm not sure which it was. The shaman stopped them, and they slipped away.

"When they were well away from the camp, the shaman said they must go to the home of the woman of the great leader who had helped them during their starvation period, and tell her."

Jack did not discount the chief's tale. Though he was a violent man, he was also a believer in God and had seen miracles and proof of the supernatural in his travels as a young man. He turned to the shaman and gave a respectful nod.

Jo hadn't finished. "Jack, that's not all. The shaman predicted they would meet us. He told the chief they would find the great leader's woman riding with a white man of their size, and we would be riding to meet them."

Jack felt a calm come over him he hadn't felt in a while. He looked at the chief, the shaman, and the other braves. From dark eyes, they all gazed at him, waiting for his reaction. He gave the chief and the shaman a solemn nod and turned back to Jo. "I've seen and heard a lot of things, Jo. I want you to know, I don't doubt a word Chief Mantotohpa says. I'm just glad they're here." He took a deep breath, his countenance changing to determination. "Now, we must go."

He gave another confirming nod to the chief. "I'll see you soon. Take good care of Johnny."

Before Jo could reply, they were off at a lope, Jack surrounded by Cheyenne. He looked around him and grinned at the chief. "There's a few folks I'd love to see me now."

Mantotohpa's dark eyes glinted with humor. *Yeah,* Jack thought, *I bet it's pretty funny to you, too.*

THE MOON WAS UP and bright. Darkness had caught them as they were reaching the ambush spot. Two of the braves rode ahead and alternately returned, informing the chief. They entered the treeline near where the bushwhacker had disappeared after Jack shot him. It was still hard to believe he had even hit the man with a handgun at that range. It was at least a hundred yards, pure luck and a good weapon. They walked their horses through the trees, crossed one canyon, and entered another. Reaching the bottom, they turned upstream, moving slowly in the darkness.

The moon was almost directly overhead, most of its light blocked by the tall pines, when Mantotohpa stopped. He said something, and his braves dismounted. Jack followed suit. One of the braves stayed behind to water and take care of the horses. The chief motioned Jack forward and held his finger to his lips. They began slipping through the timber. It was easy going, at least in comparison to New Mexico where he'd been trapped in the canyon. Under these tall pines, there was little brush, and they walked mostly on pine needles.

Ahead, Jack could see a fire burning. Moving closer, a substantial lean-to was evident, large enough for bedding, a few cooking utensils, and the fella's horse, if he needed to move him out of rain or snow. The horse stood with his head up. It was the same scrawny bay Jack had seen when the bushwhacker shot at him. Jack could see the man lying with a blanket pulled up to his arms. His right arm at the elbow was a bloody mess, as was the blanket and the ground around him.

Jack motioned to the chief for them to wait, and drew his knife. Jack knew his skill with a knife at this range. This fella might have a gun, but if he pulled it, he'd never use it. He slipped closer to the prone man and stopped. Still no movement. Then he saw the empty bottle. *He's been drinking,* Jack thought. *Good.* He slipped closer and stopped again, listening. There was no sound. He was within six feet of the man. He watched him closely, looking for his chest rising and falling—no movement.

Jack's lips pursed. He gripped his knife, took two steps, and dropped to his knee next to the killer, his knife blade against his throat. Nothing, no movement, no response. Disregarding the man's shattered elbow, he grabbed his shoulder and yanked him on his back. The killer's eyes, black in the firelight, and mouth were open. He was dead. Jack sheathed his knife and stood, motioning the Cheyenne in. Each came, stared, but stayed clear of the dead man. Jack could see the man had a Winchester, a scoped Whitworth rifle, and a Smith & Wesson similar to Jack's, in a holster.

The chief looked around the camp, stepped over to the gunbelt and handgun, and with a questioning look, held it towards Jack. Jack pointed at the gun and then at the chief. The gesture got him a nod, which Jack returned.

That's the least I can do, he thought. He watched the chief fasten it around his waist. Seeing the man's saddlebags, he opened one side, where he found clothes and two more boxes of ammunition for the revolver. He took them out and handed them to the chief. Mantotohpa pointed to Jack's revolvers. Jack shook his head and pulled one of the rounds from his gunbelt while at the same time taking one from one of the boxes. He held them up side by side. It was obvious they were of different lengths. Jack dropped the round from the box back where it belonged. Then he pointed at the revolver. The chief handed it to him, and Jack showed him how to open the revolver for reloading. The other braves gathered around, watching. Jack snapped it shut and handed it back to the chief.

The chief dropped the weapon into the holster, nodded, and held the boxes in his left hand. He extended his right, gripping Jack's forearm well above the wrist.

Jack duplicated his movement. "Thank you."

The chief, Jack's height, but not a great deal taller than his men, gave a single nod and said, his voice steady but slow and distinct, "Heammawihio, the Wise One, says we will meet again, and it will be good." He squeezed Jack's forearm hard and released it. "We go."

Chief Mantotohpa and his men melted into the trees and were gone. Jack started to follow, to bring Smokey closer, but saw that one of the braves had taken care of his problem, tying his horse near the lean-to. Jack moved Smokey near to where he planned on sleeping, stripped the tack, and made a bed on the pine needles. It was late, and he was tired.

A lot had happened since he and Jo had met the Cheyenne. Even with the dead man lying under the lean-to, Jack felt a certain peace he hadn't felt in a while. *Imagine those Cheyenne riding so far to bring me back here.*

He looked over at his grulla. "Smokey, boy, I figure the Big Man upstairs has a plan, whether we're aware of it or not. It's nice to be reminded once in a while." Jack glanced at the dead man. There wasn't anything that wouldn't wait till the morning, and he was bone-tired. Before sacking out, he checked the fire. It was sufficiently banked and low. He turned the corpse on its side and covered him to his neck with the blanket. Grabbing the dead man's saddlebags, he moved near Smokey, stretched out on his bedroll, and was soon asleep.

A LOW RUMBLE pulled him from a sound sleep. Through the trees, he could see the light of dawn breaking. Only a few coals remained in the fire. Two wolves, their hackles up and lips pulled back from white fangs, threatened a massive dog. Jack thought, *That fella's huge.* The dog's long hair was the color of Smokey's, and his teeth looked pretty threatening themselves, enough so to give the wolves second thoughts. Jack threw his blanket back. The wolves and the dog's head turned toward him. The two wolves watched Jack for only a second and silently disappeared into the forest. The dog sat on his haunches, his tongue lolling out and his eyes on the human.

Jack stretched and stood. He checked Smokey and stepped over to the dead man's horse. Scrawny didn't begin to describe him. The bay gelding's ribs stood out like the bars in a jail. Jack walked back to his saddlebags and pulled out three cookies. He gave one to Smokey, who munched appreciably, and carefully palmed one to the bay. The horse yanked it up. Two or three chews and it was gone. The animal stared at Jack and nudged the hand that held the other cookie. Jack turned and looked at Smokey. "Don't you think this'll work for you. This fella needs it." He gave the second one to the bay while scratching the horse behind his ears. "You're in mighty bad shape, fella." He lifted the animal's left front hoof. Sure enough, no shoe. The hooves hadn't had a trim for a while and appeared overgrown. Jack dropped the hoof and patted the bay on his neck. "He didn't take care of you, did he, pardner?"

He went back to his saddlebags and dug out a handful of oats. Smokey sniffed at him. Jack let him eat until the oats were gone. He scooped another handful from his bag and walked to the bay. He was a big horse. Jack had seen him run for the treeline. The horse was fast. He held the oats out to the animal, keeping his hand flat so the big teeth couldn't take a hunk out of him or take a finger off. The bay made the oats disappear quickly.

Throughout the time he had been taking care of the horses, he had been keeping an eye on the monster dog. He assumed the dead guy must be the dog's master, for the animal sat close by the man, his head following each of Jack's movements. Jack figured he should check the dead man's pockets. The fire was next to the body, and he wanted a cup of coffee. He started slowly toward what was left of the fire. The dog sat up, alert, watching him. He began to talk to the gray beast. "How are you doing, boy. Is that your master?" He slowly moved closer. "You know I've got to search him and eventually take him. Are you gonna be alright with that?"

Jack reached the fire, and so far, the dog had shown no aggression. He poked in the dead coals, finding a few still glowing red. After dragging them together, he picked up a couple of branches from the pile the man had stacked beneath the lean-to. It took only a few moments, and the dry limbs caught, small flames leaping. Jack added a few more and walked back to get the coffee pot and coffee. He had looked at the pot the bushwhacker was using and elected to stay away from it. Everything around this camp was filthier than anything at the Polings' place. He dipped his pot into the stream, moved back to, and placed the pot on the edge of the fire.

While looking for his coffee, he ran across his thick roll of jerky and had an idea. Jack looked up at the big dog. "You must weigh a hundred and thirty pounds, fella."

The dog cocked his head at Jack.

"You weigh more than any of those women back at the ranch." Jack pulled a wide strip of jerky out of his stash. "You hungry?"

The dog's ears perked up.

"You definitely know that word, don't you." He tossed the stick of jerky to the dog. It disappeared down the big throat with two gulps. "I guess you are hungry." He tossed him another with the same results. Jack stood and moved toward the man. The dog's big head followed him, but he made no threatening movement.

Jack reached the dead man and checked the dirty vest pockets. He pulled out a worn plug of tobacco, a Barlow knife, and a small ring of gold. Jack held the ring up and examined it. Nothing, no inscriptions, no markings. It was definitely a woman's ring, a small one at that, and the gold was thin. She'd worn it for a long time.

He looked at the dead man, the busted elbow, and the empty

whiskey bottle lying next to him. The man's face didn't even look peaceful in death.

"I don't know who you are, fella, but I know you killed some mighty fine folks. Why would you do it? That's what I'd like to know."

The dog had moved closer to Jack and lay down. He was almost within arm's reach. Jack sat and opened the killer's saddlebags. He pulled out the dirty change of clothes he had found when he'd retrieved the ammunition for Chief Mantotohpa from the bag. They definitely looked cleaner than what the man was wearing. With two fingers and a thumb, he pulled out a stinking set of red long johns and threw them as far away as he could. Beneath the long johns lay a bullet mold. Jack glanced over at the scoped Whitworth. "You cast your own bullets. I guess you'd have to. You're the right age. I'm thinking you were probably a sniper in the war. Since you're using the Whitworth, I'd say you were probably with the South."

Jack could hear the water beginning to boil. He moved the pot from the coals, raised the lid, and tossed coffee into the hot water. In a few minutes, he'd have him a cup. He went back to the saddlebags, opening the other side. He reached in and pulled out a heavy leather bag.

19

He hefted it and heard the clink. He didn't have to open it to know what was inside. Silver wouldn't be near this heavy. It had to be gold. Before opening the pouch, he reached into the saddlebags again and pulled out paper money, greenbacks. There were two stacks of at least five hundred dollars each. With the weight of the gold in the bag, he figured another five hundred in gold. He dropped the money back into the saddlebags, reached for the pot, and poured himself a cup of coffee. He took a sip, black. Not the way he preferred his coffee, but it was hot. It would do.

Jack turned to look at the dead man. "You collected a lot of blood money. I need to get you to town before you swell to the point no one can recognize you. Maybe there's someone there who might know you, your horse, or your dog." Jack turned to glance at the shaggy beast. He had crawled closer, within arm's reach. Jack knew he should leave the animal alone. He had three horses and a mule. He sure didn't need a dog trailing along, but he couldn't resist. He reached out and felt the big head beneath his hand. Belly still against the ground, the dog eased nearer. Jack scratched him behind the ears. "What's your name, boy? How long have you been with this bushwhacker? It can't be too long. I didn't see you when I shot him, and we haven't found your tracks around any of his."

The dog whined and crawled closer. *What am I doing?* Jack thought, yet he continued to scratch the animal's ears and neck. "We've got to get moving." Jack slapped his palms on his legs and stood. The dog leaped to his feet, his thick tail slashing back and forth.

An hour later Jack had the body loaded on the bay and was mounted on Smokey. The dog sat at the camp, watching. "You coming with me?" Jack called as he started Smokey down the shallow canyon. "Maybe we can find a good owner for you."

The dog sat for a moment longer, then stood and trotted forward.

JACK RODE into Laramie on Smokey, leading the scrawny bay with the killer's body on it, and a big shaggy gray dog trotting alongside. People stopped and watched him ride by, several turning and following. He saw the sheriff's office door open, and Sheriff Wright stepped onto the boardwalk. He watched Jack near, waved, and turned, reentering his office. Jack laughed to himself. *That sheriff does not like complications,* he thought.

By the time he pulled up in front of the barbershop, he had collected a crowd. A man called from the back, "Who is he, Marshal?"

Jack turned in the saddle. "That's what I'd like to know. I'd like to know so badly that if any of you fine folks can identify him to my satisfaction, you'll collect a reward of one hundred dollars."

A murmur went through the crowd.

Jack added, "In gold."

Several of the men stepped forward to grasp the dead man by

the hair and pull his head up so they could get a good look at him.

"Hold on, folks. I'm getting your undertaker to clean him up. He'll stick him in a box and lean him out front of the barbershop. It'll probably be only for today, 'cause this fella is starting to get a little ripe."

Someone yelled, "Well, tell Brad to hurry up. We need to take a good look. Where do we find you, Marshal, if we figure out who this feller might be, that is?"

"Leave your identification at the sheriff's office. I'll pick it up and investigate."

The door of the barbershop opened, and Brad Wilkins stepped onto the boardwalk. "Can a couple of you boys get this body into my shop so I can get him cleaned up and on display?"

Jack had wrapped the man's body in the filthy blankets he had been sleeping on. A railroad hand stepped forward, untied the body, and slid him onto his shoulder. "No need, Mr. Wilkins. I'll get him back there for you."

Brad moved quickly to his door and opened it. "Straight through. The shop's in the back, and you can expect a free haircut for your trouble."

"Morning, Brad," Jack said as the crowd began to scatter. "I'll stop by later. I've got to take care of these animals."

The barber glanced at the dog. It was sitting in the dust next to Smokey. "You pick up a friend?"

Jack removed his hat and scratched his head. "Danged if I know. He just showed up at the dead man's camp. I don't know if he belonged to him or not. He didn't seem too upset when I was messing around with the body." He shrugged and turned Smokey toward Otto's Livery. "We'll see."

The dog rose and trotted alongside Smokey into the livery. When Jack stepped down, the dog circled a couple of times in a pile of straw and plopped his hefty body to the ground.

Otto stepped out of his office and stopped. With his hands on his hips, he looked first at Jack, then the dog, and then the emaciated horse. "If this ain't the most raggedy-looking bunch I've ever seen. Where'd you get this ragtag pair?"

Jack led Smokey into a stall while tossing the lead rope for the bay to Otto. "They belonged to the fella who tried to kill Johnny and took a shot at me."

"Is Johnny alright?"

"When I last saw him, he was."

Otto stripped the tack from the bay. "Guess he's the reason the doc raced out of here in such an all-fired hurry yesterday. Is the owner of these scraggly-looking animals the one Brad's working on?"

"That's him. Do you recognize this horse?"

"I never forget a horse, and I can honestly say I've never laid eyes on this bag of bones. This pore thing don't even have shoes. What kind of man was that feller?"

Jack shook his head. "I know nothing about him except he's the man who shot Johnny and took a shot at me. I also believe he's the man who shot General Franklin and his son and tried to kill Jo."

"He's been busy."

"Yeah, but *his* business is done."

Jack stripped the tack from Smokey.

Otto stepped back and eyed the bay. "Marshal, what do you want me to do with this bag of bones?"

"Feed him. Get some shoes on him. Let him rest. Let's see what kind of horse he turns into."

Otto shot a skeptical look at the bay and shook his head. "There's no telling what else is wrong with him inside, as bad a shape as he's in."

"True." Jack picked up a brush and began brushing Smokey. "I'd like to give him a fair chance, though, before doing anything drastic. I saw him run yesterday, and as bad a shape as he's in, he was fast. If you can bring him back, he might be a mighty fine horse."

Otto shook his head. "It'll cost you, and you might be throwing away good money."

Jack's voice took on a firmer note. "Take care of him. Don't worry about the money." He finished with Smokey, picked up the two saddlebags, his Winchester, and the killer's Whitworth. "If anyone's looking for me, I'll be in the sheriff's office."

Otto stopped his brushing and turned to Jack. "You might want to know, McClain has been spreading around town that he's not letting you leave town without cleaning your clock." He grinned at Jack. "You best keep an eye open. Course, you're no stranger to his sucker punch."

Jack, passing the dog, gave a short laugh. The animal looked up at Jack and stood. "Thanks, Otto, I think." With the dog at his heels, he strode from the livery and crossed the street, dodging ore wagons and riders. Reaching the sheriff's office, he opened the door and stepped in. The dog dropped on the boardwalk next to the door.

The sheriff, his boots stretched across the corner of his desk, motioned his head toward the door. "You taking up with strays? I saw the looks of the bay you had hauling that body. It looked worse off than that monster lying outside my door. Where'd you get 'em?"

Jack dropped the killer's saddlebags on the desk and pulled up a chair. "The corpse is the bushwhacker. At least I'm sure he's the bushwhacker of me and Johnny. I'm pretty sure he's the one who killed General Franklin and Warren. He was paid to kill them, and tried to kill Mrs. Franklin."

The sheriff shook his head. "You're gonna have to explain to me how you managed to leap so far to those conclusions. Did he talk before he died?"

Jack shook his head. "Nope, he didn't, but look inside those." He nodded toward the saddlebags.

The sheriff dropped his feet to the floor and slid his chair forward, reaching for the bags. He let out a long whistle when he pulled out the two stacks of bills and bag of gold. "From the looks of that feller's horse, he wasn't a rich businessman. The money and him don't fit. What else?"

Jack laid the long, scoped Whitworth rifle across the desk. "You ever see one of these?"

Sheriff Wright reached for the rifle. "Whitworth, used by the Rebs and their snipers. It's a deadly weapon. One of these killed General Sedgwick at Spotsylvania." The sheriff shook his head. "That was a mighty bloody battle."

Jack nodded. "They all were, and I believe this rifle also killed General Franklin and Warren."

"Could be. Too bad that feller who owned it ain't alive to tell us." The sheriff looked up at Jack. "What happened?"

Jack recounted the encounter with the killer and how he found the man's hideout.

Sheriff Wright leaned back in his chair to bring the Whitworth's side-mounted scope to his eye. He tracked several riders as they passed his window. When Jack finished, he laid the rifle on his desk and gave his head a single shake. "That's quite a story. Those Cheyenne mystify me sometimes. You say this feller was dead when you got there?"

Jack nodded, saying nothing.

"How do you know them Injuns didn't kill him?"

Jack turned his cold, gray eyes on the lawman. "Are you serious? I can read sign."

Wright fidgeted under the marshal's gaze. "It's possible. You know how they are. They could've slipped in, killed him, and pilfered the camp before you got there. No tellin' what they might have taken."

Jack stood. "Sheriff, I came here expecting reasonable assistance, hoping you might be able to help me identify the dead man or come up with a reason he might have been so intent on killing the folks on the D Bar J. It's obvious all you can do is come up with excuses and sit on your butt."

The sheriff's face turned rosy red, and he jumped to his feet. "Don't you talk to me like that. It don't matter who you are, I'm the sheriff of this county, and what I say goes."

"Then start doing your job. Your deputy has been shot by that man." Jack tossed a thumb toward the barbershop. "You need to get outside this office and talk to the people. Find out all you can about who he might be or might know. While you're at it, you might try checking into who killed Toler. Have you found out anything about him? Have you examined every inch of his place? I don't know how, but mark my word, this whole mess is tied together some way."

The sheriff glanced down at his desk when Jack asked his question. He looked up. "Ain't nobody goin' into Toler's place. It stinks too bad."

Jack turned for the door. "By the way, if any of the townsfolk remember who the dead man is, they'll be coming here to let you know. Write down their information and their name. I promised a reward of a hundred dollars in gold to anyone who could come up with a solid lead on who he is."

Jack opened the door and stepped out to the boardwalk. The sheriff's mouth was running faster than a jackrabbit chased by a coyote. "You should have asked me first. I ain't no bookkeeper. I—"

Jack slammed the door shut. He was tired of dealing with incompetence. He stood there, trying to decide what to do next. The big dog had been sleeping. He looked up at Jack and then sat, his head above Jack's waist. Jack's hand found the dog's head and gently rubbed it while he pondered his next step. A quick flash of motion at the hotel caught his attention.

Roland Farnsworth had walked out the front door and was waving at him, holding a large envelope. *Ah,* he thought, *Roland may have the information I asked Carter to get for me.* He strode along the boardwalk to the hotel entrance and shook hands with the restaurant owner, taking the envelope.

"Marshal Sage, it is good to see you. Mr. Schofield left this with me yesterday evening. He asked me to tell you he had to go back to Denver City. He said that if you need him, send a telegraph message there. If it's urgent, he will come immediately."

"Thanks, Roland, I knew I could trust you."

"Always, Marshal. Why don't you come in and have a coffee while you go over your information. I have just brewed a fresh pot."

"Good idea." He started inside, and the dog moved to follow. Jack knew the smells coming through the door had to be enticing, especially for a hungry dog. He stopped. "Roland, I hate to ask, but I've picked this old boy up, and I'm thinking he's mighty hungry. Would you have anything back there you might want to get rid of?"

"Bring him around to the back, and I'll see what I can do."

"Thanks." Jack headed to the corner of the hotel and turned into the alley, the dog trotting alongside. "I'm betting you're about to get yourself a treat, boy." They climbed onto the porch, and he pointed to an out-of-the-way spot. "Sit." Surprisingly, the dog sat and looked up at him, drool dripping from his jowls.

Roland met them with meat-laden bones and other delicacies piled high in a large bowl. He set it in front of the dog, who immediately began gobbling the contents. "I think you're right, Marshal. You have a hungry dog." He held the door open for Jack. "Come in. The coffee is waiting."

Jack removed his hat, ducked, and made his way through the door frame to the kitchen and on to the dining room, where Roland indicated his favorite table. "Please, Marshal." A piece of cherry pie awaited him, along with his coffee.

"Roland, you're spoiling me as badly as that dog. You remembered my favorite pie."

The rough railroad man turned chef returned the smile. "My

pleasure, Marshal. Now enjoy." He turned and hurried back to the kitchen. Jack prepared his coffee, took a sip and a bite of pie, and opened the envelope. The package had a cover letter from Carter. "It looks like you're Bowden Jessup has an unblemished record. One thing I found, which may or may not be concerning, is his several transfers after short duty periods. Other than those possible problems, he has an acceptable record. Sorry, that's the best I could do."

Jack looked over the telegraphed copies of Jessup's military records. Like Carter said, nothing stood out to him. Also, as Carter had mentioned, if he were the commanding officer and received a transferred officer with this kind of record, he'd be concerned the man had been moved along because of some difficulty. There were a few commanding officers who would not discipline Jessup, if discipline was indeed needed, because his father was a full colonel.

He scanned the information again, finished his coffee, poured a refill, and relaxed in his chair, watching traffic move on the busy street. His mind struggled with the murders. Who might have hired the dead killer? What did they want? Were they after the ranch? Was there something on the ranch of value known only to the killers? What other reason was there to kill General Franklin and Warren? Killing the two of them certainly pointed to a valuable commodity located on the ranch. But what? Could it be silver or gold? *Check the assayer's office,* he thought. *Of course, if minerals were the reason, the killer might have gone to Cheyenne or Denver City or a handful of towns to get the ore checked. It didn't have to be here, but it is worth checking.*

Jack stood, dropped two silver dollars on the table, and headed for the back door. Roland was in the kitchen, preparing for the supper rush. "The pie and coffee were great, Roland, and thanks again for feeding the dog."

The chef smiled. "My pleasure, and you'll be glad to know your dog ate every morsel."

"Of course he did. He's smart enough to recognize great cooking when he tastes it."

Jack raised his hand in salute, bent, and slipped through the back door. He straightened and leveled his hat on his head. The dog lay on the porch, gnawing on what was left of a demolished bone. He looked up at Jack and stood, the bone clinched between his large teeth.

"Take it or leave it, but if you're coming with me, it's time to go." Jack strode down the stairs and around the corner of the hotel.

Reaching the street, the first thing he saw was the dead man in his casket leaning against the barbershop. Several men were gathered around the corpse. He headed toward the display.

The men moved aside at his approach and gave the dog a wide berth. Jack stopped to examine Brad's work. *Not bad,* he thought. *The fella actually looks almost alive, but I still don't know him.* "Any of you men recognize him now that Brad has cleaned him up?"

All the men shook their heads except for one burly-looking gentleman. "I'm from Cheyenne, Marshal, and he looks a mite familiar. I can't be positive, but I think I saw him down in Denver City, maybe four or five months ago. The wind was hollowing, and we had a blizzard going on. Seems this feller, I'm almost positive it was him, come in all bundled up from the trail, snow all over him."

"Do you remember him talking to anyone?"

At that moment, Bowden Jessup stepped from his office across the street.

20

The stranger stopped talking and stared at Jessup. He raised his long arm and pointed at the lawyer, who paused, glared at the man, and continued toward the Last Chance Saloon.

"Marshal, you ain't gonna believe this, but I swear, that right there is the feller this dead man was talkin' to." The man looked around at the other men who were standing by the casket. "Now don't that beat all. Who would've thought?"

Jack looked at Jessup and then back at the man who had just pointed at him. "Are you sure? Is he the man?"

"Well, shoot no, Marshal. I ain't one hundred percent sure, but it looks almighty like him."

Jack grabbed the man's arm and started up the street to intercept Jessup. "Come on. I want you to take a better look."

Startled, the witness pulled back at first, but in the vise grip of Jack he relented and moved with him.

Jack called to Jessup as they converged. "Hold up. I want you to meet someone who knows you."

Jessup looked like he was about to turn around and go back to his office, but he changed his mind and angled toward Jack and the stranger. Reaching the two men, he stopped. "What do you want, Sage?"

Jack turned to his witness. "Is this the man you saw in Denver City?"

The man from Cheyenne hesitated, leaned forward until his face was inches from the face of Jessup, and stared. Finally he straightened. "I'm sorry, Marshal. I think so, but I just cain't be sure. Like I said, it was five or six months ago, and it was a saloon. You know what most folks do in a saloon. I ain't any different."

Jack was desperate. He knew Jessup was involved in these murders. He stared at the lawyer's face, and he could see the fear residing deep in his eyes, beneath the conceit and arrogance. "Look at him close, man. Try to think."

Jessup stepped back. "Marshal, I could have you arrested for false accusation." He glared at the stranger. "And you, sir, I will take you to court and strip you of every single one of your material possessions. You cannot blatantly accuse an honest man for consorting with types such as him." At his last word he raised an accusing arm and pointed at the dead man in the casket.

Jack could see the stranger shrivel. He looked at Jack and then Jessup. "I'm sorry, sir. I ain't meant nothing. I just saw you come out from the building across the street, and in the glare of the sun you had a familiar look, but as I'm closer now, I can see you ain't anything like the man I saw in Denver City. I'm mighty sorry." The stranger yanked his arm out of Jack's grip, backed a few feet, turned, and scurried down the street.

Jessup turned his gaze toward Jack. This time Jack saw no fear, only pride and arrogance. "I have told you, Marshal, I am guilty of no crime. If I am guilty of anything, it is an overly kind heart. I have taken of my valuable time to help the Franklins for the simple reasons I felt sorrow for Josephine and her family, and they were friends of my parents. I promise you, if you continue to hound me, I will file a lawsuit against you for defamation of character and have you thrown into jail. I'm sure the sheriff would enjoy the opportunity."

Jack Sage had dealt with many criminals. With each of his previous experiences, he had used his guns or fists, but he had recognized the same quality in each of his opponents, an evil pride and unhealthy love of self deep in their souls. Though Jessup was different in many ways, he possessed those same qualities, and it was all Jack could do to keep from smashing the self-possessed smirk from the lawyer's face. He leaned forward, lowering his head until his face was inches from Jessup's. "Remember, I know you had them killed. I don't yet know why, but I will find out, and when I do, I'll see you stretch a rope. You'll pay for what you've done, I guarantee it." Jack held Jessup's gaze until the lawyer broke the stare, turned, and stiffly walked to the Last Chance. Before he entered, he glanced over his shoulder, saw Jack still watching him, jerked his head forward, and hurried through the saloon's doors.

Jack turned toward the corpse. It leaned alone in its casket, against the front wall of the barbershop, deserted by the crowd that had previously surrounded it. Jack walked back to the dead man. The man's expression was one of sadness. It was like his empty body was aware of the pain he had caused.

Jack gazed at the face. *I had no idea my bullet, from such a distance, would bring you here,* he thought. *I don't regret the shot, but I sure regret not being able to question you.* The barbershop door opened, and Brad Wilkins stepped out.

"Sorry, Marshal."

"You heard?"

"I think everyone heard Jessup's threat. You should have seen the crowd scurry away when the fella from Cheyenne jerked from your grip and hurried back down here. These folks are afraid of what an attorney can do. They've blown his power far out of proportion. They see Jessup as capable of stripping everything they've worked for from them if they say a word against him. He has the town's residents buffaloed." Brad Wilkins stood beside Jack, staring at the corpse. "Sure wish he could talk."

Jack nodded. "I was thinking the same thing, Toler, too. Have you buried him?"

"Yeah. Put him in the ground yesterday. I still haven't had a chance to examine Toler's apartment and business. I'll wait another couple of days and give it a try." He glanced down at the dog. "What's your plan for him?"

Jack looked down at the dog. "I have to admit, I haven't really given him much thought with everything going on. I don't know."

"You ought to at least give him a name."

"That's a good idea. I'll think on it tonight. That'll give me something to think about other than Jessup."

A DEEP RUMBLE came from alongside Jack's bed. "Easy, Ghost." One hand dropped to the big dog's head while he filled the other with his Smith & Wesson. He heard a board creak again, just outside his door, then pounding sounded against the door frame.

"Hang on." Jack swung his long legs from under the cover and glanced outside. Daylight was breaking. Still in his long johns, and holding his revolver ready, he started for the door.

"It's me, Marshal, Sheriff Wright."

Jack frowned, moved the chair from under the door handle, and opened the door.

The sheriff saw the weapon in Jack's hand. "That ain't the friendliest way to greet a person."

"When was the last time you've been shot at in your hotel room, Sheriff?" Jack stepped back, motioning for Wright to enter.

The next thing the sheriff saw was the big dog, sitting on his haunches, staring at him. Jack pulled his matches from his vest, struck one, lifted the chimney of the dresser lamp, and lit the wick. Light spread through the room.

"You keeping that dog?"

"Maybe. What's on your mind?"

"I thought you'd like to know. Jessup left town."

Jack's brow wrinkled. Leaving was the last thing he expected from Jessup. There was no proof against the man. In fact, all he had against the lawyer was suspicion and dislike. "When?"

"Sometime last night. I was making my rounds this morning and stopped in at Otto's. He opens up early. I usually grab a cup of coffee from him. He makes a mighty good cup. It ain't as good as—"

"When, Sheriff?"

The sheriff's lips pursed slightly. "As I was about to say, Otto said he pulled out around midnight. I don't know where he's headed, but Otto mentioned he took out west like the devil was chasing him."

West, the thought slammed into Jack's mind. *He's heading for the ranch, and leaving like this, he can't be up to anything good.* He grabbed his trousers and yanked them on.

The sheriff's forehead wrinkled. "You know something?"

Jack dropped to the bed to pull his boots on. "He's headed for the D Bar J, sure as I'm sitting here. Don't ask me why, but I can tell you it isn't for anything good."

Ghost had stood when the sheriff entered the room. When Jack started getting dressed, the big dog moved to a corner and remained standing, his tail slapping rhythmically against the armoire. Jack glanced at the dog. "You up for a long trip, fella?"

"You taking the dog?"

Jack slapped on his hat, shrugged into his coat, picked up his saddlebags and rifle, and stepped to the door. "You want to keep him?"

The sheriff's single laugh barked through the room. "I have a hard enough time feedin' myself. We'd both starve. I was just thinking, the way you're rushing out of here, it looks to be a hard, fast ride. You think he's up to it?"

Jack clucked. "Let's go, Ghost." He glanced at the sheriff. "You coming?"

Wright jumped forward and rushed through the open door behind Ghost, making sure he kept a safe distance between him and the massive animal. "You want me to go with you?"

Jack had closed the door and was turning to head down the stairs. He jerked to a halt and turned on the sheriff. "Why are you being so helpful?"

"Look, I thought about some of the things you said. Maybe you hit too close to home." He stopped and motioned down the stairs. "Let's go. Do you need me or not?"

Jack turned and started down the stairs, taking two at a time. The morning clerk had just come on duty.

"Good morning, Mr. Sage." He eyed the dog, but said nothing.

Jack nodded his greeting and continued toward the door. He opened it and turned to the clerk. "I'll be gone for several days, but I'll be back."

"Yes, sir, your room will be taken care of. Have a nice trip."

Jack was out the door and heading toward Otto's. Ghost and the sheriff trotted alongside. "Sheriff, I appreciate the offer. But I don't want to take you away from your town. This'll give me a chance to check on Johnny, and I'll let you know how he's doing when I get back."

"Suit yourself. I need to finish my rounds." They reached the entrance to Otto's Livery, and the sheriff stopped. "There's something else."

Jack followed suit. Ghost trotted to the watering trough and began drinking.

"You may have already heard, but Lewis McClain is spreading around town he's going to clean your plow. You should be on the lookout for him."

Jack gave the sheriff a long look. "I'm a United States Marshal. Do you think he would try something? He could go to prison for that kind of stunt."

Sheriff Wright gazed at the brightening eastern sky for a few seconds before responding, "Marshal, you have probably met men like him. He came up a really hard way, with the railroad. He's solved a lot of his problems with his knuckles, and he's pretty well off. McClain is used to getting his way, and he's used to having the railroad and the government back him on everything he does. Do I think he'd jump you?" He shook his head. "I don't think he'd hesitate. As far as he's concerned, you've insulted him, and he can't stand it. All I've got to say is watch your back."

"Thanks, Sheriff. I appreciate you being straight with me, but I've got a killer to apprehend, and I don't want him to have the chance to add anyone else to his list."

"You really think he killed all those people?"

"Killed some and had others killed, I know it. I just don't have the proof. Hopefully I can catch him before he leaves more bodies." Jack nodded and spun toward Smokey. The horse was watching him when he turned. "I hope you're ready for a hard ride, boy."

Otto came out of his office. "You're going after Jessup?"

"I am."

Ghost had trotted inside the livery door and sat watching.

"You taking the dog?"

"Up to him, not me. I'm not his boss. He'll do what he wants."

He dropped his gear and began to saddle Smokey. Otto disappeared while he worked. Once Smokey was saddled, he backed him from the stall, swung into the saddle, and walked him to the trough. "Get a drink if you want one, boy, but not too much. We've got a run ahead of us."

Otto walked up with a sack pulled closed and tied with a short rope. "Here's some oats. It'll give him a little nourishment along the way."

"Thanks, Otto." Jack took the bag and hung it on the saddle horn. He allowed Smokey to drink a bit longer, then pulled him away from the trough. "That's enough for now, boy. There's plenty of streams ahead." He looked down at Ghost. "You going with us?"

The big chocolate brown eyes stared back at Jack.

"I'll take that for a yes." He glanced at Otto. "Thanks for the help. I'll see you in a few days."

"Go with God, Marshal."

Jack bumped Smokey, and the big horse started forward. "Thanks, Otto. I hope so."

Ghost started trotting alongside as Jack walked Smokey toward the prairie.

Jack glanced down at him. "I hope you're up to this, fella. It's gonna be tough on you." He patted Smokey on the neck. "Let's go, boy," and bumped him in the flanks. The horse broke into a ground-eating lope.

While the country fell behind them, Jack's mind was on Amy, the Franklins, and Jessup. *Stay calm, Jessup. Don't do anything crazy.*

JACK SWUNG down from Smokey and loosened his cinch. The grulla lowered his head and drank greedily from the clear water rushing along in the shallow stream. Jack kneeled and scooped water from the stream with one hand, keeping his head up and watching. Indians were always a possibility, and he couldn't take the chance of being surprised today. He also looked for Ghost. The dog had disappeared a ways back. "Maybe he got tired of us, boy." Smokey raised his head from the water, and Jack stood.

"What say we walk awhile." Grasping the horse's reins, he started toward the ranch. They were about halfway there, and he was worried. When he had last seen Jessup going into the Last Chance Saloon, the man looked anxious. "Smokey, I'll never forgive myself if he's out there killing people. Hopefully, I'm wrong, and he just rode to the ranch for another meeting with Jo. We'll just have to wait . . ."

He saw dust drifting into the blue sky in the distance toward the ranch. It quickly changed to the outline of a single rider. He stopped, tightened Smokey's cinch, and stepped into the saddle. Movement in the grass to his left caught his attention. He flipped the thong from his Smith, but relaxed when Ghost trotted from the tall grass. The big dog's mouth was bloody.

"So I guess I don't have to worry about you not eating."

The dog sat and looked up at Jack with its mouth open and long, pink tongue hanging to one side. He looked as if he were giving Jack a satisfied grin.

The laugh died in Jack's throat as he turned his concentration to the approaching rider. He could clearly make out it was a single rider, and he was running his horse flat out. Jack urged Smokey forward at a gallop. The intervening distance closed rapidly. Nearing, Jack recognized the rider as Dot, Josephine's oldest daughter. Her hat was whipping behind her head, straining against the retaining string. Long, shiny black hair, escaped from its bindings, waved around her flushed face.

"Jack, thank God!" She yanked the lathered, black horse to a stop. "It's Jessup. I don't know what's gotten into the man. He's gone crazy!"

Jack stepped Smokey in close to Dot's mount and grasped her forearm. "Dot. Calm yourself. Take a deep breath, and then explain to me what's happened."

He watched the young woman's wide-open pale blue eyes focus on him. She took a long slow breath and let the anxiety slip from her body. "He's gone. He shot everybody."

"Jessup?"

"Yes, Jack. That's who I'm talking about. Bowden Jessup."

He squeezed her arm. "Slow down. Start from the beginning. Tell me what happened."

Her wide mouth opened in a shout. "I'm telling you!"

Jack swung down from Smokey and grasped Dot around the waist. She dropped her hands to his shoulders and swung out of the saddle, allowing him to lower her to the ground. "Let's walk the horses toward the ranch and allow them to cool down. You can tell me all about what happened from the beginning."

Dot reached back and pulled her hat onto her head, leaving her wind-tousled black hair hanging haphazardly across her shoulders. They started toward the ranch. Ghost trotted up to Dot and walked next to her. She looked up at Jack. "When did you get a dog? He's so big."

"He is big. It's a long story, but it looks like he likes you. His name is Ghost."

Her hand dropped to the dog's neck and shoulders, fingers twisting and rubbing in the dog's long hair. It seemed to calm her. "Bowden showed up this morning right after the men and I rode out to work the cattle. He passed us riding in. He seemed fine. Bowden has always been a little high-strung."

Jack thought, *That's not what I'd call it,* but said nothing.

"We were well away, had the branding fires going, and had branded several head of cattle when we heard the shots. We were so far out, it's a miracle we heard them, but Blaze, with his young ears, picked the first one up, then we stopped working and listened for the rest. We thought nothing of them. Somebody's always practicing. A lot of times, we shoot from the porch. It's a great place. Our trouble signal is three evenly spaced shots, but this was at least five, so we shrugged them off. Quite a bit of time went by before I began to feel something. You'd probably call it a woman's intuition, but whatever it was, I finally told the boys I was going back to the ranch to check."

Jack wanted Dot to get to the point in the worst way, but he wouldn't interrupt her. Both horses would be better served with the rest. He reined in his impatience and let her talk.

"So I headed back to the ranch. Even then, I wasn't concerned. To be honest, it gave me an excuse to raid Teresa's doughnuts and say hi to Bowden. She had just made a fresh batch for breakfast, and she always has plenty of them left over." She looked up at Jack again. "I'm babbling, aren't I? I'm sorry, this is such a shock."

Jack couldn't stand it any longer. "Did he kill anyone?"

She shook her head. "I don't think so, but Jack, he shot Mama and Lilly. Why would he shoot Mama and Lilly? Mama's tried to help him ever since he first brought Amy over back at West Point. I think she felt guilty for introducing Amy to Warren. And Lilly, she's the sweetest person there is. Why would he do something like that?"

Jack shook his head. "I don't know, Dot. There are bad people out there. Sometimes they make it into our homes."

She sniffed. "He shot Tripp, too."

"But you say he didn't kill anyone?"

"I don't think so. Doc said everyone would make it."

"What about the doc and Johnny?"

"Bowden knocked them both over the head. Doc, blood caked on his head and face, was up and helping the others when I arrived."

"Where were Amy and the kids? What about Schmidt and his men?"

"Schmidt took all of his men back to his ranch. They had work to do, but he told Amy and Mama he'd be back in a couple of days."

Her eyes had been filled with tears, but she had managed to keep from crying. Now she broke down and began sobbing. Jack stopped and took her in his arms.

Into his chest, she murmured, "He took Amy."

He felt like she had thrust a knife into his heart. He managed to keep his breath steady. "Why did he take Amy?"

21

Dot shook her head against Jack's chest. "It's so crazy. Mama told us he said Amy was his. He threatened to kill the kids if Tripp didn't saddle a couple of fresh horses for them. When Tripp brought the horses back, he tried to jump Bowden, and was shot for his trouble."

Jack eased Dot away. "We'd better keep walking."

"Yes, of course."

"What about the kids?"

"When Bowden brought the horses back, Mama sent the kids running out the back door. They got away. After he shot Tripp, Mama said Bowden was so angry. Everyone said he was screaming and yelling about the Franklins taking all that was rightfully his. That's when he shot Mama and Lilly." Tears began again. "Why, Jack? Why would anyone do something like Bowden has done."

Jack shook his head. "I can't say, Dot, but maybe we should mount up. The horses look ready."

The young woman wiped her eyes with the back of her shirt-sleeve. "Yes, you're right."

Jack waited until she was in the saddle, then swung up on Smokey. "Did anyone see which direction they took?"

She shook her head. "I didn't look for sign. Once I found out everyone was alright, I jumped on Blacky and headed for town. I passed the boys at a pretty good distance. They saw me, so I'm sure they'll be heading back to the ranch. They probably got there an hour or two ago."

Jack shot a quick look at Dot's black horse. "Blacky looks like he's got his wind back. You ready to pick up the pace?"

She nodded.

"We'll keep it down to a lope for a while." He bumped Smokey into a lope while his mind worked over the problem. *If Quint and Monty, or Blaze, take off after Bowden,* Jack thought, *they're going to wipe out all of the sign.* His mind went to Amy. *Hang in there, girl. You've been dealt a tough hand, but you've handled tough things before. You can do it.*

He remembered her smell in the barn and felt a tug at his heart. *Not now. You've got a job to do. Get her home safe, and then find out where you stand.* He glanced at Dot and nodded. They broke into a gallop. *We can't maintain this for long, or Dot's Blacky won't last.* He let them run for a mile, then he pulled the big grulla back to a walk. Amy followed his lead.

They alternated mostly between walking and loping, occasionally letting the animals run for no more than a mile but bringing them back to a walk. Time passed slowly. The sun seemed to be racing them toward the horizon, but Jack knew they were making good time. It wouldn't be much longer. The mountains were growing in the distance.

At last, the treelined ridge came into view. He knew Dot was at least as tempted as he was to put the horses into a hard run, but he maintained an easy lope, occasionally broken with a walk. Blacky was lathered and tired. Smokey too was showing signs he was reaching the edge of his endurance. Jack knew the horse would run for him until his huge heart exploded, but it wasn't necessary now. As much as he wanted to race for the ranch house, it would do no good. Darkness would be falling soon, and there was no way he'd be able to track Bowden and Amy in the dark. Since he would have to wait until daylight, there was no reason to kill two fine animals.

They made the turn into the trees. Jack could see smoke rising from the chimneys of the ranch house and bunkhouse. The sun had slipped behind the mountaintops, and cool air accompanied the darkening shadows. At long last, they stopped their horses at the hitching rail in front of the house. Jack swung down, amazed to see Ghost standing at Smokey's side. The dog's tongue was hanging out the right side of his mouth, but he looked like he could keep on going. Jack rubbed the dog's head in his hands. "I don't know how you did it, boy, but you've made it all the way."

Doc Tilson stepped out the door with Davy and Flo. The two children leaped from the porch and raced to greet them, sliding to a momentary halt upon seeing the dog.

Blaze stepped up and took the reins of both horses. "These here animals need to cool down." He walked away, leading them around the yard to cool them properly.

The kids were both clinging to Dot. Jack reached down and thrust his hands under Davy's arms and lifted him. "How are you doing, pardner?"

Davy placed his small hands on Jack's chest and pushed, leaning back against the thick arms. His young brow wrinkled in a scowl. "Mr. Jessup shot Grandma Jo and Aunt Lilly and Tripp and took Mama. You said you were going to protect us. Where were you? You're too late."

The boy's words felt like more knives driving into Jack.

Before he could respond, Dot spoke up. "Davy, Marshal Sage was on his way. He was trying to get here in time."

Tears filled the boy's swollen blue eyes. He threw his arms around Jack's neck. "I didn't help. I ran out the back door like a coward. Papa never ran during the war. I ran, and Grandma Jo and Aunt Lilly got shot, Tripp too."

Jack patted the lad's back and spoke into his black hair. "You followed orders like any good soldier. You did exactly what your grandma told you. That's what a boy your age is supposed to do. You protected Flo. That was your job." He pulled Davy away. "Look at Flo. Is she alright?"

The boy leaned back again and looked down at Flo. "I guess she is."

Flo smiled up at Davy, and Dot spoke, hugging the little girl. "You saved her, Davy. If you hadn't reacted so quickly, there is no telling what Bowden might have done. Don't you ever call yourself a coward. You're my hero."

Jack dropped Davy to the ground. "Now let me go talk to your grandma and Deputy Johnson. I need to find out what happened. Meanwhile, you and Flo can get acquainted with Ghost. Looks like he likes you."

Ghost had been standing between the two adults, watching Davy. As soon as Jack put the boy down, Ghost shoved his big head in Davy's face and started licking. Davy immediately broke out in peals of laughter while trying to dodge the big tongue.

Flo pushed close, and both of the kids lavished Ghost with love.

Jack stepped around the kids and the dog and headed for the house, Dot alongside. "I think Ghost will keep those two occupied for quite a while." Reaching the porch, Jack looked at the banged-up doctor. "Looks like you need some doctoring yourself."

"I'm fine, so's the deputy. His shoulder is healing quite well, but he still shouldn't be up yet."

Jack opened the door and strode into the parlor to meet Johnny heading out. "Hold up there, Johnny. The doc tells me you should still be in bed."

"Marshal, I ain't stayin' in a bed no matter what anyone says.

This shoulder is healing fine." He attempted to swing his arm and winced, moving his hand to his gunbelt buckle. After hooking his thumb behind the buckle, he relaxed the arm. "It'll be alright. I can leave with you right now."

Jack turned to the doctor. "Where are the wounded?"

Before the doctor could speak, Johnny chimed in, "Lilly and Mrs. Franklin are in Lilly's bed, and Tripp is in Mrs. Franklin's room."

The doctor nodded. "That's right. Tripp is hit the worst. It appears Jessup's bullet hit him in the thigh and broke the femur. I'm going to have to operate to make sure the bone broke cleanly enough to mend and doesn't have any shards around it. Mrs. Franklin has a nasty shoulder wound in her left shoulder. Lilly was only grazed on her right side. It cut a pretty deep furrow, but no organs were reached. She's already up and trying to help. She refused any laudanum. I know she's hurting, but you can't seem to stop these Franklins."

Jack saw the look of pride drift across Johnny's face while Dr. Tilson spoke of Lilly. Johnny saw Jack watching him. His lips pursed and brow wrinkled. He looked away, his complexion turning the color of a ripe apple. Jack choked off a grin. *How could a young man not lose himself in this home,* Jack thought, *with so many beautiful women?* He immediately put Johnny's plight out of mind. "When do you plan on operating?"

"As soon as possible. If there are any bone fragments in there, I need to get them out."

"I assume you're planning on doing it here?"

The doc looked surprised. "Of course. A buckboard ride to Laramie would kill him." He turned to Dot. "Your mother tells me, though you're not formally trained, you worked as a nurse, back east?"

"Yes, I did, and I have also assisted in surgeries. I can help."

He nodded. "Good, I'll need a flat surface."

"The kitchen table," Dot replied.

"It will be bloody."

"We can clean it. The kitchen table is the place."

Jack stepped toward the bedrooms. "Can I talk to Jo?"

The doctor turned from Dot. "Yes, of course. I've cleaned and bandaged her wound. She should be fine, though she will be hurting."

Lilly limped into the room. "I can help."

Johnny rushed to her side. "You need to rest like the doctor said."

"Pshaw, Johnny. There's too much that needs to be done." She looked at Jack. "I'm glad you're here. I just wish it had been sooner."

Jack stepped toward the young woman. "No more than I do, but I'm here now."

"He has Amy."

"Dot told me. I'll be after them first thing in the morning."

"Good, thanks for coming." She turned to Dr. Tilson. "What can I do to help?"

Dot answered, "Go to the kitchen and help Teresa clear the table. Tripp needs surgery, and it'll be done on the table. We'll need several sheets to cover the table and him. I'll help. Have Teresa start a big pot of hot water."

Lilly turned to Johnny and tossed him a smile, then limped toward the kitchen, accompanied by her older sister.

Jack left Doc Tilson and Johnny standing in the parlor and headed for Lilly's bedroom. The door was open. He removed his hat and stepped inside the room. Jo had leaned back on a stack of pillows. Her eyes were closed. He started to turn, but she spoke. "Come in, and pull up a chair, Jack. I'm just resting my eyes. It has been a trying day."

Jack grabbed a chair and placed it near the bed. Lowering himself into the plush blue wingback, he relaxed on the comfortable cushion. It felt much better than his saddle. "How are you feeling, Jo?"

She gave him a sad smile. "Like an old, foolish woman who brought evil into her home and encouraged it to stay. I should have listened to you."

"You didn't know, Jo. People like Jessup are chameleons. They show you the side they want you to see. They camouflage themselves, and they do it very well."

She shook her head. "But he had me fooled for so long. All this time, from West Point days, I thought he was Warren's friend, and I was helping him. He was just planning to 'get even' as he put it. It's like a dream. I can't believe I was so wrong."

Jack leaned forward. "I need you to tell me everything, no matter how insignificant. Amy's life depends on it."

She turned her head toward Jack and released a long sigh. "I killed my David and my son, Warren, just as surely as if I had pulled the trigger. They survived the war, all those battles, only to die building the ranch they both had dreamed of. How can I live with that, Jack?"

Jack's face hardened. He slid forward in his chair to where he was inches from her sad gray eyes. His voice was cold. "Listen to me, Josephine Franklin. You're a general's wife. Your son was a hero. Neither would want you lying in this bed talking of guilt you don't own and rolling around in self-pity. You've never been that kind of person. You need to straighten up, quit taking on blame for the past, and fill me in on every detail. Think of Warren and how much Amy meant to him. What would he want you to do right now?"

Jack waited. *Was I too hard on her?* he thought. *I know she's tough, if she can just pull herself out of this spiral.*

Jo remained leaning against her stack of pillows for what seemed like ages to Jack. Then she scooted back, shoving her bottom deeper against the pillows, and straightened her shoulders. With a steady hand, she wiped a single tear from her left eye, took a deep breath, exhaled, and looked at Jack.

"Thank you, Jack. Sometimes a person needs a sharp smack

to wake them up." She sighed one more time and began. "We met Bowden in his and Warren's junior year at the Point. We were throwing a little gathering for the juniors. He showed up with Amy. She was such a beautiful girl, who has turned into a lovely woman." Jo smiled at Jack. "But you're well aware of the lovely woman part, aren't you?"

Jack adjusted his position in the wingback, eyebrows pulling together. "Go on, Jo."

She nodded, her smile fading. "Yes, of course. Bowden seemed like a happy, if a slightly pompous, cadet. Warren arrived late. As soon as he arrived, he came straight to me to apologize." Jo paused and looked through the window at the darkness outside.

She took a deep breath and continued, "Amy and one of the other young ladies had engaged me in conversation when Warren entered. I remember how their eyes locked together, and from that moment I knew my son was going to marry this lovely girl. She was radiant, with her long blonde hair cascading over bare shoulders, and green eyes. Warren never stood a chance." A smile drifted across her lips. "But he would never have wanted it any other way. They were so happy."

"So how did Bowden react?"

The smile left her face. "He was bringing drinks back for Amy and me. I think he saw them the moment they saw each other."

Jo coughed. From the pitcher next to the bed, Jack filled a glass and handed it to the woman. She took two swallows and continued to hold it in her lap. "He was not a happy boy. He continued to join our parties and get-togethers. I made a point of including him. He even attended the wedding." She looked at Jack. "Did you know he never wed?"

Jack didn't know nor did he care. He had one purpose, to rescue Amy. He shook his head. "So why do you think he moved out here?"

"Until today, I thought it was to start a new life around people he knew and loved, and away from his father. Colonel Jessup was very much a disciplinarian. I always detested the man, but David thought highly of him. He was a very effective, though brutal, commander."

Jack nodded. He had known men like that, both in the United States Army and the French Foreign Legion. He didn't like bullies either in or out of the military.

Jo took another sip of her water and continued, "I'm sure he beat Bowden. As a boy at the Point, he was quiet, not very well liked, but extremely successful. He was very good at boxing, wrestling, and fencing. Quite often when he would come over, at our invitation, he'd have a black eye or swollen cheek from a boxing or wrestling match."

Jack caught himself nodding in agreement again. *I knew he had the fighter's look to him,* Jack thought. *He kept his physique hidden under slightly larger shirts and suits, but he would be tough in a fight.*

"Jo, tell me what happened when he showed up this morning."

"It was shocking, the change in him." Her head turned again toward Jack. She had it tilted as if she couldn't quite believe what she was remembering. "He stormed onto the porch, yanked the door open, and charged into the house. We were sitting in the parlor, Amy, myself, and Dr. Tilson. Tripp and Lilly were still at the kitchen table. Deputy Johnson was in Lilly's bed. At Bowden's abrupt entrance, Tripp leaped to his feet and charged into the parlor. Bowden's revolver appeared like magic. I had no idea he was that fast. Dr. Tilson leaped for the gun, but Bowden slapped him across the top of his head with his revolver, and he collapsed like a sack of oats. Tripp froze. At the noise, the kids raced into the room. I tried to grab them, but it was too late. Bowden saw them and swung the gun on them. Without hesitating, he told Tripp to saddle two good horses and bring them to the front of the house."

Jo's eyes widened in disbelief at what she was remembering. "He threatened to kill the children if Tripp didn't hurry. Tripp raced out of the house, and Bowden asked where the deputy was. Without thinking, I pointed at Lilly's room. He strode into the bedroom, and we heard him smash Johnny in the head. On the way out of the bedroom, he grabbed Amy by the wrist. She tried to jerk away. He yanked her to him, released her wrist, and gave her a powerful slap."

Jack could feel the tamped-down anger beginning to boil. Threatening kids, hitting women, this man was setting himself up for a hangman's noose, if he made it back to Laramie. "Why did he start shooting?"

"We were standing, Amy and I, and had moved so that we were blocking his view of the children. Tripp came in, and Bowden turned to him. I had already gotten Davy and Flo's attention. When Bowden turned, I pointed to the back door and yelled run. Bowden started to turn and fire. I don't know if he was planning on firing at the children or me or Amy, but as soon as he began to turn, Tripp hit him with his fist. The blow caught him on the side of his head, causing him to stagger, but only for a second. He spun around and shot Tripp, then me. Lilly was at the kitchen entrance, and he shot her. The children raced safely out of the house. After he started shooting, he was yelling at the top of his voice that it was all my fault. If I hadn't introduced Warren to Amy, none of this would have happened. He kept yelling, 'It's all your fault,' over and over till he pulled Amy out of the house. His last words were if anyone followed them, he'd kill her. I made it to the doorway, and before they left, he leveled his gun at me. I swear, Jack, I thought he was going to kill me, but then they raced away."

Jack stood. "Do you know if anyone saw which direction they took out of here?"

She shook her head. "Quint and Monty took off after them, but they haven't come back yet. Quint's a good tracker, but he can't track a man in the dark. I look for them to be showing up soon."

Even as she spoke, Jack heard the sound of hoofbeats approaching the house. He jumped to his feet, leaned over, and patted her hand. "Thanks, Jo. You did real good. Don't you worry, I'll get her back."

She gripped his hand, pulling him close, and whispered in his ear, "Jack, Hank Schmidt has asked her to marry him. He's a good man, and Davy likes him. She said yes."

Jack commanded his lips to form a smile. "I'm happy for them, Jo. From what I've seen of Schmidt, he'll make her a good husband. Now I've got to talk to Quint and Monty."

Jack stood to his full height and took a deep breath. He was tired. Tired of chasing bad men, tired of chasing Jessup, of all the killing and violence, and tired of losing good women. He took a deep breath and put the feeling in a vault, hidden deep inside, to be examined at a future date.

Quint charged through the front door, followed by Monty.

22

Quint, smelling of horse and covered in dust and dirt, strode toward Jack. "It's good to see you, boy. We followed him until midafternoon. Weren't no sense in trying to trail him after that. Our horses were beat. They almost didn't make it back. I know where he's headed, but I need a hot cup of coffee." He glanced into the kitchen for the first time.

Quint stared. "What's goin' on?"

"Doc is operating on Tripp's leg. Jessup's bullet broke the bone. He's checking for pieces."

Monty stared at Dot. "In the kitchen?"

Teresa walked in toting a large tray with coffee, cups, the trimmings, and doughnuts. "Sit in the parlor, *Señor* Quint. You can have your coffee and anything else you want as long as it does not require cooking."

Jack sat, mixed himself a cup with extra sugar, and grabbed a doughnut. He hadn't eaten today, and besides being tired, he was hungry. Between chewing, he asked, "Where's he headed?"

Quint reached for a doughnut. "A watering stop for the train, almost due north. If he makes the train, we'll never see her again.

He'll take her to San Francisco. He can disappear there. No one will ever find them."

Jack listened as Quint talked. *Jessup won't stop there,* he thought. *He'll catch a ship and sail to South America or the Orient. He's trying to leave everything and everyone behind, but he'll have to kill Amy. She'll never give in. She'll fight him every inch of the way.* Jack swallowed his last bite of doughnut. "Quint, is it possible to catch him before he gets to the train?"

Quint thought for a moment. "Nope. Not even a little chance. We swung in to Schmidt's place on the way back and told him. He'll head out from there in the morning. He's got a good tracker, but he ain't gonna make it in time. Jessup has too big a lead and knows the country."

Monty interrupted. "He sure does. We could tell, following him. He skirted the deeper gorges and picked his way through the rough country. He's familiar with the trail and where he's going. He's planned whatever he's up to. You ain't never gonna see him again."

Jack remained silent. Schmidt would definitely hit the trail as soon as the tracker had enough daylight to see. Hopefully, he wouldn't catch them. *Hank Schmidt is a bull,* he thought. *He'll ride straight in, and Jessup will kill Amy before he'll let anyone else have her.* He pulled out his watch, opened it, and checked the time, eight o'clock. "You say the train leaves at five in the morning?"

"Yeah," Quint said, "from Laramie, but Jessup ain't pickin' it up in Laramie. He's headed for the water stop."

Blaze stepped into the house. "Fellers, I'm getting almighty tired of taking care of worn-out horses." He saw the coffee, hurried to the table, and poured himself a cup. "Whew, I'm about as tired as them horses y'all brought in." He dropped to the divan, bit off half of his donut, and glanced toward the kitchen. "What's going on?"

Quint was watching Jack. "The doc's cuttin' on Tripp's leg. I think they'll be a while. What's on your mind, Jack?"

Jack snapped his watch shut. "I may not be able to catch up with them on the trail, but I've got time to hightail it back to Laramie and catch the train. That way I can be waiting for him when he comes aboard."

Quint thought about it and gave Jack a conspiratorial grin. "Why, I think we could do that, boy. I surely do."

Johnny hadn't said anything, but he'd been listening. Now he chimed in, "Yes, sir, we could do that for sure if we left right now."

Blaze took a long swig of his coffee, set his cup down, and headed for the door. "Alright, how many horses?"

Jack beat the others. "Two. Pepper and Thunder. I'll start out with Pepper. Saddles on both so I don't have to waste time changing tack."

Johnny jumped to his feet. "Marshal, I'll go along. You might get hurt on the way. You'll need someone with you to finish the job if you do."

Quint nodded. "The deputy's right, Jack. If something happens to you, someone else needs to be there to carry on. Otherwise, Amy's gone forever."

Jack looked around for Davy and Flo. They were still outside with Ghost. *Good,* he thought, *they don't need to be hearing such things about Amy.*

"But," Quint continued, "he ain't in shape to make that ride." When Johnny started to protest, Quint held up his hand. "Johnny, we ain't doubtin' yore sand, boy, but you've got to look at it realistic like. You won't be halfway there before that shoulder'll start bleeding. You just can't do it." He turned to Jack. "But I'm the perfect one. I can ride you into the ground any day of the week."

Quint grinned at Blaze. "Saddle two more for old Quint, boy. You know which two."

Jack stood. "Alright, Quint. You've sold me. I'm gonna talk to Jo, then I'll be out there to help."

Monty and Quint rose. Each grabbed another doughnut and accompanied Blaze out the front door.

Jack stood and gently patted Johnny on the shoulder. "Heal up, boy. There'll be plenty of work for you back in Laramie." He glanced toward Lilly. "And it looks like there might be some around here."

Johnny missed Jack's meaning. "I'm right sorry, Marshal."

"You've nothing to be sorry about. You're a good man. Now, I've got to talk to Jo."

He stepped into the bedroom. Josephine Franklin lay on the bed, still propped up, her head turned toward the door. "I heard it all. Good luck, Jack. Bring her back."

"I'll do that, ma'am. You get better." He turned and strode past Johnny and Lilly. She whispered, "God bless you, Jack." Dot looked up and called, "Good luck, Jack. Thank you."

He pushed the door open. "Take care of yourselves."

To his left, Ghost lay sleeping on his side. Davy and Flo lay next to him, arms thrown across the dog's wide chest. His eyes opened, and he raised his head. Jack stopped and knelt, rubbing the big dog's head in his hands. He spoke softly to prevent waking the children. "You best stay here, fella. It looks like you may have found a home. I envy you." He gave Ghost one last scratch behind his ears and stood.

The dog watched him walk down the steps, then laid his head back on the porch deck, between a blonde-headed little girl and a black-headed little boy. His eyes closed, and he gave a deep sigh.

Turning to the barn, Jack could hear the soft breathing of the children and their dog.

JACK PULLED out his pocket watch and held it so the light of the Last Chance Saloon fell across the face. In the shaft of light, he was able to read four fifteen. "Let's head for Otto's. He'll be up by now. These horses are near as worn out as we are."

"Speak for yourself, boy. I'm raring to go."

Jack looked at Quint and chuckled. "That's only because you slept through the whole trip."

The corners of Quint's mouth drew down in mock sadness. "I'm hurt, boy, but I guess that's all I can expect from a young whipper-snapper."

The two men grew serious at the sight of the train. It sat with its headlight piercing the darkness, occasionally puffing blasts of steam. Men hustled around the cars, loading freight and passengers. Those passengers who had come in from Cheyenne and farther east had stepped from the train to stretch tight leg and back muscles.

Jack wheeled Thunder in at Otto's Livery. Quint sat watching the bustle around the station. "Looks like we made it in time."

Jack swung down as Otto walked from the barn. "You're back again? You must have the grass pretty well beaten down between here and the Franklins' place."

"We need to catch the train. Jessup shot Josephine, Tripp, and Lilly. He also pistol-whipped Johnny and the doc. Doc Tilson is fine, and he says everyone else will make it. If you wouldn't mind, let the doc's wife and Johnny's ma know."

Jack handed the reins for Thunder and Pepper to Otto, snaked out his Winchester and untied his saddlebags, throwing them over his shoulder. "I've got to go see McClain. Where would I find him this early?"

Otto stared at him. "He's always in his office when the train comes through. He likes to be ready if there's a problem. You planning on starting something?"

Jack shook his head. "No, I need a favor."

Otto's eyes grew wide. "I don't think you'll get a favor from him."

Jack started across the street to the railroad offices. He could see lights on in the windows. He pushed through the door and turned directly toward McClain's office. The clerk looked up at the rifle-packing marshal and stood. "Marshal, you can't go in there."

Jack ignored the man and pushed McClain's door open. Inside, the railroad executive sat behind his desk, and another burly-looking character sat across from him in a less than comfortable wooden chair. Both men leaped to their feet. The burly man made a move to step between Jack and McClain.

Jack stopped and held up his hand. "I'm not here for trouble. McClain, I need your help."

McClain's chest swelled, and he gave a sharp laugh. "It'll be a cold day in the nether world before you'll be seeing any help from me, Marshal. You're mighty brazen even to be asking."

Jack pointed a finger at the big railroad man. "You owe me, McClain. I could've marched you out of here in irons, but I didn't because you asked me not to."

McClain waved the burly man from the room. When he had gone, pulling the door closed behind him, McClain said, "What's your request?"

"Your lawyer, Bowden Jessup, has shot Josephine Franklin, her daughter, and foreman, and kidnapped her daughter-in-law."

McClain's mouth gaped open, and his eyes bugged out at Jack. "He couldn't have. I just met with him two days ago. He was calm and relaxed. He assured me we'd have a contract with Mrs. Franklin in a few days."

Jack shook his head. "I don't know anything about contracts. What I do know is that Jessup has Amy Franklin and is high-tailing it up to the water station north of there. It looks like he's figuring on boarding your train and going to the west coast with his captive. I need to get to the station to meet him."

McClain's head began to nod. "You need to hop this train to catch him."

"Exactly. I've got one other man with me, but that's not the favor. I know the train is headed on west. When we rescue Mrs.

Franklin, we'll need to get her back here and bring Jessup back for trial."

McClain peered at Jack. "Or to bring him back for burial."

"That, too, but I'd prefer to see him hang. I think he also killed Toler."

"He couldn't have. I don't think the man has it in him."

"Believe me, McClain, he is capable of that and more, but I don't have time to discuss it with you. We need to catch that train."

McClain dropped to his seat, picked up a pen, a piece of paper, and began writing, but suddenly stopped and glared up at Jack. "There's one more thing this'll cost you."

"Well?"

"A fight. You owe me an honest-to-goodness fight. You knocked me down and threw me in jail. You can't do that. I want satisfaction, and, by all that's holy, I'll get it."

"Just write your paper, McClain. I'll give you your fight, but I can promise you, it'll be more than you want."

McClain started writing again, a smile on his lips. "Ahh, the big man talks big, too. We'll see how big you're talking when I'm through with you." He finished writing, dropped his pen in the holder, and blotted the paper. Still grasping the paper, he rose and charged for the door. "Come with me."

McClain yanked his door open and stepped into the lobby, Jack on his heels. The clerk jumped up. McClain yelled at the man, "Get over to the station and hold that train till I get there. Have them bring up an empty passenger and freight car. Don't let him leave, or you and the whole crew are fired."

The clerk yanked on a cap and dashed from the lobby, disappearing through a side door.

McClain didn't look back. He turned left and exited the front door and turned right for the station. Jack looked around for Quint. When they approached the train, he saw the cowhand standing on the train platform, rifle in hand, waiting. McClain turned to Jack. "Wait here."

The conductor and engineer were talking to the clerk on the platform. McClain strode over to them and gave several orders, handed the paper he had written to the conductor, and continued to talk. There were several questions and answers, and finally both men nodded to McClain. He turned and came back to Jack.

"Alright, this is what's going to happen. We have started a spur to run down to the Franklin ranch." Jack frowned, and McClain waved his questions away. "I'll explain it to you when you get back. We have an engine and several flat cars at the spur. It's located about three miles before reaching the water stop. It's in scattered timber, so there's no way Jessup will even have a hint of anything going on. The two cars you see being connected will be switched to the engine at the spur, and he'll take you up to the water stop. That way none of my passengers will be exposed to gunfire. There's a siding for watering and trains passing, so when you get your business taken care of, the engineer will blow his whistle, and the train with the passengers will come up, water, and be on its way, and the spur train can bring you back here. Of course, I'll be billing the U.S. government for all these shenanigans, but I'm thinking it should fool Mr. Jessup."

Jack watched the additional cars being connected while McClain talked. "Bill what you will. I'll sign it when I get back. Thanks." He extended his hand.

McClain slapped it aside. "Keep your worthless handshake. Don't forget our deal."

Jack gave McClain a cold grin. "Believe me, McClain, I'm going to enjoy it."

The conductor called, "All aboard." Passengers stared at the additional cars behind the caboose, but climbed onto the train.

McClain pointed at the conductor. "Go with him. He can answer any questions you might have."

Jack nodded and motioned to Quint. The two of them strode

to the conductor. He pointed to the front of the first car. "Find a seat up there. I'll be along shortly."

Jack and Quint climbed aboard. They moved forward to the front and took an empty seat on the left. Jack leaned his rifle against the sidewall and leaned back. There wasn't a lot of cushion, but there was more than his saddle. They had been sitting only a couple of minutes when the coach jerked and jerked again.

Quint grabbed at the armrest. "I ain't never gotten used to these confounded gadgets. They've got to follow these doggone rails. Give me a good horse anytime that can leave the trail anytime you want him to."

Jack leaned back and watched Laramie's buildings slowly move past the train. "You're just old and set in your ways. Relax and enjoy it." The buildings disappeared behind them, and the click and clack of the passing rail joints grew faster and faster until it became hypnotic. Jack was almost asleep when the conductor stepped to the front of the seat.

"Marshal Sage, we will be at the spur in one hour and thirty minutes. It will take no more than fifteen minutes to switch the cars to the other engine. At that point, you'll be on your way. Please do not take more time than necessary. We have a schedule to keep."

Jack started to say something, but held his tongue. McClain and the railroad were helping him, so he had little right to be reprimanding this man for wanting to do his job. He gave the conductor a tight grin. "We'll do our best."

The man replied with a sharp nod and moved down the aisle, collecting tickets.

Quint leaned toward him. "Friendly feller, ain't he?"

Jack pulled his Stetson over his face. "Friendly enough to let us ride on his train."

Quint said nothing. The old cowhand was snoring before Jack.

23

"Mr. Sage." The insistent voice repeated itself. He felt a hand grasp his shoulder and shake.

With his left forefinger, he slid his Stetson back and looked up at the conductor. The man was leaning close enough for Jack to smell his rotten breath. "Yes?"

"We're slowing for the spur. We'll be there in five minutes." He cast a jaundiced look at Quint, who was still snoring.

"Thanks." He shoved an elbow into Quint's ribs. The old cowhand hardly moved, but from under the crumpled, sweat-stained hat came, "The last feller who did that is in boot hill."

"Wake up. We're almost there."

Quint shoved his hat back from his face to his head and looked out the window. "That was fast. I just went to sleep."

The train continued to slow. Through the window, Jack saw the engine on the spur slowly pass by the window. "Come on, let's get moving." He stepped from between the seats into the aisle. The train jerked to a halt. Jack and Quint exited from the front of the car, to the voice of the conductor. "Please keep your seats, folks. Do not exit the train."

Jack strode over to the man who appeared to be in charge of the other locomotive.

The man watched him approach. "You the U.S. Marshal?"

"I am. How long will it take for you to attach the cars and get us on our way?"

He shook his head. "Not long." He held up the letter McClain had written. "I understand you're after an outlaw."

"That's right. A bad one, but I don't want anyone involved other than the two of us." He indicated Quint and himself. "We'll need a conductor to make this look like the regular train, and the water loading needs to look just like it would be for the train coming in from Laramie. This man is sharp. Anything out of place, and he might take off."

"No problem. We're offloading water right now. It'll be just like the one that brought you in."

Jack watched the men hooking the two empty cars to the train. "You're also attaching the caboose?"

"Yes, sir. You want them the same. That's what we're giving you."

Jack turned to Quint. "I forgot one thing. I need to swear you in."

"Well, what're you waitin' on, Mr. Marshal?"

"Raise your right hand."

Quint raised his hand. His forearm jutted out from his elbow at about a forty-five-degree angle.

Jack shook his head and said, "You swear to uphold the law and do what I say?"

"I sure do."

"Good, you're now a deputy." He opened his saddlebags, searched around in them, and finally drew out a badge, tossing it to Quint. "Pin it on."

Quint looked at it while the clank and bang of the cars slamming and locking together reverberated across the plains. "Well, ain't that fine. I've been a city marshal, a deputy sheriff, and a constable, but I ain't never been a U.S. Marshal."

Jack grinned. "And you're not one now. You're a *deputy* U.S. Marshal who takes orders, and don't forget it."

Quint frowned at Jack. "You're a mighty uppity boss. If you ain't careful, I'm liable to quit on you."

"Just wait until we get Jessup back to Laramie, then I'll be glad to take that badge back."

The conductor on the new train waved at the man standing with Jack and Quint. The man turned to them. "You can board. They're ready. Good luck to you."

They trotted to the front car, where the conductor stood, and swung aboard. The conductor waved to the engineer, and the train jerked forward. Jack asked, "How long before we get there?"

"Fifteen minutes at the most. We'll pull up to the water tank, and the fireman will start taking on water."

Jack checked his watch, six forty-five. By seven thirty this would be over, and Amy would, hopefully, be safe, with Jessup captured. "Are there any buildings there?"

"Just an equipment shed with a ramp. When we stop, the ramp will be at the front of the rear car."

"Alright, thanks." Jack turned to Quint. "Take the back entry of the front car. Jessup is tricky and smart. Don't forget to check the offside. Be alert and ready for anything."

Quint winked at him. "Yes, sir, and you be careful."

"Quint?"

The old cowhand had turned away. He stopped and half-turned back to Jack.

"Don't kill him if you can keep from it. This is one man who deserves to hang. I want to take him alive if at all possible, but the most important goal is to save Amy. If the only way you can do it is by loading Jessup up with lead, then go for it."

Quint gave Jack a knowing nod and headed forward to his position. Jack turned back to the conductor. "Your job is to act normal and save yourself. If bullets start flying, which they very well might, get to cover, and don't come out until the shooting stops and Jessup is either tied up or dead."

"Yes, sir. I can follow those orders. We're pulling in, and I don't see anyone around."

Did I guess wrong? Jack thought. *Has Jessup gone to the mountains? Maybe he headed south to Colorado, but, no, Quint and Monty trailed him north. He's got to be coming here. Did a horse break a leg?*

He saw the dust, two horses racing hard toward the train. He yelled so both Quint and the conductor would hear him. "They're coming, still south of here and running hard. Mr. Conductor, when they get close, have your man shut down the water and start the train slowly moving away. That should force him to try to board from the back of the caboose. I'll be back there waiting for him."

The conductor hurried to the fireman to give him the lowdown, then worked his way back, acting as if he were checking the wheels. Jack could see Amy and Jessup. They were pushing the horses, and the animals were lathered something fierce. He expected one or both of them to stumble at any moment. Just when Jessup started slowing, the fireman signaled and the engineer blew the whistle. A moment later the train jerked.

The riders were close enough for Jack to hear Jessup yelling and see the desperation in the man's face. "That's the way I want you, Jessup, reacting, not thinking." He moved into the caboose and walked quickly to the back window.

Jessup had started toward the second car, but when the train began pulling away, he was forced to aim for his only chance, the caboose. The man yelled something unintelligible to Amy, and she shook her head. Jack's heart jumped when he saw Jessup pull his sixgun.

From inside the caboose, Jack centered his front sight on Jessup's chest, but the man yelled again, and Amy angled toward the back of the caboose. Every fiber of Jack's being was telling him to step outside on the platform and give her a hand up, but he couldn't. Jessup would recognize him and shoot Amy. She had to make the leap herself. Once she was on board, he could yank her inside, not before.

From the corner of his eye, Jack caught the conductor, who had followed him back, along with Quint staring at him when he said, "Come on, Amy, you can do it."

She angled her horse closer. The engineer was accelerating perfectly. Jack made up his mind, he was going to give a healthy tip to the whole crew if they pulled this off.

She was even with the back step, but Jack could hear her horse laboring. He gave her a whispered command. "A little closer."

As if she were listening to his direction, she eased the horse closer. "Now!" Jack shouted. "Jump!"

She did and grabbed the bars, but her feet hung down near the rails, which were passing faster and faster.

Her horse slowed and fell back, allowing Jessup to pull close to the rear of the caboose. He cursed his horse and thrust the spurs to the animal. It leaped forward. At the same moment, Jack yanked the back door open, grabbed Amy, and threw her past the open door of the caboose into the arms of Quint.

Jessup recognized Jack immediately and began screaming, cursing at him. The lawyer's usually aloof face was twisted in a grotesque mask of hate. He brought his revolver up, and Jack launched himself from the caboose steps straight into Jessup, passing under the raised weapon. It exploded into the roof of the caboose while Jack's impact drove Jessup from the galloping horse. The two men sailed away from the caboose and crashed on the rocky ground. Airborne, their bodies had tangled, and Jessup managed to twist Jack beneath him just before they struck.

Jack tried to pull his body tight, tucking his chin to his chest. The last thing he wanted was to hit the ground on his head or neck. He could feel Jessup's weight. Just like he had figured, the man was bigger than he appeared in his loose-fitting suits. The combined weight of the two big men slammed into the rocks on Jack's right thigh, directly on his old wound. Through the pain, he could feel his leg go numb. Jessup still held his revolver.

Jack had multiple problems. His entire body screamed in pain from the rocks cutting and gouging into his muscles, Jessup was strong and attempting to bring the revolver to bear on Jack's head, and Jack's leg was numb. He probably wouldn't be able to stand, so he couldn't let Jessup get away from him. He'd tried to holster his right Smith & Wesson before grabbing Amy, but there had been no time. He'd turned it loose and let it fall on the platform of the caboose. His left one had managed to stay in its holster through the jump and fall, even though he'd flipped the loop from the hammer, but he couldn't get to it. Both hands were wrapped around Jessup's wrist, controlling the direction of the muzzle of his weapon.

Jessup managed to get to his knees and with his free hand smashed Jack in the jaw, but he hardly noticed, he was concentrating on Jessup's gun hand. He tightened his grip and twisted, rotating in opposite directions with each hand. He could feel the tendons and bones in Jessup's wrist grating against themselves. He bore down with every ounce of strength he could muster.

Jessup screamed and hit him again and again.

Jack felt wrist bones break, and the revolver dropped from Jessup's hand, the fingers reflexively extended like claws. Jessup tried to scramble away from him, but Jack wasn't turning loose of his opponent's right hand. Using Jessup's wrist for leverage, Jack jerked himself to his feet, his right leg completely numb. He stared into the deranged attorney's hate-filled eyes, held tight to the man's wrist, and released a smashing right-hand blow to Jessup's left temple.

Jessup's eyelids fluttered and closed, and his body collapsed to the ground. Jack, his leg still numb, and his left hand gripping

Jessup's right hand, went to his knees with the lawyer. He released the unconscious man's mangled wrist and picked up the killer's Colt.

He took a deep breath and looked around. The train was backing up. Quint, Amy, and the conductor stood on the platform of the caboose. Quint had one arm around Amy and was holstering his Colt with the other. He'd picked up Jack's Smith and had it shoved behind his belt. His mouth was spread wide in a grin, showing a broken front tooth.

That was fast, Jack thought. *It couldn't have been more than three minutes ago I was standing on the caboose.* He chuckled. *And now I can't stand at all.* The train jerked to a stop, and Amy leaped from the back and ran past rails and rocks to Jack.

She knelt next to him and threw her arms around his neck. "Oh, Jack. I thought my life was over, and you've saved me again."

Jessup stirred.

Jack looked up at Quint still standing on the platform with the conductor. "You think you could earn your money and get Jessup out from under me? He's waking up."

Quint stepped down from the train and strolled over to Jack. He stood there with his thumbs in his gunbelt, looking down at the three of them. "You mean I'm getting paid? I didn't even think about that. How much?"

Jack motioned to Jessup. "Get this killer out from under me and on the train. We'll take him back to Laramie for a trial and the gallows."

Amy stood and provided Jack a brace to lean on. He cautiously got to his feet. His leg was beginning to tingle and burn. Quint drew his Colt with one hand and dragged the semi-conscious Jessup to his feet. He shoved the muzzle under Jessup's chin and, in a soft but ever-so-threatening voice, said, "Give me a reason, Jessup. There's nothin' I'd like better than to save the hangman the trouble." He pressed the muzzle deeper into the flesh until Jessup was standing tall.

"Easy, Quint. I'd like to see him make it to trial."

"More than I would, I'm sure."

"Just get him on the train." He glanced at the conductor. "You can signal your engineer."

The conductor waved to the engineer, who, along with the fireman, was hanging onto the engine, staring back at the action. Immediately the engineer disappeared, and there were three long blasts of the train's whistle. A moment later, a like response was heard in the direction of the spur, but closer than Jack expected. He looked quizzically at the conductor.

The man gave him a sheepish grin. "In that note Mr. McClain sent, he said to move the passenger train as close as we could without spooking Jessup here. You remember that grade we came up just before we got here?"

Jack nodded.

"That's where they waited."

Even as he was explaining, the train came puffing past the water station. The engineer and the fireman waved as they went by. Jack watched the passenger cars go by, faces plastered to the windows. "I guess those folks coming from back east will have plenty to tell their families about the wild west when they get home." He looked to see Quint with the revolver still jammed under Jessup's chin. The old cowhand was staring at the train as it creeped by.

"You might want to get that hogleg out from under Jessup's chin, or they could think you're the bad man."

Quint grinned at Jack and, with his hand still full of Colt, waved to the passengers going by. "What they don't know, Jack, boy, is that I am a mighty bad man." He handed Jack his Smith & Wesson and jerked Jessup toward the caboose.

Jack watched the train. It wasn't stopping. He dropped his revolver into its holster and looked at the conductor.

Before he could ask, the conductor said, "We have a temporary water station at the spur. Since he was there, we figured to save time and fill him up. We are on a schedule."

"I noticed when we arrived, we pulled on to this siding. Is that normal?"

The conductor looked uncomfortable. "We did that so the passenger train could sail on by, with no delay, when you were done."

Jack nodded. "Was that your idea or McClain's?"

"Oh, that was Mr. McClain's. He thinks of everything. He's a hard man to work for, but he knows how to run a railroad."

And that little touch, Jack thought, *could have blown this whole deal. But it didn't, and we have Jessup.*

Jack hopped around to move toward the train, with Amy supporting him. "It all worked out." He grasped the back rail of the caboose and tried lifting his numb leg to the first step. It took a bit of work, but he got it there. Then pulling with his arm, pushing off with his good leg, and Amy's help, he made it to the first step and into the caboose. He dropped into a seat, but before he could lean back, the conductor said, "Wait, don't lean back, Marshal. Give me just a second."

"What?"

Amy looked at his back. "Oh, Jack, your back is covered with blood. You must have cut it up really badly on the rocks."

The conductor hurried back. In his hands he held two large towels. He draped them over the back of the seat. "Alright, Marshal, you can lean back all you want. You'll need to get that back looked at. We've got a doctor at the spur. We can stop if you like."

Jack shook his head. "No, let's get this killer to jail, and I'll get it looked at then."

"As you wish."

He saw Quint standing, then bending over to look out the window to the south. Jessup was doing the same.

He looked through the smudged glass. Dust. A lot of dust, and it was coming fast.

Quint looked back. "You know who that is, don't you?"

Jack stared out the window, thinking, and then it hit him. "Schmidt?"

Quint nodded. "I'd lay money on it. He's coming hard, but if we hadn't of been here, he wouldn't have made it. Jessup would been on the train and long gone."

Amy was concentrating on the dust. She looked forward. "Quint, do you really think that's Hank?"

"I'd bet a gold strike on it, ma'am. Monty and I followed you past his place, and when we knew we couldn't catch you before dark, we turned around to head back to the ranch. You know, to check on Mrs. Franklin and Lilly. We was mighty worried."

"I understand, Quint. I'm so glad you did. Somehow you and Jack managed to get here. You wouldn't have if you hadn't turned around."

"No, ma'am, I reckon we wouldn't, but we stopped at the Schmidt place and told him about what had happened and that Jessup was headed this way with you. He was all for taking off at night, but his tracker was trying to convince him to wait until morning when we left."

Amy looked up at Jack. "I need to tell you something."

24

Jack shook his head. "You don't need to explain anything to me. Jo told me about you and Hank, and I'm happy for you."

Her bright green eyes stared deep into his. "Are you, Jack?"

He looked at the backs of Quint's and Jessup's heads. Lowering his voice, he responded, "Amy, I'm not a good catch for any woman. My life is the law, and after Jessup is taken care of, I'll be moving to wherever I'm needed. It's no life for a woman or family. You and Davy need stability. Hank will provide that, and from the speed of that dust cloud, I'd say he's mighty committed to you. Don't worry about me. I'll be fine."

Jack looked past her. The dust had changed to individual riders, and they were coming fast. "Quint, why don't you go out there and wave them down. They're killing those horses."

The cowhand deputy stood. Jessup shot a nervous look first out the window and then to his right. Jack drew his revolver and eased back the hammer. The clicking was loud inside the empty caboose. "Don't get any ideas, Jessup. Just because I haven't shot you yet, don't think I won't if you give me a reason."

He glanced at Amy. "Why don't you go on out there and calm your man down. It'll be good for him to see you're safe. Tell Quint to bring him in when they get here but only him. I won't have this turn into a hanging party."

She slipped past him, and her long fingers touched his cheek for the last time. "You're an amazing man, Jack Sage. I will never forget you."

His voice had turned gruff and hard. "Go ahead on. Tell Quint before there's problems."

She smiled past the gruffness, and tears filled her eyes, but she hurried out the door of the caboose.

The conductor, standing by the back door, spoke. "How long will this take? We have a line to run, and these rails are blocked until we get back to Laramie."

Jack was no longer feeling agreeable with anything or anyone. "As long as it takes."

He kept his eyes on Jessup. *You've brought pain and grief to a lot of people,* he thought. *I won't be the only one who'll be glad to see you ended.* Then his mind drifted south. *I wonder how Bronco Fenn and Montana Huff are doing. It'd be good to see them and get into warmer country. It's pretty up here, but it's too blamed cold.*

The door banged open. Schmidt charged in the back door and stopped, staring at Jack's back. "You're not looking too good."

"Thanks, you don't look so great yourself."

Schmidt was covered with dust. "We've been riding hard."

Jack looked out the window at the horses. "Yeah, they look the worse for wear, but you made it, and Amy's safe." He watched Schmidt eying Jessup.

"Vat is your plan for him?"

"I've arrested him, and I'm taking Jessup to Laramie to stand trial and hopefully hang. He's got enough against him."

"Ve can take care of the hanging part right here."

Jack tapped his badge with his left hand and held his revolver up with his right. "This badge and gun say he goes to Laramie. Does that present a problem for you?"

Jack kept his eyes on the big German. He could see the man wanted to get his hands on Jessup and conduct a little frontier justice, but he was here to ensure his prisoner made it to the courtroom. He said nothing and waited.

Finally Schmidt took a deep breath and blew it out. "No. It is no problem. We need law in this country, but I will be at the trial to make sure he hangs. I'm taking Amy with me."

Jack nodded. "Is that what she wants? She's had a long ride, and it'll be a long ride back. We'll be in Laramie in a couple of hours. She can get a hotel room, a bath, and some rest."

Schmidt shook his head. "No. Last night, before we left, I sent a rider down to get clean clothes for her. She'll have everything you say at my ranch."

Amy stepped through the door. "I want to go, Jack. Hank's not forcing me."

Schmidt's thick eyebrows jerked together, his forehead wrinkled, and his eyes tightened. "You think I make her go?"

Jack shook his head. "No, Hank, I don't think you make her do anything."

The German smiled, and his sun-browned cheeks seemed to turn a little pink. "You know me well, Marshal Sage." He pointed at Jessup and spoke directly to the lawyer. "You are a lucky man, Mr. Lawyer. If I had caught you, you would no longer be breathing the same air as my Amy." Turning, Schmidt dropped his big hand to Jack's shoulder and squeezed. "Thank you for saving my Amy, Marshal. You are welcome at our ranch anytime."

Jack looked up. "Thanks, Hank."

Amy's soft voice carried through the caboose. "Goodbye, Jack."

"So long, Amy. Be prepared to testify. It might be necessary."

Schmidt moved past him. He heard the back door of the

caboose close. Moments later it jerked with the release of Schmidt's weight.

The conductor gave Jack a pointed look. "Now?"

"You bet. Move it out. We can't get to Laramie fast enough."

He saw Amy and Schmidt wave as the train began to back down the tracks. He felt a slight bump as it moved onto the main tracks. Minutes later, it began accelerating. He watched Amy and the group of horsemen slowly shrink in the distance until the train dropped over a hill and they were gone.

Quint moved past Jack and turned around, dropping in one of the seats. "This has been a long couple of days."

"Yeah, and it isn't over yet." He turned to the conductor. "How long do you think it'll take us to get to Laramie?"

The conductor did what conductors do. He removed his pocket watch and examined it. "It is eight o'clock. We will be arriving in Laramie at nine twenty-five."

"Thanks. Do you happen to know where my rifle and saddlebags are?"

"Yes, Marshal. I took the liberty of moving them back here." He opened a closet, removed them, and handed them to Jack. He turned to walk forward.

Jack had opened the saddlebags and looked up when the conductor moved away. "Hold on, before you go. I don't know your name."

The conductor smiled. "Granger. My name is Raymond Granger. I go by Ray."

"Nice to meet you, Ray. You folks made all the difference. I really appreciate what you did." While he was talking, Jack thumbed through his saddlebags and opened a leather pouch. "So there were three of you involved in this, you, the engineer, and the fireman?"

"Yes, Marshal, that's correct."

From his pouch Jack removed three double eagles. He held

them out, but the conductor stood stiff, not reaching. "Marshal, we are all professionals. We work for an honest wage. I dare say, all three of us were happy to assist you."

Jack smiled. "Ray, take this. It's not payment. It's an acknowledgment of a job well done. Take your wife out to a good dinner, or buy your son or daughter a present. Enjoy it with my gratitude."

The conductor held out his hand. The gold coins clinked into his palm. "I will see that the engineer and fireman receive theirs."

Jack nodded. "Thanks, I'm sure you will."

The conductor moved forward, exiting the caboose.

Quint yawned and nodded at Jessup. "You watching this cow pie?"

"I am. Get some sleep. I'm wide awake."

Quint nodded, slid down in the seat, stretched his legs, and pulled his hat over his eyes. Within minutes he was snoring.

He had been asleep for no more than fifteen minutes when Jessup spoke. "My wrist is swelling. You did something to it."

"That was my intention."

"I could lose my hand."

"Where you're going, you're not going to need it. Now shut up."

Jessup was silent for a few minutes. "You know you can't get a conviction for murder because I haven't killed anyone."

"Of course you have. You killed Toler, and you paid to have General Franklin and your friend, his son Warren, killed."

Jessup shook his head. "All lies."

"Shut up, Jessup."

"Or what, you're going to hit me like you hit Mr. McClain? You are a dangerous man, Marshal Sage. You've killed more people since coming to Wyoming than you claim I have. You killed Leander Hull and two of Henry Schmidt's cowhands, Cain Walker and River Jordan. The last one was only a boy, and you shot him down like a dog. How many others have you killed, Marshal, we don't know about?

"I think I'll mention that at the trial. Warren talked about you all the time. You were in the French Foreign Legion before the war. Is that where you learned to kill, or was it as a ship's officer, traveling all over the world into dangerous exotic ports and having to deal with mutinies? Maybe I should also mention that."

Jack let out a light snore. Jessup leaped to his feet but froze when he saw Jack grinning at him. "No, no, no, Bowden." He waggled a finger at the man. "Mustn't try to escape. All I have to do is wake up Quint, and I think he would be more than happy to satisfy your death wish." His voice changed to cold and hard. "Sit down. Don't even think about whatever it is you have in mind, because the more you talk, the more I'm inclined to allow Quint to take over."

Now Jack saw the face he had seen outside of the train, full of hate. Jessup continued to stare at Jack. It was as if he couldn't take his eyes from him. "Turn around, and sit down."

Jessup stared for almost a full minute, then faced forward and slowly lowered himself to the seat.

Jack had brought men in he didn't like, but this Jessup. He was loathsome. *Does he have any saving grace?* he thought. *I haven't seen it. With his attitude, I'd sure hate to be headed to meet my maker.*

The metronomic click of the wheels over the rail joints was hypnotic. Jack could almost see the demonic expression Jessup had had in the train yard. His eyes blinked open. Jessup had creeped to almost within reach of Jack, and the expression he had just been picturing was on the killer's face. Jack smiled at him, and Jessup smiled back.

He wagged his finger in the same manner Jack had earlier. "Almost got you, Sage. You would have been a dead man."

Jack held his smile. "And yet I'm not. You might want to move back to your seat, or you can have a .44 slug move you. Your choice."

The train whistle blew, and the train began slowing.

"Get in your seat, Jessup."

The man moved back to where he had been sitting and dropped into his seat. At the same instant, the forward door of the caboose opened, and the conductor stepped inside. "Coming into Laramie. We'll be at the station in three minutes."

Quint stretched and sat up. "Now that was nice. I feel like a new man." He looked at Jessup and then Jack. "What?"

Using his revolver, Jack motioned toward Jessup. "Mr. Jessup has been contemplating doing us harm."

"He's gonna have to work fast, because I see a hangman's noose in his future."

The train jerked to a halt, and holding his right wrist, Jessup groaned. "I've got to see a doctor. My wrist is killing me."

Jack stood and moved toward the man. "Stand up." He motioned to Quint. "Keep him covered while I get my gear."

Quint pulled his Colt and leveled it at the lawyer. The back door of the caboose banged open, and Lewis McClain walked in with Sheriff Wright trailing him.

Before either Jack or Quint could say anything, Jessup leaped from his seat, his voice now filled with pain and fear. "Help me, Sheriff. These men are trying to kill me. They've already broken my wrist and refuse to take me to the doctor. Please don't leave me alone with them."

The sheriff looked at McClain and then Jack. "What's going on here?"

Jessup tried to say something else, but Quint's rugged fist slammed into his jaw, knocking him to the floor of the caboose.

"Oh, help me, Sheriff, Mr. McClain. You can see what they're doing to me."

Jack's attention was fully engaged by Jessup until he heard a weapon cocking.

"Alright," the sheriff said, "everybody just calm down and let Mr. Jessup explain to me what's going on."

Jack was looking at Jessup, prone between the seats and hidden from the sheriff and McClain. The man gave him an evil, triumphant grin, then, as the sheriff moved forward, his expression changed to one of a man in excruciating pain. He cried again, "Oh, thank you, Sheriff. Please, I need to get to the doctor's office immediately."

Jack glanced at Quint. "Keep him covered," and grabbed Jessup's collar, yanking him to his feet. "One more word out of you, Jessup, and I'll gag you. Go ahead, try me."

Jessup closed his mouth and remained quiet. The sheriff looked at Jessup and at Jack's back. "I don't understand what's going on here, Marshal, but you can't be manhandling prisoners."

"Put that gun away, Sheriff. This man has shot Mrs. Franklin, her daughter, and her foreman. He also kidnapped Amy Franklin. Thanks to Mr. McClain, we were able to apprehend Jessup before he forced Amy to board the west coast train. No one would have ever seen her again."

Wright looked around. "Where is she? Is she alright?"

Jack kicked himself for not bringing Amy back to Laramie. "She's fine, Sheriff. Hank Schmidt followed Jessup and Amy and was able to escort her back to the ranch."

Jack sensed movement and turned toward Jessup to see him vigorously shaking his head.

The sheriff's face was a complete contradiction. His lips turned up in a faint grin, his brow was wrinkled, his eyes were scrunched together so he could barely see. Finally, he made up his mind. "I don't know what's going on, but I can see Mr. Jessup's arm. He needs a doctor. I'm taking him to the doctor."

Jack shook his head. "Look, Sheriff, I agree with you. He needs a doctor, but a doctor can see him in the jail. That's where he belongs. Let's both take him. That way he'll be locked up, and the doctor can take care of him. We'll both be satisfied."

The sheriff slowly shook his head. "No, I'm taking him to the doctor. The man's in pain, and he needs a doctor right now. Afterwards, Marshal Sage, you and your deputy can come to my office and explain this far-fetched tale."

Jack stepped out of the aisle, allowing Jessup to walk toward the sheriff. He motioned for Quint to lower his weapon. "Where are you taking him, Sheriff? Doc's out at the Franklin ranch. He's also been pistol-whipped by Jessup."

Wright paused, then looked at McClain. "You've got a doctor for your railroad folks, don't you, Mr. McClain?"

McClain shook his head. "He's not a doctor. He's a nurse, employed by the railroad."

Sheriff Wright thought on it for a second. "But he can fix breaks and sprains, cain't he?"

McClain sighed. "I suppose he can."

"He sees patients in your offices?"

"He does, but why don't you take Jessup to jail, and I can bring my man down there."

Wright shook his head. "No, I've made up my mind. Look how swollen Mr. Jessup's arm is. I don't want him losing a hand because I was in a hurry to get him to the jail."

"Alright, follow me." Jessup stepped out behind McClain, looking confident again for the first time since he had spotted Jack on the caboose platform.

Jack moved in behind Jessup, but Sheriff Wright stepped in the aisle and stopped him. "I'm the sheriff in this county. I'll take care of this. You ain't needed."

Jack, doing all he could to rein in his temper, leaned toward the sheriff. "You listen to me close. I'm going to let you take him because I don't want to have to shoot a sheriff for being stupid, but I'm going along. You aren't going to stop me or my deputy. Do you understand me, Wright?"

Wright stepped forward behind Jessup, his revolver lowered. "Do as you please. Just don't get in my way."

Jack motioned Quint to follow and fell in behind Wright. His leg almost buckled when he made his way down the steps of the caboose, but he managed to hang on to the railing. It was a short walk to the executive offices where the station's medical office was located. The lawmen and killer entered the building behind McClain. A number of gawkers were following, but stopped at the entry doors. Jack motioned for the clerk to come over. "Does the infirmary have an outside entrance?"

"Yes, sir. It sure does."

Jack looked at Quint. "Get back there and guard that entrance. I know Jessup's going to try something. Be ready and be careful."

To the clerk, he ordered, "Show him where it is."

"Yes, sir."

Jack watched Quint and the clerk dash through the front door. Once they were gone, he hurried to catch up with the others. Rounding a corner, he saw McClain pull an office door closed. He hastily strode to the railroad man and pointed at the closed door. "Did they go in there?"

McClain nodded. "They're with Wyatt Carter. He's the medical specialist here in our Laramie office."

Jack reached for the latch.

"Sheriff Wright said I'm supposed to tell you to wait here."

"McClain, I've just about had enough of Wright." Jack pulled on the latch. Nothing happened.

"I guess Carter must've locked the door. He usually does to keep people from barging in on an examination."

Jack heard a muffled cry from inside. "I knew it." He lifted the massive boot on his injured leg and drove it into the door latch. Pain plunged deep into his battered thigh, and the door flung open. Forcing the pain away, Jack's brain took a picture of the stark interior and imprinted it forever.

A man, who Jack assumed was the medical technician, was on the floor, his hands desperately attempting to stem the blood spurting from his throat. The sheriff leaned with his back against a table, a scalpel protruding from his chest, and Jessup stood backlit in the open door, raising what Jack figured was Wright's revolver. Jack, who still held his Smith in his right hand, jerked it up and fired. His revolver crashed, and Jessup's spouted flame from its muzzle. Jessup staggered back into the alleyway, and another weapon discharged. The lawyer was blown sideways out the door and from Jack's vision.

He turned to McClain.

"I'm fine," the railroad man yelled.

Another shot blasted outside. Jack limped across the room to the exit door. Jessup was on his back, Wright's Colt still loosely gripped in his hand. Jack caught movement and jerked around to see Quint holding his smoking weapon. He spun back to Jessup, who, strength gone, was futilely trying to raise the revolver. Jack kicked it from the man's left hand and knelt beside him.

"I . . . win." Jessup gasped through a grotesque grin.

"How do you figure?"

"No . . . hanging."

"Don't bet on it. I'm taking your body outside of town and hanging you in a high tree. I'll strip you naked and cut traitor in your chest. How do you like that?"

Jessup's eyes spread wide. "You can't."

"Who'll stop me, you? You'll be in hell, burning forever."

The dying man's smile was gone. "No, no . . . you—"

Jack watched the light fade from the man's eyes. "If there's any justice on the other side, Jessup, you're already feeling the heat."

He stood.

Quint was standing over him. "That was pretty cold, pardner."

"Yeah, I suppose sometime in the future I'll regret saying it, but right now, all I can think about is Warren and the general, Jo and Lilly and Amy, and those kids, who'll have to live with the picture of the man who they thought was a friend trying to kill them. And look at that poor man in the infirmary. He did no one any harm, and now he's bleeding out, and the sheriff, all because of this pile of cow dung." Jack kicked Jessup's corpse. "Yeah, I'll probably feel bad about what I said to him sometime in the future, but it's a long way off." He looked down at the corpse again. "A long, long way." Jack turned back into the infirmary to check on the injured men.

EPILOGUE

August 3, 1873

Jack Sage, Davy gripping his left hand and Flo his right, stood on the Laramie Train Station platform with the rest of the family and watched the train slowly accelerate into the distance. He glanced over his shoulder to see Carter Schofield leaning against the station wall, and nodded to him. Davy saw it and asked, "Who's he?"

"Just a friend," but Jack mulled over his statement. *Is he a friend? Maybe, like a working associate is a friend, but not like Quint had become. He's a real friend, like Bronco Fenn and Montana Huff, or old Sully Johnson in Cherry Creek. Those are friends.* He glanced back at Carter, who gave a slight motion toward the hotel, pushed from the wall, and walked toward the Gleason.

Jack looked around at the happy faces. Jo Franklin stood ostensibly leaning on her foreman, Tripp Singletary, but she had healed quickly, and was, in fact, providing support for him. His leg was healing, but it was a bit shorter than the other, although Doc Tilson swore it wouldn't be long before he'd be riding like he used to, but with a shorter stirrup on that side.

Lilly had her arm through Johnny's, and Dot stood with

Monty. The loss of the general and Warren and then their own brush with death had brought the realization to all of them life was short. A person should grab happiness when they had the chance, because it could disappear like wisps of early morning fog on a mountain stream.

The train dipped below the horizon. Only the smoke could be seen.

Flo looked up at Jack. "Will Amy and Hank be gone long, Marshal Sage?"

Jack shook his head. "Before you know it, they'll be back."

She looked over at Davy. "When they get back, I don't want Davy and Amy to leave. I'll miss them." She looked at the big dog sitting by Davy. "I'll miss Ghost, too."

Jack gently squeezed her hand. "You're a lucky girl. They'll be close, and you two will be able to play on your mama's ranch and on Hank's. Just think how much space you'll have."

She grinned at Davy. "I never thought of that. Let's go to Otto's and look at the horses."

"Good idea," Davy said. "You want to go, Marshal?"

"No, I've got some business to take care of. Flo, you best ask your mama first."

She jerked her hand from his. "Alright," and ran to Jo.

Ghost waited, looking up at Jack. The lawman knelt and held the dog's head in both hands, staring into the big brown eyes. "I don't know where you came from, but you're a wonder with those kids. You take care of them, you hear?" The long tongue lashed out and wiped a fistful of slime on Jack's cheek. He laughed, wiped his cheek with his sleeve, and turned to Davy.

Davy was gazing at Jack, his little face fighting back the tears marshaling in his eyes. "You're leaving, aren't you, Marshal Sage?"

Jack could feel the tightening in his own eyes and blinked. "Reckon I am, Davy." He tapped the badge on his chest. "This means I have to go where people need me. You're safe now, and other folks still need help. I've got to go protect them, but you've got Ghost. He's big like me. He'll be with you for a long time."

Davy's hand rested on Ghost's back, and he looked at the dog. "I love him." He looked back at Jack. "I love you, too, Marshal Sage." The pools in his eyes broke and streamed down the little boy's cheeks. He continued to gaze at Jack.

Jack Sage, the tough U.S. Marshal, held his face stiff and scooped the boy up in his arms. "I love you too, Davy. Someday we'll see each other again."

"Promise?"

"I promise." He gave the boy a big hug, set him back on the platform, nodded at Flo, and winked at Davy. "Your aunt is waiting on you."

Davy's face widened into a grin, his sadness forgotten. He spun and raced toward Flo, tossing over his shoulder, "Bye, Marshal Sage."

Moments later the two kids and the dog were dashing across the street, dodging between wagons and riders. Jack heard someone yell at them, and he jerked his head toward the offender, but they were across the street, and the rider was moving on.

Dot stepped up beside him. "That boy loves you, you know."

Jack nodded, not trusting his voice.

She looked at his tight jawline and smiled. "I know you love him, too, Jack Sage."

Jack stared at the horizon where the train had disappeared and cleared his throat. "Reckon I do."

"I understand you'll be leaving us."

Her faint enticing fragrance enveloped him. "Yep."

"It was nice of you to stay for Amy and Hank's wedding."

Jack shook his head. "I had some loose ends to clean up. It worked out."

She nodded. "Yes, it certainly did. Do you know where you're headed?"

Jack smiled. "I'm planning on heading back to Texas. I've found these old bones can't handle this cold weather. Warmer days are what they need, though, on occasion, it can get a mite biting in the winter."

She weaved her arm in his and squeezed. "We'll miss you, Jack. I like Hank, but personally, I think Amy made a huge mistake." When she said huge, she squeezed his arm tighter against her. "He's good and solid and definitely a man, but he's not you."

Jack laughed. "You be careful, you'll have me chasing you." She looked up into his face, locking her sky-blue eyes on his, and Jack was sorry he'd made the comment, even jokingly.

"I just might let you catch me."

"Dot, you don't mean that. Monty is a good man."

She gave Monty a wistful smile and relaxed her grip on Jack's arm. "Yes, he is. When are you leaving?"

"In the morning."

"So soon?"

"Yep. I've got to be heading south." He grinned. "Got to get out of here before these nighttime temperatures get any lower and it starts snowing."

She pulled his head down, planted a long kiss right on his lips, and stepped away. "Remember us." Dot turned and walked back to Monty, who stared, frowning at Jack.

Jack grinned at him and shrugged.

Lilly and Johnny eased over to him. "How's your shoulder, Sheriff?"

Johnny grinned. "It's fine, but I cain't get used to being called sheriff."

"You're a good man, Johnny. Wright was lucky he lived, and smart to step down. You carry the title well. Just remember to treat everyone fairly, no favorites, and never let your guard down. The nicest, most friendly guy could kill you."

"Thanks, Jack. After Jessup, I reckon I'll never forget." He looked at Dot and back to Jack. "From the looks of it, I'd say you're about to pull out."

"Yep. In the morning."

Lilly spoke in her usual soft voice. "You best talk to Mama Jo before you go."

"I'll do that, Lilly, girl. You take good care of my sheriff, here."

She smiled at Johnny. "I'll take very good care of him, Marshal." She stood on her tiptoes and kissed Jack on the cheek.

Johnny gripped his hand in both of his. "Thanks, Jack. Good luck to you." Lilly flashed him one last smile, and the couple moved away toward the wagon.

Jack looked around the station. The train was gone, and so were all the folks seeing others off. Besides Tripp and Jo, he was the only one remaining on the platform. He walked over to the two of them. "You folks better be heading on out. It's a long ride back to the ranch."

Tripp nodded. "That it is." He moved his cane and extended his right hand. "So long, Jack. It's been a real pleasure knowing you. Take care of yourself, and speaking for myself, you're always welcome. You deserve a passel of good." He released Jack's hand and slowly made his way back to the wagon.

Jo watched him like a protective mother hen. "That leg is still giving him great difficulty, and to think, he got that bullet trying to save us."

"He's a good man, Jo. You're lucky. You're surrounded with good men and women. You've raised some strong females. It takes a strong person to do that."

Jo made a fist and lightly struck Jack in the chest. "Why, Jack Sage, I do believe you're becoming a philosopher."

He shook his head. "No, ma'am. I just know I was lucky to be influenced by your son and your husband. I'm a better man for it. And your daughters. I think they've all found strong men, including Amy. You'll have grandchildren to fit this land. You can't hope for better than that."

She turned to face Jack. "I could hope for one thing better, but I fear it will not be happening. You would have made any of my girls an extraordinary husband." She shook her head. "But it is not to be." She stared down the disappearing tracks before turning back. "Believe me, Jack, I give you all of my gratitude for everything you've done. I love you, young man, and like Tripp said, you will always be welcome here. *Vaya con Dios*."

Tears were in her eyes, but her back was straight. She turned and walked slowly toward the wagon. Tripp sat on the wagon seat, holding the reins, and Monty gave her a hand up before swinging into the saddle. The rest of the troupe were mounted and ready. They turned and waved. Jack waved back, watching Tripp guide the team to Otto's and stop only long enough for the kids to dash out and leap into the wagon, followed by Ghost. He could hear Jo complaining, but only a little, as the big dog lay down with the kids. Riding out of town, their laughter floated back to him. At the last minute, her face solemn, Dot turned and raised a hand. He watched them until they were out of sight.

That's surprising, he thought. *Usually it's me riding out of town.* He felt a touch of melancholy. *I wonder what Carter wants. If it's another assignment from the president, it better be in Texas, but whatever it is, Carter can wait. I need a haircut and to thank Brad before I leave.*

Crossing the street, he could see through Otto's wide-open door. Pepper and Thunder stood with their eyes closed. Smokey was eating. Only Stonewall stared at him as Jack walked by. It was like the mule could read his mind.

He stepped onto the boardwalk in front of the barbershop and reached for the latch. The door was yanked open, the latch jerking from under his hand. McClain charged out, head down. "Not you again," Jack roared.

McClain stopped and stared at Jack. He punched Jack in the chest with a stiff finger. "You still owe me a fight."

"You keep doing that, and you're liable to get it."

McClain put his hands on his hips, chest swelled, and neck thrust forward. "Don't tempt me. I don't like you, Sage."

Jack frowned at the big man. "That makes us even. You don't rate too high on my friends list."

McClain shook his head. "But you know what? I've lost my desire to whip you. I know I can, but we've been through too much. I just don't want to fight you."

Jack shook his head. "You are so wrong. Fighting me would be the worst mistake you've ever made, but I've never wanted to fight you."

"But you promised."

"I promised, and I'll go through with it, but I'd prefer not to."

McClain shouted, "As would I." He spit a big glob in the palm of his hand and held it out to Jack. Jack did the same and slammed his hand into McClain's. Jack felt McClain bear down, and he followed suit, but the contest lasted only seconds before the two men simultaneously broke the grip. Each nodded to the other. McClain stepped off the boardwalk, and Jack started to move into the barbershop and stopped. He turned to the departing back. "McClain?"

The big bully railroad man turned to stare at Jack.

"Thanks for the help."

He gave a single wave and marched straight across the street to his office, forcing wagons to stop and riders to detour.

Jack stepped into the shop. Brad stood grinning at him. "So it's over?"

Nodding, Jack looked around the shop. He had it to himself. He removed his hat, tossed it on the tree, marveling the Stetson had made it through all the shooting without a hole drilled through it, drew his Smith & Wesson, and stepped to the barber's chair. He laid the revolver in his lap as Brad Wilcox threw the sheet over him. "I need a good haircut and shave. I'll be hitting the trail in the morning."

Brad opened his cabinet and removed his best badger-hair

shaving brush, mixed the soap with the brush, and when it was lathered, spread it over Jack's face. When he was finished, he placed the cup and brush on his counter and picked up the straight razor. He stropped it a couple of times, dropped the strap, pulled Jack's cheek tight, and made a smooth stroke from sideburn to jawline.

Jack let his eyelids close, his mind drifting down the trail. *In a month or so, I'll be crossing the Red, then it won't be long to the ranch. It'll be nice to see Montana and Bronco. I'll plop myself into a rocker, prop my feet up on the bannister, listen to the cows, and enjoy a peaceful cup of coffee just the way I like it. No lying, no shooting, and no killing.* A faint smile spread the big man's lips, and the corners of his eyes crinkled a touch. *I'm getting out of this cold country.*

A vagrant thought slipped through his mind, jerking his eyes open and bringing wrinkles to his brow. *I wonder what Carter wants...*

Ride with Jack Sage as he continues his dangerous adventures into frigid country.
Book 6:
THE LOYAL STAR

AUTHOR'S NOTE

I hope you've enjoyed reading *Five Women and the Star,* the fifth book in the Jack Sage Western Series.

If you have any comments, what you like or what you don't, please let me know. You can email me at: Don@DonaldLRobertson.com, or fill in the contact form on my website.

www.DonaldLRobertson.com

I'm looking forward to hearing from you.

BOOKS

A Jack Sage Western Series
STRANGER WITH A STAR
WITHOUT THE STAR
RETURN OF THE STAR
THE HANGING STAR
FIVE WOMEN AND THE STAR
THE LOYAL STAR

Logan Mountain Man Series
(Prequel to Logan Family Series)
SOUL OF A MOUNTAIN MAN
TRIALS OF A MOUNTAIN MAN
METTLE OF A MOUNTAIN MAN

Logan Family Series
LOGAN'S WORD
THE SAVAGE VALLEY
CALLUM'S MISSION
FORGOTTEN SEASON
TROUBLED SEASON
TORTURED SEASON

Clay Barlow - Texas Ranger Justice Series
FORTY-FOUR CALIBER JUSTICE
LAW AND JUSTICE
LONESOME JUSTICE

NOVELLAS AND SHORT STORIES
RUSTLERS IN THE SAGE
BECAUSE OF A DOG
THE OLD RANGER

Printed in Great Britain
by Amazon

57986943R10152